THE LUCKY ONES

EVERGREEN BOOK 3

MATTHEW S. COX

DIVISION ZERO PRESS

The Lucky Ones
Evergreen Book 3
© 2019 Matthew S. Cox
All Rights Reserved

Cover and interior art by: Alexandria Thompson

ISBN (ebook): 978-1-950738-04-5

ISBN (paperback): 978-1-950738-05-2

CONTENTS

WE'RE ALL A LITTLE BROKEN

Somber thoughts followed Harper on her patrol route, gnawing at her wandering mind. Eight months ago, she never would have imagined herself shooting anyone, much less multiple people, much less doing so before finishing high school.

In all fairness, she also never imagined a roving gang of thugs would try to kidnap her after the total breakdown of society either.

She didn't really feel like a cop. Police never had to protect their town from organized raids, or worry about citizens from another town coming to loot whatever they could get away with, even if it meant randomly killing people in their way—probably why Walter and the others decided to call themselves the militia and not police. Most of the original Evergreen militia had been sheriff's deputies before the war. They also had a few big city cops like Roy Ellis, and a few military vets trickled in later—like Cliff, the man who'd essentially become a new dad to her.

The Evergreen Militia dispensed with much of the 'paperwork' as Walter Holman (the commander) called it, since no official legal system remained. However, they had been teaching her tactics, how to negotiate with bad guys, and so on. Plus, Cliff worked with her a couple times a week on hand-to-hand training. Mostly, he taught her techniques from a modified form of jiu-jitsu he'd learned during his days as an Army Ranger.

Going into law enforcement hadn't even been the last thing on her mind before the war. Then again, she *hadn't* gone into law enforcement—she'd gone into 'not dying.' Ever since she cowered with her family in their basement while nuclear fire reshaped civilization, Harper flew down the long slope of a rollercoaster in a car without brakes, on a track with big holes, her life going wherever circumstance pulled it.

The girl voted sweetest in class... most likely to kill.

She eyed the quiet houses on either side of South Hiwan Drive, the trees swaying in a gentle late-May breeze. The clear sky overhead had a few clouds, plus a noticeable haze above them that hadn't been there before the nukes. It didn't look *too* bad, more like the artist who painted the sky had spilled a little grey into the once-rich blue. Except for the complete silence—no car engines, helicopters, or jets—her immediate surroundings didn't give off any visual indications that the worst disaster in human history had happened. All the houses in sight stood quiet, windows dark. Lawns had grown a bit wild, but not *too* bad. No one had a working mower since all the gasoline had been used or rotted. A few people had old school push mowers or scythes, and they'd essentially become professional landscapers. Their 'job' entailed going around the entire city and dealing with grass. At least, wherever the occupants of homes hadn't decided to replace their lawns with vegetable gardens. Lawns might look nice, but no one could eat them.

Harper marveled at the big houses with tons of room between them. Her family hadn't exactly been poor, but she doubted they could've afforded any of these houses so near the former golf course and country club. Few of the original residents remained, which made her wonder what happened to them. Would the people who lived in walking distance of such a place be horrified that their playground had turned into a farm? All the resources that had once been used to keep grass picture perfect for golfers had been put to work feeding survivors of a nuclear war. The long, narrow strips of open land nestled in and among these houses had become lush with corn stalks.

This new world had little respect for former wealth, perhaps even the reverse—contempt. Someone accustomed to the finer things would be ill-equipped to handle their absence. An executive could wind up starving in an alley right next to a girl like Lorelei whose drug-using mother barely noticed she had a child in the house.

Harper paused, studying the Mossberg in her hands. Dad's shotgun. The same shotgun she'd been using since thirteen. Back then, she only killed paper targets, clay pigeons, or sometimes bottles of water, achieving a modicum of YouTube fame for being a marksman prodigy. The gun people adored her as a rising star, some found a child of thirteen winning timed courses against grown men a bizarre curiosity, and of course, others called her parents all sorts of awful things for letting her handle a gun at all. From the first day he took her to the range at like seven, her father had drilled respect for firearms into her head. Intellectually, she'd known she wielded an instrument of death, but it never felt like anything more than a piece of sporting equipment, something to plink targets with and earn points. The idea of pointing it at a living person went against everything she'd been taught and every fiber of her conscience.

The girl who wouldn't squish bugs had killed roughly ten people. Of course, they had all been trying to hurt her or Madison. Most of the deaths blurred together in her mind, faceless 'bad guys' from a video game like *Call of Duty*. Perhaps thinking of them that way helped her brush aside guilt. She hadn't murdered anyone—she'd defended herself, and protected her ten-year-old sister. That she hadn't freaked out yet over shooting people worried her. She'd been too busy freaking out over her parents' deaths, nuclear war, the loss of everything she'd known and everything she'd ever hoped for. So, yeah, killing a few thugs trying to kidnap her didn't really rate.

Today, however, she dwelled on a more depressing thought: her imminent birthday.

Next week on June second, she'd turn eighteen. She wouldn't be graduating high school. There'd be no awesome party with her friends, no cute cake from Mom. Dad wouldn't pretend to have forgotten, then surprise her like he always did. Madison wouldn't spend half the day complaining about having to stay home for the party instead of going to hang out with her friends.

Harper almost couldn't even picture her little sister acting like that anymore. Mom had kept her so busy with activities, she barely had time to just be a kid. So, whenever she didn't need to rush off to dance class, or gymnastics, or soccer, or whatever else Mom got her signed up for, she wanted to spend time with Becca, Eva, and Melissa, her three closest friends.

Only Becca had resurfaced after the bombs. The other two could be anywhere, if they even remained alive. She had no idea how much of the area around Denver kinda survived like her home had, or wound up flat as a parking lot. The difference of a quarter mile could have changed survival to vaporization.

A lump formed in Harper's throat at that thought, growing when she thought of *her* friends. Mellow pothead Darci, Christina Menendez the genius, Andrea Orton also known as 'Perfect Girl,' and Veronica Jackson, karate enthusiast. She'd wanted to become the female Wesley Snipes, with dreams of going into action movies. If any of her friends could've handled the apocalypse, it would've been Veronica.

Not scaredy-cat Renee. That girl would never last on her own... most likely how she ended up with the Lawless, or the 'blue gang' as Harper had thought of them at first. At least she'd gotten her friend away from those bastards *before* they violated her. Renee had pretended to be younger than seventeen, and it fooled them for a little while. Evidently the Lawless weren't *total* monsters, but Harper couldn't find the least bit of respect for them. When they tried to kidnap her little sister, they reassured them by saying they'd let her get old enough first.

Harper squeezed the shotgun. The girl who carried insects outside alive wanted to shoot Lawless on sight. *Lower than bugs.*

But... birthday next week. The brief burst of anger faded under a morass of sorrow.

She resumed walking, trying not to think about June second, trying not to think about all the big plans she and her friends had floated around for 'the big one-eight.' Having her first birthday without her parents around shouldn't have happened until she'd grown old. It definitely shouldn't have been her eighteenth.

Quiet tears ran down her cheeks while memories of birthdays past played in a loop across her thoughts: her parents smiling, various cakes, Madison going from oblivious infant to happy toddler, to happy little kid to begrudging tween. Friends, a safe home, a normal world, gifts, no thoughts about *if* they'd have enough food or if she'd have to take someone's life to protect hers.

This year, despite it being the big eighteen, she wanted her birthday to go by unnoticed, wanted not to think about her parents and friends who wouldn't be there for it. What did eighteen even matter anymore? The world didn't have a legal system. Having to kill to protect herself, having to survive—that made her an adult long before some arbitrary number of spins around the sun did. The town already allowed people her age to have beer, so turning twenty-one no longer held any significance at all, either. Well, no significance beyond 'holy crap I'm still alive.'

Jonathan Chen, her brother of circumstance, turned eleven a few weeks ago on May eleventh. She and Cliff claimed a couple toys for him that the militia collected on various scavenging runs from stores like Walmart. Since no one could eat toys, Elizabeth Trujillo, the quartermaster, didn't ration them too strictly. She wanted to be fair, so one kid didn't get too many. Considering video games and computers had all mostly died to the EMP flash, the town management decided to add non-electronic toys to the priority list after food, clothing, and medicine due to something about mental health for the kids.

The boy had worn a happy face most of that day, only succumbing to grief over his dead parents at night after he'd crawled into bed. Harper comforted him until he fell asleep, somewhere between big sister and replacement mother.

Carrie Rangel, the woman who lived next door to them, had been flirting with Cliff, who—up until only two weeks ago—remained either oblivious to it or overly polite. Perhaps Harper wouldn't need to be 'Mom' as well as big sis for too much longer. Watching the man who had essentially become her stepdad test the waters of a romantic relationship felt awkward and endearing at the same time.

It also made her question how she felt about Logan. Before the war, she'd been dating this kid Micah mostly because he asked her out and her crew all had boyfriends. There hadn't been much of a spark between them; she merely didn't want to be the only one of her friends without one. The short time she'd known Logan felt entirely different, but she also didn't trust her feelings anymore. After everything she'd been through, what appeared to be affection could have simply been wanting to cling to any source of reassurance—like with Tyler. And that didn't exactly end well.

Jonathan's birthday had been a 'match day,' as Mom used to call it. He'd turned eleven on the eleventh of the month. The thought brought a spontaneous chuckle and a wave of longing for her parents. Her match day happened when she'd been two, before she'd become old enough to even comprehend what a birthday was. At least Madison's match birthday occurred before the world went nuts. October ninth, a touch over a year before some heartless piece of shit pushed the button.

Harper walked onward, gazing left and right past dirt hills at big houses set back from the relatively narrow road. Madison's ninth had been a major party due to the match day thing. The parents had taken an entire pack of tweens out to Elitch's theme park, barely squeaking in before they closed at the end of October. After the park, they'd gone to a restaurant for dinner with cake at home.

Memories supposedly lasted a lifetime, but in that moment, Harper wanted to forget them all. Bad enough they'd lost both parents, but the entirety of civilization had gone with them. She grumbled to herself, trying to think about nothing, trying to reset her brain to blank out everything that happened before the Lawless killed her parents.

A few minutes later, she regretted her desire to forget. All she had left of her parents and friends were memories. Even if they hurt more than anything, she'd cling to them. Her mind swung the other way, diving headlong into the happiest times she could remember throughout the years. In short order, thoughts of her parents and friends, moments she'd never have again, brought quiet tears.

"Madison's gonna turn eleven this year... right around the anniversary of the nukes falling." Harper kicked a rock off the road. *I hope she doesn't like start associating her birthday with Mom and Dad dying.*

Overcome by sorrow at that thought, Harper strayed off the road, hiding in a shadowy grove of trees at the corner of someone's front yard. She sat with the shotgun across her lap, head bowed against her knees, arms wrapped around her legs. Alone with her sadness, she retreated from the world.

For about an hour, one memory of her parents led to another and another, each progressive snapshot of the past driving her deeper into a hole of apathy. Her grief took the form of silent staring rather than tears, of withdrawing into a shell of not giving a crap. Grace, a new friend she'd made, had been disassociated from reality when she'd first arrived in Evergreen, refusing to accept the war happened, worried she'd fall behind in school and not get into a decent college. Despite knowing it pointless, Harper couldn't help but feel weird about missing the last eight months of high school. She'd only gone to school for a few weeks before the bombs fell.

I don't care if I get held back. I'll repeat the year if it'll fix the world.

The school here in Evergreen, a mish-mash of grades all thrown together, would officially take a summer break soon. Any kid twelve or older would need to spend a few hours each day at the farm learning and doing stuff. Ten- and eleven-year-olds could go if they wanted to. Somewhere, Harper picked up that the tradition of summer break started due to rural communities needing the kids to work on family farms. Like so much else, another relic of 1800s life appeared to have returned.

We're all just going in circles.

At least Madison stopped complaining about school. The teachers here decided to abandon the 'traditional' structure and present more practical and useful subjects instead of preparing kids for colleges that no longer existed. Mr. Simon worked with a few of the older kids who wanted to learn more advanced math, but they didn't force algebra on kids who'd spend the rest of their lives pulling potatoes out of the ground or building houses by hand.

Madison once dreamed of becoming a veterinarian or zoologist. She'd fantasized about possibly becoming a professional dancer, but never really took that seriously. Now, she'd probably end up taking care of chickens and cows—if she could tolerate the idea that most of those animals would end up on a dinner plate. Her friend Christina got accepted at UCLA. She'd wanted to work at NASA. Andrea still hadn't figured things out officially, but everyone expected she'd end up being a teacher. Renee wanted to go into nursing, but her likely path now appeared to be seamstress. Darci, on the other hand, had already been accepted at a graphic design school. She intended to pursue some sort of artistic career to pay the bills while trying to make it big as a rock musician on the side. Darci played decent guitar and could sing okay, and always bragged she'd be the first of their friends to meet a celebrity, probably a musician.

The more Harper thought about all the dreams vaporized in nuclear fire, the more she had to struggle to care about anything, least of all her birthday.

We're only repeating the same stuff. If society even recovers, they'll just nuke each other all over again a couple hundred years from now. What's the point?

Soon after she began to shed tears over the future they'd all lost, she thought of Madison and Lorelei snuggling up with her at night, both staring at her like some form of superhero who could protect them from all evil in the world. It bothered her that Madison still sometimes acted like a girl half her age, but what ten-year-old could watch *both* of her parents murdered six feet in front of her and not have an issue or six. All things considered, Madison handled it well.

I shouldn't dwell on crap I can't change.

Harper pulled out of her depressive dive, sitting up and forcing her tears to retreat back into her eyes. Where sorrow receded, anger bloomed, fury at whoever started the war. What possible reason could anyone have had to use weapons like nukes? Brainless, heartless, or insane…

With a sigh, she forced herself to her feet and resumed patrolling her assigned area, trying to cling to good memories. She pictured the moment Madison finally put her dead phone down, or her reaction when her friend Becca arrived in town. Even gloomy Mila Cline had eased off on the morbidity. With the threat of the Shadow Man (men) removed entirely, the girl had stopped trying to deliberately alienate herself from other kids by saying dark things. Acting super creepy had been her way to protect them from the men she expected would show up to kidnap or kill her. Surprisingly, the girl admitted to the rest of the class why she'd been so weird. However, she retained a precocious dark humor more befitting an adult than a girl of nine.

Harper spent a few minutes trying to remember when that girl's birthday fell, wanting to say July, but not entirely sure. Maybe they *should* still celebrate birthdays. Only, it had a totally different meaning now. Congrats on *surviving* for another year. Will you see another one?

"Dammit. Now I sound like Mila."

She proceeded down the road, muttering, "Rainbows and bunnies" to herself for a few minutes.

THE STRONG FRAGRANCE OF GRILLED FISH HUNG IN THE AIR AROUND THE house.

Harper sat on her front porch step, Logan on the porch behind her. She reclined against his chest, content to trust the .45 handgun in a belt holster and leave the shotgun inside. Her friend Renee sat beside her on the step with Grace cross-legged on the ground facing them.

Cliff and Carrie cooked on the backyard grill, which made her feel all too much like a kid in a functional family with parents again. Madison, Jonathan, Lorelei, Becca, and Mila ran around kicking a ball, though whether or not they attempted any sort of organized scoring remained a mystery. Other than a little extra dirt and frump to their clothes, they didn't appear to be survivors of a nuclear war… not unless Harper looked them in the eye and saw the hollowness where joy and innocence once dwelled.

Except for Lorelei. She still brimmed with both, laughing and giggling enough for everyone.

Harper watched her zooming around after the big red ball, no doubt 'borrowed' from the school gym. *Her mother was so horrible to her. Except for nearly starving to death, nuclear war* improved *her life.* Though far less energetic and giggly, even Mila appeared to be enjoying herself. *What did that crazy wanna-be ninja do to her?* The girl hadn't spoken much of what those men put her through other than keeping her locked up and trying to train her into some kind of assassin. At one point, they tried to make her shoot a man in the head, but she refused.

Both of them lived in their own personal hells. I got nerve feeling sorry for myself.

"What's on your mind, Harp?" asked Renee. "You look like you wanna kill someone."

Grace winced. "That's not funny anymore."

Logan reached around and took her hand. "You okay?"

"Just being moody. Spent most of the day thinking about my parents. But we really had a great life up until the war. I was just thinking about Lore and the bullshit she had to deal with at only six. Or Mila. Who seriously tries to brainwash a little kid into being a killer?"

"Bad things happen to a lot of people," said Logan. "Awful stuff happening to them doesn't make your pain any less real. You and Maddie saw crap no kids should ever see. I lost my parents, too. And Luisa."

"You didn't watch them die. They didn't die because you hesitated…" Harper filled her lungs through her nose, held the breath for a few seconds, and let it out. Everyone in town had suffered loss. Maybe he had a point. "I guess you're right."

"It's okay to be sad." Grace fidgeted at the grass by her foot. "How twisted do you think I feel that my first reaction to learning my parents died was relief? Not like they were awful parents, just super strict and demanding. Making every decision for me, telling me exactly how my life would go. I feel like I escaped a cage."

Renee wiped tears. "Great. Now you guys got me thinking about my mom. I have no idea what happened to her or where she is."

"We're all a little broken." Logan squeezed her hand.

"Some more than others," whispered Harper.

"Maddie still talking to her phone?" asked Renee in a hushed tone.

Harper shook her head. "No. And I meant me. What am I doing running around with a gun? How twisted is it that I've shot people and no one seems to mind?"

"You've always been good at it." Renee picked up her water glass. "Now you're helping keep us all safe. I couldn't do that. I screamed every time the stupid thing went off that time your dad took me to the range with you guys."

Harper laughed at the memory. "Yeah. You threw his Beretta over your head when the guy in the next lane fired that hand cannon."

"Loud noises get me every time." Renee blushed. "Oh, hey... next Sunday."

The better mood brewing inside Harper crashed into her lap, along with her stare. "I'd rather just forget it."

"Aww, why?" asked Renee.

"Forget what?" asked Grace and Logan at the same time.

Harper shot Renee a 'don't you dare' look.

Her friend bowed her head, seeming about to cry.

That made her feel like she'd kicked a puppy. "Ugh. Sorry. My birthday's on the second."

Renee lifted her gaze off the ground, managing a weak smile.

"Oh, nice." Grace reached for a high-five.

"Happy birthday," whispered Logan.

Harper begrudgingly mashed hands with Grace. "Thanks. It's just... my friends and I had all these glorious ideas for the 'big one-eight,' but they're all gone except for Renee. And... parents."

"They're not dead. They can't all be dead." Renee covered her face with both hands. "We all lived fairly close. Our area wasn't hit *that* hard. They would've survived the bombs. I gotta believe they're okay, somewhere. "

"I'm trying to believe that, too." Harper leaned her head back against Logan's shoulder, gazing up at the clouds. If the war hadn't happened, by the end of this summer, her friends would have all gone in different directions anyway for college. Not like they would've been hanging out constantly anymore. At least, not all of them would be. Mom said she hadn't seen her high school friends in years. "All we can do right? Try to stay positive."

"Pretty much. Keep smiling and save the random fits of intense crying for when no one's watching." Renee made a face like she only half joked.

"Better not lose it too bad." Harper poked her in the side. "All the therapists have been vaporized."

Her friends chuckled.

Jonathan shouted, "Look—"

The giant red kickball walloped Renee in the head, knocking her over backward off the porch steps.

"—Out."

Mila and Lorelei erupted in laughter. Madison waited for Renee to sit up in good spirits before she, too, laughed.

"Sorry." Becca jogged over. "My fault."

"Ow." Renee rubbed her nose. "I hate taking balls to the face."

Logan and Grace snickered. Harper bit her lip, fighting not to laugh.

"Oh, funny." Renee rolled her eyes. "I meant I hate the big red balls like from grade school dodgeball."

Harper cackled. "That's even worse! So you don't mind the other kind hitting you in the face?"

Grace and Logan continued laughing, while the kids stared in confusion.

"No. Argh!" Renee tried to growl, but wound up laughing, too.

"You're impossible. I hated dodgeball. This kid Ricky Myers always threw it at my face, trying to knock me off my feet."

"Oh, I remember that. He was such a douchebag." Harper sighed at grade school memories.

"Kids?" called Carrie. "C'mon inside. Food's ready."

"I should get back to the house. Anne-Marie's going to want me to help cook." Grace scrambled to her feet. "See you guys later."

Renee got up and hurried inside. Technically, Carrie had adopted her. Having her best friend living next door would have been awesome if not for such a situation requiring the end of civilization. Logan stood to leave and hugged Harper, respecting her not being ready for kissing yet. He shared a house with three other farm workers: two other boys from the Colorado Springs hockey team and a slightly older twentysomething guy, Juan. Though, the guys all slept under the same roof, they didn't have organized meals like a family.

Harper stood. For a brief, but intense moment, she wanted to scream at Carrie for not being Mom. How dare she act like the world remained normal, like they had a family... but the resentment imploded into a dense nugget of guilt that broke apart into acceptance. Both she and Madison could've been killed in their home. They could've died on the way to Evergreen. Lorelei might have starved in the street if Tyler hadn't found her. Renee might have suffered horrible abuse at the hands of the Lawless gang if not for one well-timed scavenging trip to a hospital. Had Harper not been on that trip, one of the Evergreen militia may well have even killed Renee, mistaking her for a member of the gang.

But they'd all managed to end up here, together.

Family didn't care so much about genetics anymore.

With a smirk, she snagged Logan's arm before he could walk away. "Where do you think you're going?"

"Umm..." He pointed toward the house he slept in, a decent way across town from there.

"C'mon. Time to eat." She pulled him inside with the rest of the family.

FATE AND CIRCUMSTANCE

Two days later on Thursday night, Harper slipped away to meet Logan at Earl's bar, formerly the Evergreen Brewery and Tap House.

Having a date, naturally, caused the expected good-natured teasing from Madison and Lorelei. Fortunately, Cliff didn't do the douchebag thing of making a joke about shooting Logan if something happened. Dad used to do that every time she introduced a new boyfriend. He'd usually be cleaning one of his rifles when the boy walked in and would invariably say something like the boy would get a good close look at it if Harper wasn't home by nine. The first kid she brought home, Marc, barely said two words their whole movie date and never even looked at her again after that night, thinking her Dad a psycho.

Madison teasing her about a boyfriend sounded so damn normal that she teetered at the edge of crying the whole walk to Earl's. The oddity of walking into a bar at seventeen let her keep her emotions on an even keel. The place didn't appear much different from how it had probably been before the war, with the exception of light coming from several oil lamps instead of electricity.

Logan met her by the door and they walked in together, taking a booth seat among tables mostly populated by the forty-plus crowd. She slipped into the bench, sitting nervously while gazing around.

"What?" Logan sat opposite her. "Something wrong?"

"Just feels strange being in a bar. Like we're not old enough. I keep waiting for someone to scream at me and kick me out." She glanced to her left at the actual bar, where six guys ranging in age from fifty to seventy all wore handguns on their belts out in the open. "Especially with everyone carrying a gun."

Logan eyed the men. "They have guns? But they're not militia."

"Nah. Walter only asks people with rifles to turn them in or join. They have plenty of handguns from the old sheriff's armory. We're not trying to disarm everyone, just put military style rifles to more practical use defending the town."

"Ahh." He nodded, then picked up the pepper shaker, turning it over and over in his fingers while watching the grains tumble.

A twentyish woman with shoulder-length auburn hair, green eyes, and a warm smile approached. "Hi, you guys. I'm Andie. You two are adorable. Is this your first date?"

Logan opened his mouth, but demurred to her, perhaps unsure if she considered it a date as opposed to merely hanging out with a friend.

"Second actually." Harper managed a weak smile. "But I'm not nervous because of the date. Feels weird being in a bar."

Andie grinned. "Yeah. Lot of things these days feel weird. Never thought I'd end up waiting tables at my dad's place. Never thought my dad would wind up running a bar either, but he got a great deal on the property."

Logan chuckled.

"So, how's this work?" asked Harper.

"You two are both old enough for the beer, but if you don't wanna go there we, of course, have water. Food's available, but it's whatever we got's ready. Tonight, grilled veggies and potato burgers."

"Umm." Harper tilted her head. "What's a potato burger?"

Andie held her hands together, making a disc with her fingers. "It's a hockey puck of potato on bread like a hamburger. Meat doesn't exactly keep long enough to store without electricity."

"Right." Logan shrugged. "Sounds interesting."

"Cool. So, water or beer?" asked Andie.

"How high octane is it?" Logan smiled.

"A bit stronger than big brand beer, but it shouldn't knock you on your ass."

Harper fidgeted. "Sure, why not? One won't kill me."

"Sounds good." Logan nodded.

Andie smiled at them and whisked off into the back room.

Harper sat in silence for a moment, listening to the older people talking about various things from hunting to their theories on who started the war to wondering if anyone would try to resurrect the Pony Express. The response that there'd have to be enough other places to take crap to didn't sound reassuring. One old guy thought the place needed a piano and whores. Harper went scarlet in the face.

"Wow," whispered Logan. "This feels like we're halfway between the 1890s and a post-apoc video game... except no one's using bottle caps for money."

"What?" She blinked at him. "Bottle caps?"

"Something from a computer game I used to play. They use bottle caps like coins."

"Why not use actual coins?"

"No idea." He looked over at the bar. "I feel underdressed for the place."

"This isn't exactly a fancy restaurant." Harper tensed at motion coming up behind her, but relaxed upon realizing Andie approached.

The woman set their beers in front of them, then pointed back over her shoulder with a thumb. "Food should be out in a minute. Doesn't take too long to grill veggies."

They thanked her, and she headed off once again to the back room.

"I mean... I'm the only one in the room except for Andie who isn't carrying a weapon."

Harper became acutely aware of the weight of the .45 on her hip.

She squirmed. "Yeah, well... some geniuses decided to light the sky on fire."

"Wonder how she'd react if I put a handful of bottle caps on the table when she brings the food."

"Probably think you're littering." Harper grinned. "No one's using money at all anymore. It's useless. Everyone lost it all anyway, except for the cash they had in their pockets. Money was all just numbers in computers that melted. People aren't even really bartering. We're just kinda helping out whoever needs it and everyone's working together. I guess once we start feeling like death isn't around every corner, we'll probably start trading again... then someone will reinvent money."

Logan sipped his beer and his eyes nearly crossed. "Whoa. Okay, yeah. One of these is going to be plenty."

She leaned close to sniff her glass, a continuous spritz of cool foam at her cheeks. The high alcohol content made her eyes water. "Wow, you're right. So, yeah. You know Lucas Garza?"

"Sounds kinda familiar."

Harper took a sip of beer. Despite the strength of its aroma, it didn't taste bad... well no worse than any other beer she'd ever tried, but it definitely had an after-burn in her mouth. "He used to be a celebrity. Had millions. Now he's just like anyone else in town."

"Yeah." He twisted his glass back and forth, peering at her past a flop of dark brown hair over his eyes.

Laughter erupted from a man seated at the bar out of sight behind her, but an older man let out an enraged howl. A heavy *thud* preceded the clonks of several heavy glasses falling to the floor. Harper twisted around in her seat. A greying man in his early sixties she knew as Mr. Halliday repeatedly hammered the face of a younger Hispanic man into the bar top. The fortyish man—Bryson—got his legs under him the third time his head bounced off the wood. He shoved the older guy away and tried to back up from the bar, but tripped over the stool he'd been sitting on and landed flat on his back.

Mr. Halliday stumbled from the shove, also falling over—due to being drunk.

"Hey, knock it off!" yelled Harper. She leapt out of her seat and ran over, putting herself between them. "What the hell are you guys doing?"

Bryson backed off, hands up. "Just a joke, Graham. Calm the hell down."

"I'll show ya who's old!" Graham Halliday pushed himself upright, but stumbled into the bar, knocking over an empty stool. He wobbled to his feet again and stared at her. "Get outta the way, missy."

Logan scrambled to his feet and started toward him, but stopped when Harper raised her hand.

"Mr. Halliday. You've had too much beer. I think it's time you should go on home for the night." She tried to herd the old guy toward the door.

"Bah. I don't take orders from no potbellied plumber. I ain't 'bout to take orders from no snot-nosed kid either." Mr. Halliday lunged at Harper, trying to grab her.

She caught him by the arms, shifted her hips the way Cliff taught her, and lightly tossed the old guy into the bar again. He knocked two more stools over and grabbed the countertop to keep from falling completely over, ending up hanging by his grip, his knees inches from the floor.

"Mr. Halliday, you—"

He shrieked in anger, finding his feet and whirling around with a right hook.

Harper twisted under his arm, grabbed him by the wrist, and flipped him to the floor, before dropping on top of him with one knee on his back and his arm chicken-winged up behind him.

"Gah! My damn arm," howled the old man.

"Look, Mr. Halliday. You're drunk. You need to go home and sleep it off. I might be a kid to you, but I'm still on the militia. Swing at me again, and you can spend a couple days chilling out at the sheriff's station." Harper relaxed the tension on his arm a little. "C'mon, don't be a dick. Just go home. Sleep it off."

Mr. Halliday muttered something incomprehensible, but nodded before emitting an onion-and-beer-scented belch.

Harper stood and helped him up, keeping his arm pinned to his back while ushering him out the door. The old guy staggered off down the highway when she let go, swaying, but evidently not too drunk to walk. Once she felt sure he'd make it home on his own, she went back inside.

Bryson Soto walked up to her. His face appeared red, but he didn't bleed from anywhere. "Sorry about that. Just made a little crack about him being a bit old to carry a gun. Geriatric cowboys and whatnot. No idea he'd flip like that."

"Are you hurt? If you want to complain, we can treat it like an assault."

He waved her off. "Nah. No big deal. Graham just got a bit too much beer in him. I, uhh, could've handled that, but thanks."

The row of men sitting at the bar all looked at her with varying degrees of 'what the heck did I just watch?' or concern.

"You're welcome. Didn't want that to turn into another fight. This place is starting to get a reputation for brawling." She smiled and headed back to her table.

Bryson picked up the stools, then sat where he'd been before, chatting with three other men.

"Whoa." Logan chuckled, then sat again. "Impressive. You threw that guy around like a rag doll."

She slid back into the booth seat, rested her elbows on the table, and exhaled. "Not that impressive. He's like sixty-three and drunk."

"Still. Just because a guy's old like that doesn't mean he's weak. Like three years ago, a couple younger guys tried to mug my grandfather and he beat the snot out of them."

"Wow." Harper sipped her beer. "Was he former military?"

"Nah. Just a semi-professional boxer back in the day. He still works —umm, work*ed* out."

She reached across the table and put her hand on his. "Sorry."

"Not your fault. So, where'd you pick up moves like that? Let me guess, taekwondo classes since you were nine?"

"No." She laughed. "I was too lazy for that as a kid. Cliff's been showing me some jiu-jitsu techniques he learned in the Rangers."

"Ranger?" Logan made some weird martial-artsy hand motions like from a bad movie. "Which color was he?"

"Dork." Harper stuck out her tongue, but grinned at the stupidity of it. "Not that kind of ranger."

"I love seeing you smile."

Harper stared into her beer, certain she blushed as red as her hair. "Your smile's kinda cute, too."

"So you like this militia thing?"

"It's okay. I like helping people but I could *really* do without having to get into gunfights sometimes."

He rubbed the back of her hand with his thumb. "So why do you do it?"

"Didn't want to give up Dad's shotgun. I'd never forgive myself if anything happened to Madison or the others if I didn't do everything possible to protect them."

"You're a fascinating girl, Harper Cody. Sometimes, when I look into your eyes, I see this fierce creature. Sometimes, I see innocence. Life."

"Yeah, well. I guess I'm complicated." She nodded to the side to get her hair out of her face. "I kinda like that you're uncomplicated."

He chuckled.

"Do you enjoy working on the farm or is it just where they asked you to go?"

"Yes to both. I didn't have any real experience at anything except high school coursework and hockey, and I kinda like not starving to death, so I agreed to work on the farm. This town is starting to grow on me."

She stared at the table, mostly because if she looked up at him, the faint tickling sensation in her stomach would likely grow into a massive pack of butterflies. They spent a few minutes talking about life in Evergreen. He expected to work on the farm until he became too old for it. Not exactly the grandest plans for the future, but the world had changed. He didn't mind busting his butt so people could eat. Their conversation about how long she planned to stay with the militia paused when Andie brought out the food. Except for there being an inch-thick disc of potato on two pieces of bread, it sorta resembled a hamburger with a side order of grilled cucumber, tomato, bell peppers, and onions. The notion that Harper might never again see a real hamburger bun in her life made her feel strange. Not quite sad, more unsettled and worried about the future.

"Hope you like it." Andie smiled. "And let me get you two some water."

Harper turned her head to look up at the woman, her skull feeling as though it floated on a neck made out of gummi bears. "Thanks. Yeah, water would be good."

Andie walked off.

"Not like I have any issue with you being on the militia besides worrying about you, but you're not really going to be able to do that when you're sixty."

She nibbled on a bit of grilled tomato. "Yeah, I know. But sixty's a long way off and I'm still kinda scared I won't make it to that age. We had nukes go off only a few miles away. Every one of us might get all sorts of messed up cancer and there's no real hospitals left."

"Oh, there's a happy thought." He slid his arm across the table to take her hand. "Elevated risk isn't a guarantee. And besides, we're on a new all-natural diet. We're not eating all those dyes, preservatives, and other chemicals that caused cancer."

"Would you rather be a disappointed optimist or a surprised pessimist?" asked Harper.

"I'd rather worry about things within my control and try to find happiness where I can." He picked up the 'burger.' "Like this thing. Never had a potato sandwich before."

Harper picked hers up as well. "Maddie used to spread mashed potatoes on bread at Thanksgiving dinner. Mom always yelled at her not to do it. Something about 'combining starches,' but she still put bread on the table with mashed potatoes. My grandfather insisted on having bread at the dinner table all the time. All the food's going to end up in our stomachs anyway. Does it matter if we put them together before we eat them?"

He chuckled and took a bite.

"How is it?"

Logan gave a thumbs up while chewing.

She took a bite... *Mmf. Basically a baked potato sandwich with Cajun spices.*

"Do you ever wonder if fate is steered by desire?" asked Harper.

"Huh?"

She waved the potato-burger around while trying to think of how to explain what she meant. "Umm. Like if enough people want or believe something, the universe reacts to it. All those post-apoc movies and shows and stuff, what if everyone thinking about that all the time made it happen?"

"Oh. Nah. I don't think so." Logan ate a whole hunk of green pepper in one bite. "If reality changed based on what people thought about most, there'd be zombies."

She laughed.

They ate without speaking for a minute or two.

"Pretty sure hate or greed caused it. Maybe even a glitch in a computer. Stuff like that has happened before, but didn't go all the way to war. Years ago, an error in an early warning system made it look like we'd been attacked. I think we came pretty close to launching weapons until someone figured out the whole thing had been a problem with the system. Something like that could've happened again. Maybe they upgraded the defense network to Windows and it crashed."

She chuckled.

"Seriously, though. All military contracts are won by the company willing to work as cheaply as possible in the shortest amount of time. With that kinda policy, I'm surprised it took this long for something big to go wrong."

"Wow." She stared at her food, not sure if she should laugh at that or break down. "That's really sad to think about... a typo wiping out the world."

"Yeah. Assuming it *was* a glitch and we didn't get legit attacked. But the news didn't really have anything too scary in the couple of weeks leading up to it. So if someone attacked us, it would have had to be spontaneous and random." He finished off the last quarter glass of his beer, then gasped. "Whoa. Maybe the guy at the console was drinking this stuff."

That got a weak chuckle out of her. "I'm seeing vapor trails and my head feels like it's floating around away from my body."

"You finished the whole beer this time, and kinda drank it fast. Surprised you're still sitting upright. This stuff is hectic."

"Me too." She took a few fast bites of the potato-burger hoping it would soak up some alcohol. "Maybe the computer didn't make an error. What if it did it on purpose? Like, calculated humans had gotten out of control and needed to be culled down to a manageable population."

"Heh. Could be, but that sounds more like science fiction. I'd like to think the government wasn't dumb enough to connect an AI to the big red button."

"Seriously," muttered Harper. "So I guess that brings us back to people being shitty human beings. If there is such a thing as karma, I hope whoever made the decision to fire the first nuke dies painfully."

Logan stared at her for a while. "When someone as sweet as Harper Cody wishes death on a person, it sends a ripple across space and time. If the guy who did it is still alive, he probably just stubbed his toe."

She chuckled. "Stop. I'm not that sweet..." Her smile died. "Not anymore."

"Sure you are. But you've had to grow an armored shell. We all have."

"Yeah."

He finished off his veggies. "I dunno. I kinda have trouble believing a person ordered the first strike. What kind of insane moron would do something like that? They'd have to understand what would happen. One gets fired, everyone blows their entire arsenal. Nukes weren't supposed to ever be used, just exist as a deterrent."

"Deterrent?" She downed a few gulps of water. "To what?"

"To using nukes."

Harper sighed. "That doesn't make any sense."

"Exactly. Nuclear weapons are pointless when everyone has them. They basically become a shield and a threat at the same time. Countries only kept them around because other countries had them."

"So stupid," muttered Harper. "The ultimate penis envy. Couldn't world leaders just put giant tires and a lift on their trucks like normal guys with adequacy issues?"

He laughed. "Hey, my father had one of those."

"Oops." She cringed.

Logan looked off to the side. "I can't stop wondering if Ana and Luis are still alive. I hate not knowing."

"I'm sorry." Harper reached over and held his hand.

"At least my parents and Luisa went fast. Didn't feel a thing." A tear ran down his cheek. "She was only fifteen. If I wasn't on the hockey team, I would've been vaporized with them. Who decided civilians needed to die? What kind of monster wages war with nukes? That's not war, that's just murdering everyone."

She bowed her head. A moment later, she got up and moved around the table to sit on the same bench with him, leaning into an embrace. He shook as if crying, but made no sound. Contagious grief stole her voice, so she merely held him until he collected himself a few minutes later.

"I'm sorry," whispered Harper. "So stupid of me. Shouldn't have talked about that stuff. We're supposed to be on a date."

"It's okay. I've been holding that in too long. Needed to come out. Thanks." He continued holding her. "I don't have anyone else I can talk to about real stuff."

Harper studied her lap. She couldn't deny the squirmy feeling building in her gut. *Is this anxiety? Depression? Am I really starting to fall in love with him?* She rested her head against his. *Am I being pushed to seek out a mate by some primal species-conscious reaction to the near eradication of humanity? Okay, now I know I'm overthinking.* A silent sigh escaped her nose. After what happened with Tyler... Sure, she'd thought him the last boy in the world around her age, and his odd quirkiness endeared him to her. But she'd kissed him so fast. Totally unlike her. She'd also been in a crazy headspace at the time. Part of her worried that as soon as she let herself attach to a boy, something horrible would happen to him. Another part only wanted to be sure her feelings were genuine, and not—as Cliff said—wanting to jump on the nearest boy because the airplane plummeted toward the ground.

I'm going to be eighteen in a couple days. Not that anyone gives a crap. Beth and Jaden have been doing it almost every day for weeks. Everyone knows and no one seems to care. She's still a sophomore. Or would be if school existed. Dating Logan doesn't mean we instantly go to bed together. Am I being cautious or chicken?

"Feels weird going out for food and not having to pay for it," said Logan.

She pushed aside thoughts of nuclear death and summoned a tiny smile. "I wonder how long that will last before someone ruins it by reinventing money."

"Probably not long. Humans have had money almost as long as we've had the ability to speak. They used to use salt like money. Anything rare or precious. Hell, maybe people will use food or water as money."

"I hope not. That's just cruel. It's much nicer like this. Everyone helping everyone. I like this way more." She sighed. "But I'm not that naïve. I know it won't last forever."

He tossed the last bite of his potato-burger in his mouth, mumbling agreement.

"Wow." Harper looked around at the room, noticeably dimmer than when they'd arrived. Nimbuses of light danced on the walls behind the lamps set up here and there around the room. She hadn't consciously noticed the pervasive smell of burning oil until she looked at them. They didn't give off too much light, creating a dark, cozy—and kinda romantic—ambiance. "This almost feels like a date."

"Is it a date?" He smiled at her.

Harper turned her head toward him. Sitting shoulder to shoulder, she found herself almost close enough to kiss him. His eyes simultaneously radiated joy and sadness, hope and pain... pretty much a mirror for how she felt. Another pull, another moment of doubt. The instant she admitted to herself she might have feelings for him, he'd go crazy or decide not to like her, or something bad would happen.

We're all a little broken inside now. Do we give up and stop trying to live? The beer-soaked butterfly in her stomach decided to start tap-dancing. *Screw it.* She exhaled.

His eyes widened.

"Yeah. It's a date."

A broad grin spread over his face. "Cool."

"Still not quite ready to do more than hold hands or cuddle. And no, it's not you. I'm… I gotta know that what I think I'm feeling for you is real and not something else. Like reflexively clinging to the first boy who talks to me."

Logan put an arm around her. "Makes sense. I love spending time with you no matter what we're doing."

"Do you mean that or are you just saying what you think I want to hear so you can get into my pants?" She grinned.

"I'm being sincere. Otherwise, I'd be using the accent on you." He wagged his eyebrows.

"The accent?" She looked him up and down. "You don't have an accent."

"Joo have the most beautiful blue eyes," said Logan with a thick Spanish accent and a slight deepening of his voice. "More beautiful than the ocean in Barcelona."

"Wow." She blinked. "My jeans almost flew right off by themselves."

He laughed. "My brother didn't have an accent either, but around his dates, he'd always talk like that constantly. Luis had a new girl almost every month. My family spoke some Spanish at home, mostly for the grandparents. But none of us have ever been to Spain—or even Mexico where my great grandparents came from. Most people can't tell the difference between a Mexican Spanish accent and a Spaniard's accent."

"I'm most people." She held up a hand.

"Let us find a nice quiet place and count the stars," said Logan in the accent.

"Hon, if you don't go with him, I'm about to." Andie paused on the way by to wink at them.

Logan blushed.

"That sounds sweet." Harper took his hand and scooted out of the bench seat. "But I can't stay out too late."

"Let's go to your backyard then. It'll give us the most time."

"Okay." She followed him outside, still holding his hand.

If he'd hoped something might happen off in a quiet little private spot by the creek, he'd clearly given up on that hope by suggesting they hang out in her yard. No way would they do anything there. Harper bit her lip, surprised by a boy not putting any pressure on her to go faster, even after the world fell to pieces. Most confusing of all, she found herself ever so slightly frustrated. Between that strong homebrew beer and her increasing urge to trust Logan, had they gone off somewhere alone…

She just might have tried to kiss him.

BARISTA

H arper drove Dad's new SUV with all her friends in it, plus Madison, Jonathan, and Lorelei.

She stared at the dashboard, watching the speedometer needle wobble around fifty. Driving felt unusually strange, and not merely because she hadn't done it often. Anxiety built up, as though she'd stolen the truck without permission. Even though she'd gotten her license a few weeks ago, it felt somehow wrong to be driving without Mom or Dad in the passenger seat.

Her friends wanted to go to the mall. They'd all been hanging out at the house, and everyone randomly decided to pile into the Explorer. Madison, Jonathan, and Lorelei popped up to peer at her over the rearmost seat, smiling. The tiny platinum-blonde sprite and the Chinese boy shouldn't be there. Why had they called her parents 'Mom and Dad' too? She kept staring at them in the rearview mirror, trying to figure out how she knew them.

A few minutes after they left home, whole city blocks pulled away on both sides, flying off into the sky like pieces of a movie set being removed by the hands of invisible giants. Soon, she found herself driving along a desert highway, all signs of civilization having vanished.

Harper realized she dreamed. Surprisingly, not a nightmare—at least not yet.

With that realization, she understood why the kids in the back looked familiar. Also, Darci, Veronica, Andrea, and Christina changed... fading out to ghosts rather than real solid people.

Christina and Andrea yelled about not having any cell reception to check maps. Veronica nagged her to turn around and go back. Darci sat silently in the middle of the rearmost seat smoking a joint. The kids in the far back all pulled their shirts up over their noses, glaring at her.

"Dude, you're gonna get her in trouble." Renee grabbed Darci by the arm and shook her. "If her parents smell that crap in here, she's going to be grounded until she's out of college."

"It's legal," muttered Darci, the smoke leaving her lips shifted to form the word 'legal' in midair.

"I still can't believe her father let her take the new car," said Andrea.

"They didn't," whispered Harper. "Dad wouldn't let me drive it at all. None of this is really happening."

"Harp!" called Madison. "Lorelei's streaking again! She won't listen to me."

Lorelei giggled.

Harper drew in a breath to yell at her, but didn't bother. *I'm dreaming.*

The stink of pot changed in an instant to the aroma of toast and wood smoke.

Everyone started looking around for the source, opening every compartment, cup holder, pocket, and handbag. Harper noticed a glint in the side mirror and glanced at it... only to see Logan riding up from behind them on a mountain bike that he somehow pedaled as fast as she drove.

"I don't have the toast," said Logan once he pulled alongside her window, then pointed. "He does."

Harper looked out the passenger window at Cliff, on a big Harley, dressed in his mall security guard uniform, holding a big plate of toast up to the Explorer like a waiter. He turned his head toward her and flashed a giant, cheesy smile.

The absolute oddity of that shocked her out of the dream.

Her eyes snapped open to the now-familiar sight of her new bedroom in Evergreen, in a house that used to belong to someone she'd never met, a house they'd been assigned to. Lorelei cuddled up against her left side, back to the wall. Madison lay half on top of her on the right, her head at Harper's chin.

Sharing the bed with the girls reminded her of the time they'd visited Mom's sister in Nevada when Harper had been about eleven. The woman had three large dogs, and the golden retriever decided to sleep with her at night, an immovable weight pinning her down.

She'd grown to adore having the girls with her in bed at night for two reasons. One, her little sisters took on the role of teddy bears without the obvious embarrassment of a seventeen-year-old clinging to stuffed animals so she could sleep. Second, having them close reassured Harper of their safety. If anything happened, she wouldn't have to wonder about them. Eventually, they'd outgrow co-sleeping. By modern standards, they already had... but modern standards had gone out the window. Emotions aside, sooner or later, physical size would get in the way. Three adult women couldn't fit in that bed together without piling on top of each other. And that wouldn't be comfortable at all. Not to mention, some day, Harper might prefer the company of whatever passed for a husband in a society without actual laws.

She wondered how long it would take Madison to want a bed to herself. They'd already used up all the space they really had in the house. A second bed *could* be squeezed into their room, but it wouldn't leave much open floor. They'd end up sitting or standing on beds to get dressed.

Whenever she's ready, she'll want space. Harper smiled, finding she didn't mind how long that may take. Lorelei, on the other hand, would likely want to cling to someone at night for the rest of her life. Eventually, she'd move on from Harper to someone she fell in love with. Considering the girl's vulnerability, any potential boyfriend—or girlfriend if it happened that way—would need to be watched. Someone could easily take advantage of her. Dr. Hale said Lorelei fit the criteria for attachment disorder. The kid would run up and hug anyone no matter how dangerous or shifty they appeared. Would she ever grow out of that?

She'd walk right into a horrible relationship and not even know it. Harper exhaled out her nose. *I got her covered. I won't let anyone hurt her again.*

Soon after she stirred, the girls woke up.

"Hey," said Madison in a sleepy voice, not bothering to move.

"Morning." Harper lightly scratched at her sister's back. "Sleep okay?"

"Yeah."

Lorelei sat up, blinking dazedly around at the sunlight. "It's too bright."

"Time to get up," said Harper, right before yawning.

"I hate this," muttered Madison into Harper's shoulder.

"What?"

"I gotta pee but I don't wanna move."

Harper chuckled.

Lorelei crawled over them, slithering off the bed to the floor. She pulled open the dresser drawer containing her clothes and rummaged.

Cliff knocked on the door but didn't open it. "'Bout time to get up. Breakfast's ready."

With a resigned groan, Madison rolled off Harper.

"Okay." Harper sat up and swung her legs over the side of the bed, sitting on the edge while the girls changed from their nighties to day clothes—a simple dress for Lorelei, jean skirt and tee for Madison.

Jonathan ran by in the hallway outside.

Madison pulled the door open and the girls raced out. Despite the frustrations of having to share one small bathroom with five people, Madison hadn't yet complained even once, a stark change from how she'd been back home before the war. Somehow, in a house with two-

and-a-half bathrooms, Harper always ended up in the one Madison *had* to use. Part of her wanted to hear her sister scream hurry up just one more time.

Heart heavy, she pushed herself up to stand and traded her nightgown for the jeans-and-T-shirt outfit that had become pretty much her uniform on weekdays. By the time she exited the bedroom, the bathroom lay open, the kids' voices all murmuring from the end of the hall to the left.

I hate that a still-working toilet feels like a luxury.

A few minutes later, Harper entered the kitchen. The kids sat around the table feasting on toast slathered in brown stuff. Cliff had splurged with a small fire to make frying pan toast for a treat. A far cry from pancakes, but it still satisfied Madison's request for the occasional warm breakfast.

"Heading on a scavenging run. Probably be out most of the day," said Cliff. "Expecting to be back tonight, perhaps a little late."

Harper diverted course from an open chair to go around the table and hug him. "Please be careful."

"Hey, if the internet still existed, and you looked up careful, you'd find my picture." He winked. "Now, eat."

She smiled and took her seat. "What's that brown goop?"

Madison *mmm*-ed her approval past a full mouth.

"Good!" chirped Lorelei.

Jonathan grinned. "Yeah. I never had it before, but it's awesome."

"Apple butter," said Cliff. "Last time I had this stuff, I was like your age."

She took her three pieces of bread and smeared some of the stuff on a corner to test it. It tasted quite a bit like applesauce, only with a consistency slightly runnier than jam. Deciding she liked it, she liberally smeared it over the rest of her toast.

"What's the scav?" asked Harper.

"Checking on a bunch of pharmacies up around Wheat Ridge and so on."

She lost her appetite. "Lawless."

"We're expecting contact." Cliff nodded. "Not going hunting, but we're going to thin them out if we can. Makes no sense letting them build up to an unmanageable number."

Mixed emotions swirled around inside her. She didn't want the blue gang to take away the man who'd essentially become her second dad. On the other hand, she didn't mind the idea a few thugs would be removed from the gene pool. Cliff didn't show the slightest bit of worry, so he either expected minimal risk or knew something she didn't.

Deciding to trust him and try not to worry *too* much, she resigned herself to eat in silence.

"Did you have fun on your *date?*" asked Madison in a tone that almost sounded teasing.

"Yeah."

"Kiss him yet?" asked Madison.

"You should know. You were watching us the whole time." Harper started smirking at her but ended up smiling. "Not yet."

"He seems cool," said Jonathan.

"Yeah. He is. Just making sure I trust my feelings before listening to them."

"Good advice." Cliff stood and moved his plate to the sink. "Sorry for running out the door so fast, but we need to get going."

Harper and the kids swarmed him with hugs. He pretend fought the little ones off like Godzilla battling smaller monsters.

"Be careful," said Harper.

He clasped her shoulders, stared into her eyes, and almost seemed to be fighting a grin. "I will. You keep the little ones safe 'til I get back."

What's up with him? He's acting real weird for a scav run. "Okay."

Once the kids finished the last of their breakfast, Harper sent them off to get their shoes and collected the Mossberg from the bedroom. She returned to the front to find all three standing by the door wearing flip-flops. She stared at them for a second, shrugged, and headed out the door with her last piece of toast in her teeth.

The sunny late-spring day greeted her with the chirps of birds, a surprisingly cool breeze, and the continuous thwapping of small flip-flops behind her. Her siblings eagerly chattered about the imminent end of school, looking forward to summer break almost as if no nuclear war happened. Jonathan didn't sound too thrilled with the idea of farm work during the vacation, but Madison countered that none of them had turned twelve yet, so they didn't *have* to this year.

She guided them up the highway, taking Route 74 past the bus wall as usual since it offered a much faster route than weaving around the curvy streets by houses. The little green 'Bergen Park' sign on the side of the road up ahead let her know they'd reached the school. They scaled the chain link fence beside the highway, then crossed a short bit of woods to the athletic field and track, went past the baseball diamond, and around the side of the school building to the front.

Harper hugged each kid in turn and waved as they scurried into the building. She lost herself in a momentary daydream, imagining lines of buses stacked up on the road in front of the school, rushed parents zooming in to drop their oversleeping kids off. After a moment, the scene of ghostly morning chaos gave way to the near total silence of reality.

Lorelei paused at the doors to smile back at her. The poor kid looked as grimy as a child from the news in some foreign country suffering endless war or famine. Hair wild, face smeared with dirt, she'd become the very picture of a post-apocalyptic feral survivor—except for the big grin.

"Have fun today." Harper returned the girl's wave.

"'Kay!" she darted inside.

How is she so damn happy after everything she's been through? Harper kicked her sneaker at the sidewalk, trying to understand how a six-year-old could disregard so much awfulness and bounce back like that. Why couldn't *she* be the same way? Granted, Lorelei probably didn't miss her horrible mother, and in all truth, her present circumstances *were* better than before the war.

"How sad is that?" whispered Harper. She turned away from the school, gazing out over the empty parking lot at the tree-lined streets. "What kind of world did the politicians leave us?" A dark chuckle escaped her lips. "Well, I guess since no one's driving anymore, carbon emissions are way down."

It happened. We're still here.

A chorus of childish laughter came from deep within the building.

Harper managed a smile. "Okay. Enough thinking about sad stuff. Time to play cop."

She crossed the lot to the road and proceeded to walk the streets of the residential area surrounding the golf-course-turned-farm. Her birthday still weighed heavy on her mind, mostly the guilt of still being alive while her parents had died. Tegan, Dr. Hale, said that such 'survivor's guilt' happened to people all the time and she shouldn't be ashamed of feeling that way. Harper didn't consider herself undeserving of life, though. More, she'd become furious with whoever set off the war.

Thinking about Lorelei chipped away at her gloominess. It would probably be a long time before Harper felt truly happy about anything, but perhaps she could allow herself a few moments of joy here and there. She distracted herself with pleasant thoughts, like Madison abandoning the dead phone or finding Renee alive and okay.

People waved from various houses as she passed. By now, all the residents of her assigned area knew her. They all smiled, except for Rachel who eyed her warily. That woman probably still blamed Harper in part for her husband Tommy's death even though she'd been nowhere near him when he died. The guy beat the hell out of his wife. He died because of his own stupidity. No one forced him to pull a gun on Walter. Though, Rachel tended to give everyone the eye these days, so Harper didn't feel too singled out.

An odd—and quite unexpected—sense of contentment came out of nowhere.

Harper had never asked for this life she'd crashed into, but in that moment, surrounded by trees and the quiet of a late-May morning, it almost seemed possible she could accept it.

A LITTLE AFTER MID-DAY, HARPER FOUND HERSELF IN THE MIDST OF A pleasant conversation with Doreen Mack, a former day care owner who also used to live in Lakewood. The woman had a short but stocky frame and a squarish chin that gave her an intimidating presence completely at odds with her personality. Like many people in Evergreen, she'd lost a considerable amount of weight owing to the food shortage from a couple months ago, but remained a little on the thick side. Due to her experience, she'd been asked to look after a handful of orphaned children too young for school.

Three infants and five toddlers made for quite a handful.

A brief rapid peppering of gunfire went off not too far away in the residential area, trailing off to three stray bangs.

"Oh, that doesn't sound good." Doreen's face paled. "Excuse me."

She ran inside to collect the toddlers.

A long 911 air horn blart came from the same direction as the shots.

Shit.

Harper swung the Mossberg off her shoulder and ran down the street. At another series of gunshots, she instinctively ducked. A bullet hissed far overhead, nipping at branches. She spotted Marcie Chapman hunkered down behind a thick tree across another street and up a short hill, taking cover from a building she recognized as the home of Katherine Bowden. A dark figure in one of the windows aimed an AR-15 type rifle past the curtains. Staying low, Harper sprinted up the hill, ducking behind a tree wide enough to shield her, as close as she dared to Marcie's position.

"Marcie," whisper-shouted Harper.

The woman looked back, cringing at another shot from the house blasting splinters from the trunk above her head. "Christ... Stay down!"

"What's going on?" Harper peered briefly around her tree at the house, but didn't trust using a shotgun at that range.

"Ran into two guys carrying rifles, not ours. Didn't recognize them. Asked who they were. Right in the middle of me explaining how stuff worked here, they tried to shoot me, ran into that house, and kept right on shooting at me."

"Lawless?" Harper sounded an alarm tone from her air horn.

"Don't think so. No blue scraps. Kathy's still in there. Heard her screaming."

Grr. First those kids steal from her, now she's a hostage... that poor woman is going to want a different house.

Another shot kicked up dirt by Marcie's foot. A man in a second window fired at Harper, blasting a shower of bark over her hair and face.

"Gah!" Harper jumped back and flattened herself on the ground behind the tree. "What the hell is wrong with them?"

Darnell and Ryan appeared, jogging down the road from the southwest. The same shooter who fired on Harper sent a few bullets in their direction, forcing them to dive for cover.

"Yo, what the hell?" shouted Darnell.

Harper waved until he looked at her, held up two fingers. He nodded. She mouthed 'one hostage,' to which he also nodded.

Dennis and Roy approached from an angle off to the right that would force the shooters to lean out the window to be able to fire. The one who put a bullet into Harper's tree disappeared into the house. The other fired again at Marcie's position, kicking up more dirt.

"Marce!" whispered Harper.

When the woman looked back, Harper made a circling gesture with a finger.

Marcie gave a thumbs-up.

Shots came from the right side of the house. Dennis and Roy dove out of sight.

Harper shifted up into a squat, leaping to her feet the instant Marcie stuck her Beretta around the tree and opened fire at the guy in the window. She ran in a curve across Katherine's side yard, stopping by a huge tree that lined up with the corner of the house. Thicker than an industrial refrigerator, this one looked like it could stop bullets, even 5.56.

Shots came from Dennis and Roy's direction. Inside the house, Katherine continued screaming. Fortunately, she didn't sound pained, merely terrified. Marcie shouted at them to stop shooting and talk.

"Hell with this," yelled an unfamiliar man inside. "There's too many."

Harper sprinted from the tree to the back corner of the house, raising the Mossberg up to cover the back door—which burst open.

A thirtyish guy in dingy suburbanite clothing scrambled out, carrying a Colt M4.

"Drop it!" shouted Harper.

He turned his head toward her, the color draining from his cheeks at the sight of the shotgun pointing at him.

Recognition flickered across Harper's brain. She knew him from… somewhere. Why did he look so familiar?

"C'mon. Drop the gun. Let's talk," said Harper, tensing her finger on the trigger. If that Colt moved even a quarter inch higher…

He blinked. "Skinny mocha."

Two gunshots inside the house accompanied a spurt of blood leaping forward from the man's chest. Dead on his feet, he collapsed in an unceremonious heap.

She cringed, but pushed her feelings aside and advanced to the door, peering around.

Roy Ellis, in the living room, aimed down the hall at her for a half-second before lowering his weapon. Another man she didn't know lay dead on the floor by his boots. Katherine's rapid whispery mumbles came from under the kitchen table.

Harper stepped inside. "Ms. Bowden, are you okay?"

The woman looked up at her. "I think so."

"Clear," shouted Roy.

Dennis, Darnell, and Marcie entered the house via the front door.

Harper relaxed, bowing her head. "What the heck just happened?" She slung the shotgun over her shoulder and crouched to check on Katherine. The woman appeared to be on the verge of passing out from fear, but didn't have any injuries.

Roy walked and checked the guy on the ground outside. He

crouched, set the man's rifle aside, then searched his belt and pockets. "The hell gets into people?"

Satisfied Katherine was okay, Harper crept out to stand by Roy. "Why'd you shoot him? I think he would've given up."

"Both of these guys were firing on us. That doesn't encourage me to talk to them." Roy took an ammo belt off the dead guy. "And yeah, I know you talked the supermarket sniper down, but that guy was defending his stash. These two invaded a home."

"I knew this guy." Harper pictured him in a green shirt, talking to Mom. "He worked at the Starbucks we used to always go to. Scott, maybe. I can't… why the hell is he shooting at us?"

Roy winced. "Sorry. Guess that explains why you didn't take the shot."

"I would have if he tried to point his gun at me. Had him from a blind angle. I… think he was gonna give up, but…" Images of the guy handing her coffee, handing Madison hot cocoa, and trying to tempt Mom with cake pops clashed with the sight in front of her. She had no idea which of the two men had tried to shoot her, and both of them had been trying to kill Marcie.

"No damn idea." Marcie stepped out the back door. "You okay, Harper?"

"Yeah. Just, wow. This guy used to make coffee for us. We saw him a couple times a week."

"People change." Roy stood from his crouch, gathering the confiscated weapons and ammo. "People change faster during war."

"He remembered I always got the skinny mocha." She looked over at Marcie. "How'd it start?"

"Just walking down the street, see these two carrying rifles. They're not militia, so I approached to talk. Told 'em this place ain't for scavenging, settled and such. The guys seemed reasonable until I told them about checking in and they'd have to surrender the rifles to the militia or join it. The one inside didn't like that one little bit. I barely got behind that tree before your barista could shoot me in the face. Kept me pinned there 'til you showed up."

Harper whistled. "That's just so weird. You weren't going to take their guns, they could've walked away and not stayed here."

"Yeah." Marcie closed her eyes and let out a long, slow breath.

Dennis dragged the dead guy out of the house. "Probably means these two weren't interested in settling."

"Yeah." Darnell frowned. "These dudes just opened fire like that? Whatever they wanted, it couldn't be good."

Harper stared at Scott's face for a moment before turning away with a shudder. *So much for things feeling normal.* She clung to the scant comfort that she hadn't been the one to take the life of someone she knew. Still, watching him die jarred her back to a state of lingering unease. No matter how ordinary things in Evergreen had started to feel, running into a man she sorta knew who tried to shoot her offered a stark reminder that the world had forever changed.

Darnell and Ken comforted Katherine inside the house.

"You okay?" Roy put a hand on her shoulder.

"Depends on what you mean by okay. In general, no not really. My life is pretty damn far from anything I ever imagined. But, if you mean here and now? Yeah, I'm okay." She patted his hand. "Guess I'll go grab the cart for the bodies. Should get them out of here before school's done for the day. Don't want kids seeing this. Katherine's got a son."

"Good idea. Need a hand?"

She glanced back at him. "I'm bringing the empty cart here. You can haul it when it's not empty."

"Heh. Fair enough."

Head down, Harper trudged past the house and headed south toward the former municipal road crew garage. Someone had repurposed a flatbed trailer once used to transport small excavators into something that could be dragged along by hand. When Jeanette and her people didn't need it for moving solar panel stuff around, the militia mostly used it for transporting bodies. They'd improvised a new cemetery in the empty land southwest of the Safeway like something out of the Old West, with wooden grave markers—though outsiders killed by the militia usually ended up being cremated.

She stopped in the middle of the road, bent forward, hands on her knees, shaking. The reality of being shot at finally pierced the adrenaline wall. It took her a few breaths to calm down, clinging to the thought she hadn't killed anyone or even fired a shot. Harper straightened, exhaled, and kept walking, hoping that she'd live to see a day where the idea of having to collect random bodies once again felt like something from a movie rather than just another day.

SURREAL

C louds slid across the sky overhead, puffy and peaceful, as if the Earth had forgotten entirely about billions of lives lost only eight months ago.

Her siblings ambushed her on the way out of school with word that the town decided to open the giant swimming pool at the former country club located in the middle of the golf-course-turned-cornfield. Naturally, the kids all begged to go. Not one of them had a swimsuit, but Madison countered with 'no one did,' suggesting they'd swim in their shorts, or in Lorelei's case, dress.

Since she had nothing in particular to do other than keep an eye on her younger siblings for the rest of the day, Harper relented, figuring an hour or two at the pool might offer the kids a much-needed escape. Every one of them could use as much potential joy as possible to hold back whatever mental damage they'd suffered.

They followed a line of kids—pretty much the entire class—straight from the school into the cornfield and past the rows of cornstalks planted on the former golf holes to the country club area. The kids had heard the gunfire from the school, but taken it mostly in stride—except for this girl Emmy who thought the 'sky fire' came for her and had a panic attack. On the walk to the pool, Harper gave them the basic explanation that a couple of bad people started trouble. She didn't tell Madison about Scott the Barista, since she kinda knew him. The guy had sometimes talked with her about dance class while they waited for their order.

Harper made her way around the giant pool and sat cross-legged on a lounge chair, marveling at how the day could start off with a home invasion and gunfight in the streets then proceed from there to the kids wanting to go swimming. Real life decided to compete with her 'toast dream' for surrealism. Corn stalks surrounded the pool area on three sides. To the north, paving led out to a parking lot repurposed into a solar farm.

The pool managed to survive both the past winter and nuclear war in reasonably good shape. Its water even still smelled like chlorine, though no one expected it to last too much longer since they couldn't exactly buy more chemicals, though the attached maintenance garage had a decent amount of supplies stocked up.

Despite a lingering chill in the air, the kids had summer fever with the idea of school ending next week. It seemed every resident of Evergreen between the ages of six and sixteen had learned the town decided to remove the pool cover today and wanted to jump in.

Only a few people wore actual swimsuits as they hadn't been a high priority for scavenging. Most of the kids had on shorts or jumped in wearing their skivvies, except for Lorelei the extreme case. She decided to go full on nature child and toss *all* her clothes on the ground by the lounge chair, running off giggling fast enough to avoid Harper's attempt to grab her. Two boys a little younger than Jonathan took inspiration from that and decided to keep their clothes dry as well.

Harper inhaled a breath to yell at her about putting her dress back on, but chickened out. She still couldn't bring herself to do 'angry mom' with her. *She's had such a crummy life... I really shouldn't be letting her run wild, but I can't stay mad at her.* The other kids didn't seem to react much except for a few laughs. Some parents shot Harper disapproving looks, but no one said anything.

I'll talk to her once we're home.

Mortified, Harper kept quiet, watching the kids playing in the water. Some threw an improvised Frisbee back and forth, others swatted a volleyball around. Sadie Walker from the militia kept an official eye on things. She'd come prepared for lifeguard duty in a one-piece blue swimsuit, though she wore a towel around her shoulders to ward off the chilly breeze.

Mrs. Wheatley, mother of seven-year-old Robin, walked up, chuckling. "That girl of yours sure is a free spirit. She's going to rekindle the hippie revolution."

"Yeah. We've apparently gone hillbilly." Harper blushed again. "She had it rough before. Her mom neglected her pretty bad. Basically ignored her. Kinda think she was allowed to run around with nothing on most of the time. That poor kid has no idea what normal is. I'm trying like hell to fix her, but I just don't know what to do. Yelling at her makes me feel so damn guilty. It's a battle keeping clothes on her."

Mrs. Wheatley laughed. "Robin was the same way at three, but she grew out of it. She absolutely *hated* clothes."

"Oh, Lore doesn't hate them. She just… doesn't care one way or the other." Harper smirked off to the side, remembering Mom embarrassing her with stories of how she'd been a 'nature girl' too as a toddler.

"Kids, right?"

"Yeah. I should probably yell at her for ignoring me, but she's so brittle I'm afraid to. I don't want her being afraid of me like she feared her mom. And look at her… she's so happy. I'd feel like a complete monster if I made her cry."

Mrs. Wheatley pondered. "Definitely going to have your hands full with that one."

"Yeah." She smiled. "That's true."

"It's a bit cold today. Might not want to let them spend too long in the water." Mrs. Wheatley gazed up at the sky. "Can you believe we're having a day at the pool after everything?"

Harper chuckled. "I know, right? I'm still not convinced I'm awake right now. Of all the things we could be doing to survive, this feels so weird. Like we're wasting time we should be doing something else."

"Time spent to soothe the soul is never wasted. It does them good. No point always being glum, even if that old Grim Reaper is hiding around the corner. Surprised you're not going in."

"Nah. Wet jeans suck. And... my underwear is white. I'm a little too old to pull a Lorelei. Skinny dipping is cute at six, feels totally different for adults. Besides, I don't want to leave this shotgun sitting here unattended."

Mrs. Wheatley grimaced. "Ooh. Yes. White would be a little, erm, revealing when it got wet."

Harper chatted with her about the school, the summer break, and the oddity of Evergreen's particular mixture of surreal and normal. Aside from the majority of kids not having actual bathing suits on, no one looking at the scene in front of her could have imagined most of the world's population had been incinerated so recently.

It made no sense how a seemingly normal guy like Scott the barista who'd handed her coffee countless times with a smile or a joke could have ended up trying to kill Marcie, possibly even shooting at Harper. She didn't know which one of the men fired on her since both had M4s. Mostly, she thanked whatever powers that be for not making her kill a man she knew. He appeared to remember her at the last minute, but if Roy hadn't shot him, Scott might very well have called her bluff and pointed his gun at her.

She didn't want to think about that, knowing she would have shot him if he made her.

As much as she thought Roy should have waited to see if Scott surrendered, she felt grateful to him for sparing her the need to kill a man she sorta knew.

Madison leapt up out of the water and punched the volleyball back over an imaginary net, whooping and laughing at making a save. The sight of her having fun got Harper crying from relief and happiness. Whatever moments like this they could find, she'd savor. And, she'd fight as hard as she could to give her siblings every chance at innocence the world had left to offer them.

This is so weird. I can't believe we're sitting at a pool right now. What's normal supposed to be anymore?

A slender dark-skinned boy of about twelve walked by, a pair of soaked khaki cargo shorts struggling to cling to his hips without falling off. He paused to look at her with a hint of recognition in his eye, backed up, and sat on the chair to her left. "Hey."

She nodded in greeting... *He's one of the boys who'd been stealing food.* "Hey. T-Bone, right?"

"Naw. Just Terrence now." He grinned. "Dropped the old street name. The 'hood's gone. So, you think them rich bastards what used ta run this place be looking at us kids contaminating their pool and freakin' out?"

Mrs. Wheatley smiled at him. "Hello, Terrence."

Harper tracked the volleyball zooming around the pool. "Maybe. But it's not like money means anything now."

"Yeah, exactly. My Momma said the greedy sons o' bitches what nuked us did it 'cause they got all the money and didn't need us no more."

"The bombs killed them, too."

Terrence stretched. Water trails ran down his bony chest past a set of dog tags, clearly not his due to his young age. "'Cept the ones with big-ass underground mansion-bunkers."

She chuckled. "You really think that's true?"

"Maybe." He offered a noncommittal shrug. "The one-percent wouldn't have let them hit the button if they didn't have a place to hide. What I heard, the East Coast didn't get much warning. Even bein' two hours ahead of us, they didn't even have 'nuff time ta panic before the skies burned."

Harper looked down. The nukes hit Lakewood minutes before six in the morning. People in the East Coast would've been on the way to school and work if not there already when everything went to hell. "Yeah. Maybe that ended up being better. Everyone on the road trying to escape the cities would've caused traffic jams. They all would have been right out in the open with no cover."

"You gotta figure the government knew shit was goin' down. Kinda messed up of them they didn't give us no warning."

"At that hour of the morning, who would have noticed?" Mrs. Wheatley shook her head, frowning.

Harper stretched her legs out straight. "Yeah, but what would've been the point? Everyone would have had what, fifteen minutes of complete panic and terror before dying anyway? Though it is kinda strange that so many people are missing from Evergreen. Didn't this place have a couple thousand people in it? Now it's like 400. Where'd they all go?"

"They had some warning," said Mrs. Wheatley. "I forget their names, but this couple who lived here had a son or something in the Air Force. The boy called with a warning to get somewhere safe. Good number of people figured this area would get lit up big due to Cheyenne Mountain up north, so they wanted to get on the far side of the Rockies. Army came through a couple days after the blast, took more people off to survivor centers. We lost a bunch more when the prisoners attacked."

"Prisoners?" asked Harper, wide-eyed.

Mrs. Wheatley's eyes brimmed with tears. "About a week after the strike, a couple hundred inmates from the SuperMax showed up to loot. Walter Holman calls it the First Battle of Evergreen. He and some of the sheriff's deputies put up enough of a fight that the inmates moved on, but we lost around ninety people. A lot more didn't feel secure here after that, so they picked up and left. My husband Neal died keeping Robin and me safe."

"I'm sorry." Harper bit her lip.

"There isn't anyone in this place who hasn't lost someone. Thanks, hon. You don't have to feel sorry for us. You got your own sorrows to live with."

"Them Lawless sons of bitches got my momma," said Terrence in a voice barely over a whisper.

The patter of small feet approached.

Lorelei walked up, dripping. "I'm tired."

Harper tried to grab her with a towel, but she zipped away, running around the end of the lounge chair to hug Robin's mother. "Hi, Mrs. Wheatley." She darted back to hug Terrence. "Hi!"

He chuckled. "Hey, kid."

Lorelei grinned and plopped down to sit beside Harper, casual as anything.

Harper wrapped her in a towel-hug. "Your lips are blue."

The girl peered up at her with an expression that said 'duh, it's chilly.'

Jonathan climbed the ladder and walked over, having to hold his waterlogged shorts up. He still looked underweight, but at least neither he nor Madison remained dangerously thin.

"Maddie," called Harper. "It's been about two hours… time to go home."

"Okay!" Madison dove under, swimming toward the ladder.

"Well, you folks have a good rest of the day." Mrs. Wheatley stood and approached the pool edge, calling for Robin to also get out of the water.

The kids waved at her.

"See ya later." Terrence got up and jumped back into the pool.

Yeah. What a day all right. Harper toweled Lorelei off then dressed her like a toddler. The child's quiet shivering made her worry the girl had gotten more of a chill than she admitted.

Crap. Please don't get sick.

A SMALL LIGHT IN THE GREAT DARK

Lorelei tolerated becoming a blanket burrito after they got home. She snuggled up on the sofa while Madison and Jonathan played a board game on the living room floor. Harper rattled around the house doing her best to clean without a working vacuum and limited supplies. The house had some cleaning products from the former owner, but they wouldn't last much longer. Someone, somewhere had to know what people used before the invention of Lysol.

She paused in scrubbing the kitchen sink to wonder how far back civilization would slip before recovering. Two generations forward, would anyone even remember things like computers, airplanes, working cars, or video games? Or would society revert to a bunch of barely-dressed primitives running around with spears and living in tents? Everyone laughed at Lorelei streaking the pool before, but sixty years from now, would that be normal? Did enough people inside the former United States even remember *how* to make clothing? Or cloth? Harper couldn't think of where cloth even came from besides 'the store.'

Dad used to complain that no one made anything here. Everything came from like China or something.

Of course, people made their own things back in the day, but the colonists also came from a world where that had been the norm. Everyone alive in the US at the moment simply went to a store or ordered stuff online. One thing going to a new country and bringing knowledge along. Totally different to be dependent on industries that ceased existing. Eventually, perhaps not in Harper's lifetime, there wouldn't be any more clothing to scavenge. At some point, the houses would eventually collapse. People would have only what they could make out of scraps.

Why am I depressing myself by worrying about crap like this? I won't be around. She frowned, picturing herself as a barely mobile old woman navigating the overgrown streets of Evergreen while teens in animal hide ponchos carrying spears emerged from tents to run off on a hunting expedition.

Okay, now I'm taking things a little too far. This isn't a movie. Society will rebuild itself. We're more likely to recreate the Wild West than turn tribal.

Becca and Mila arrived, which precipitated the kids all migrating out to the backyard.

She didn't expect Cliff would be home early enough for dinner, so she planned on cooking at the normal time. They had a few things in the cabinet he could eat without too much prep, or he could always stop at Earl's for whatever they had available. That place had taken on the burden of feeding single people. The quartermaster instituted a policy of issuing limited food to people without families, basically providing breakfast they could eat at home but asking them to go to Earl's for lunch and dinner. It both made distribution of resources easier and saved on firewood.

After a passable attempt at cleaning out the bathroom, Harper flopped on the couch to rest. She stared down at her hands, wondering how on Earth her mother had managed a real job plus chasing two kids around, plus her half of the housework... until Harper hit about twelve and the chores began mounting. Her mother had been superhuman, even willing to grab a pistol and kill people to protect her children.

Dammit, Mom. I miss you guys so much. Harper grabbed a pillow off the couch and cried into it for a while, trying to stay quiet so the kids didn't hear her and become sad, too. Every argument or fight she'd ever had with her parents came to mind and set off another wave of grief. She apologized over and over in her mind.

At the creak of the back door, Harper hurriedly composed herself. Figuring her eyes would be red, she fake sneezed a few times to generate a believable excuse for it. Madison walked around the end of the couch, sat next to her, and clung.

Oh, no. "What's up?"

"Nothing," muttered Madison.

Harper put an arm around her. "Okay." *Maybe this is SUC. Spontaneous unexplained clinginess. No, 'suck' is a bad acronym.*

Madison squeezed tighter.

"Did something scare you?"

"No."

"Not a bear, is it?"

Madison shook her head.

"Did someone say something mean?"

"No. I'm sorry."

"What for? You don't have anything to apologize over."

"Your birthday is in a couple days." Madison sniffled, then peered up at her. "I'm sorry 'cause I'm happy you're not gonna ever move out to college or get married and go away somewhere I'll never see you again."

"Aww." Harper hugged her tight. "I'd live at home forever if it would bring Mom and Dad back."

"But it won't… I know they're gone." Madison wiped her eyes. "Is it okay that I'm happy you're gonna stay with me? I feel bad 'cause it's kinda like also being happy they died."

"Not the same thing at all, Termite. And yeah, you can be happy that I'm gonna be here for you."

Madison smiled. "Sorry for being a little baby."

"It's okay to be emotional. We had a rough year."

"Yikes." Madison rolled her eyes with a teary chuckle. "Just a little.

We had *way* more than just a 'rough' year. I should be in therapy, but all the therapists are dead."

Harper snickered. "Well, that works. We don't have any money to pay them."

"Heh."

"Seriously, if you want to talk to someone, Dr. Hale's there."

Madison peered up at her, pale face framed in long jet-black hair. "Nah. I've made a deal with my mental trauma. It's only allowed to bother me in nightmares now. Not when I'm awake."

Harper ruffled her hair. "Right."

The floor lamp by the front window came on.

Madison went wide-eyed, staring at it. "Harp..."

"Whoa. Is that light on?"

Cheers rang out in the distance. Something went *bang* like a celebratory firework, but she doubted whatever exploded had been meant to.

"Ooh!" Madison spun around, kneeling on the couch while facing backward. "The stove's lit up."

"Eep!" Harper leapt to her feet intending to sprint for the kitchen, but stopped herself once she realized her little sister meant the clock, not the cooking coils. She ran to the wall and hit the nearest light switch. Ceiling lights in the kitchen came on. Madison dashed down the hall to the bedroom, emitting a squeal of delight when the lights worked. She zipped across the hall and turned on the one in the bathroom.

"Hey," called Harper. "Don't waste elec—holy crap, the electricity's on."

Madison dashed to Jonathan's bedroom and turned that light on, then ran down the hall to the living room, crashed into Harper, and started bouncing around in circles with her, cheering. They ran around the house together for a few minutes, turning stuff off and on. Predictably, the television didn't have any signal—but it came on.

"Oh, whoa... the EMP didn't fry this TV," whispered Harper. "Lucky."

"Not so lucky." Madison turned it off. "TV's no use without channels."

"Yeah."

Madison looked up at her. "Are we seriously freaking out like we won a free trip to Disney World because light bulbs work?"

Laughing, Harper said, "Yeah, we are. Wow, turning on the light used to be such a nothing thing to do."

"How messed up is that? We're screaming about the lights." Madison frowned. "They nuked Mickey Mouse, didn't they?"

"No idea. Nothing's on the news."

"Butt." Madison stuck out her tongue.

"Maybe they did. Symbol of capitalism and all that."

"Huh?"

Harper headed down the hall to turn off unneeded lights. "Something Cliff said. But I guess that would only be true if some communist country nuked us."

"How long is the power gonna stay working?" Madison stood in the hallway, watching her go from room to room.

"Not sure." Harper leaned into the bathroom to kill the light and stared at the bathtub. *Hot water. No more bucket boiling.* She closed her eyes. *Oh, please let the solar system work for years.* "Umm. We probably shouldn't expect it will last forever. I think solar panels go bad after a while... and the whole power grid is basically loose wires run around town by people taking their best guess at what to do."

"Dad would've said the same thing about before." Madison emitted a mirthless laugh.

With the wasteful lights off, Harper headed back to the couch... and stared in disbelief at the floor lamp. "I wonder if this is how people felt in 1800-whatever the first time they saw electricity."

"Probably not." Madison trailed in and sat beside her. "They wouldn't have seen electric lights before. We grew up thinking it's no big deal, then lost it. To us, it's like a sign the world isn't completely broken anymore. To them, it would've been something new and weird." She did a funny 'old person' voice. "I don't need that new-fangled electricity. My candles and oil lamps work just fine."

For the second time in ten minutes, something happened that made Harper gawk. Madison displayed her old sense of humor. The kid had cracked a joke. Her goofy side poked out from under the cloud of gloom. Harper laughed despite the tears welling in her eyes, and made a silly face.

"What in tarnation is that infernal thing?" asked Harper in a 'little old lady' voice.

Madison laughed.

"That's funny." Harper wiped her face.

"What are you crying for now?"

"Laugh tears."

"Harp, you're still a bad liar."

She poked Madison in the side. "I don't want you to make fun of me for being squishy."

"But you *are* squishy. You cry when people step on bugs or kill mice in traps."

"Mousetraps upset you, too."

Madison folded her arms. "Stop changing the subject."

"I'm just happy the lights came on… and seeing you happy kinda got me."

"Aww. You're right. You're squishy." Madison flopped against Harper.

Harper raspberried her.

They sat together for a few minutes in silence. Madison seemed happy or content, Harper's mood swirling between joy, guilt, and worry. *I really need to stop feeling like I'm doing something wrong whenever I catch myself being happy. Losing Mom and Dad wasn't the end of the world… Oops. Yeah, it was.* She bit her lip at the dark humor.

"I hope it keeps working for a long time." Madison fidgeted.

"Me, too. We're good until the solar panels quit. Or something else goes wrong."

"Do you think the entire country is gone or are there enough people left to fix it?"

Harper gazed at the ceiling, trying to piece together an opinion based on things she'd overheard here and there. It didn't sound terribly good in terms of getting back to anything resembling the civilization they knew within their lifetimes. The Army people said the East Coast had been wiped out, same with major cities on the West Coast. It make little sense for anyone to waste nukes on Third World countries, so perhaps enough civilization remained in parts of the globe to seed the redevelopment of certain technologies. But, even then, it would take a long time. What had been the USA could evolve into multiple different nations as easily as attempt to put the Union back together. Perhaps they'd even be invaded by the military from like Nicaragua or Guatemala or one of those places. Or even Mexico if no one sent nukes down there. Perhaps the old government had thought about such an eventuality and nuked Central America out of spite.

"Hard to say, Termite." Harper fussed at her sister's hair. "Everyone is probably still just trying to survive at this point. Cliff said the biggest threat after nuclear war is starvation. Most of our food came from the Midwest, the fancy stuff from overseas. There's no ships anymore, most of the cars are dead, smashed bridges, no trains." She shuddered at the idea of survivor groups possibly resorting to cannibalism if they had no other source of food. *The blue gang is going to need to start farming or they'll die out. If they find out about Evergreen, they're gonna attack us. Maybe that's why Scott went nuts. Starving people do crazy things.*

Madison clutched the small sofa pillow. "That's kinda scary."

"Yeah. We're kinda isolated in the mountains, so who knows what's going on in the rest of the country. I don't really care to go exploring, either."

"Me neither. I just wanna be safe."

"Yeah. So do I." Harper sighed at the ceiling.

"Are people gonna work together or steal from each other?"

"Both. There will always be people who think stealing is easier."

Madison looked up at her. "Should I be scared?"

"We shouldn't live in fear all the time, but we need to be careful."

"Okay." She huffed. "Nuclear war is stupid."

Harper poked her again. "Talk about understatement."

"Are we gonna run out of food? Mr. Rollins said the smoke shortened the growing season."

"What?" Harper asked, trying not to sound as frightened as that question made her.

"During farm school, he said the explosions lit fires and made a lot of smoke and stuff. It's gonna make everything a little colder and less rain, so plants won't grow as long. That's why they made the farms so big even though there aren't that many people here. An' there's no bug killing stuff anymore."

"I think he's talking about what could possibly happen, but it might not be that bad. The corn is growing, and the sky isn't *too* hazy. Might not be that way all over the world, but we could've been lucky here."

"We'd be luckier if stupid people didn't push stupid buttons."

"That, I agree with."

Jonathan walked in. "Maddie?"

"Here."

He came around the side of the couch. "What's up? Oh, holy crap! The light's on!"

Harper smiled. "Yeah."

"Guys!" Jonathan ran to the back door. "Guys, come here. Check this out!"

"I should get started on dinner," said Harper. "About that time."

Madison grinned. "Hey. We have clocks again, but I don't think it's one in the morning. What time is it?"

"No clue." Harper patted the cushion twice, then stood.

Lorelei, Becca, and Mila walked in, grilling Jonathan about what got him shouting. He pointed at the bulb.

The house filled with squeals.

Harper cringed, though couldn't help but laugh. She headed to the kitchen to get started on dinner, leaving the kids to run around the house again. As soon as she opened the cabinet to stare at the dwindling supply of cans, she found herself dreading that something horrible would happen soon. Madison had acted silly. The power came back on. Too many good things too close together. This new world always seemed to punish happiness. Nothing nice occurred without subsequent punishment. She'd thought the only teenage boy left in the world liked her, then he tried to kill Madison. Later, when a whole busload of teenage boys arrived, she avoided all of them. Except maybe one. But what would go wrong next? What would the world do to jam the knife in a little deeper because she'd dared to smile today?

Cliff went out on a scavenger run. She bowed her head. *No. Please, no.*

HIDDEN THREAT

Three long air-horn blasts sounded outside.

"Dammit," whispered Harper. "Fire."

The kids rushed into the kitchen, all staring up at her in fear.

She spun to face them. "Calm down. That's a fire alarm. I gotta go check it out."

Madison grabbed her arm.

"No one's shooting at anyone. It's only a fire." Harper squeezed her. "C'mon. I gotta go."

She rushed outside, not bothering to grab the Mossberg from the bedroom. The .45 on her belt would provide enough defense for a fire scene... hopefully.

"Carrie?" shouted Harper.

Their next door neighbor appeared in a window of her house. "Yeah?"

"Fire call. Can you please watch the kids?"

"Of course. Be right there."

Another three-long tone sounded in air horn.

Harper waited the minute or so it took Carrie to hurry outside and cross into the yard, told her the Mossberg sat in the bedroom if she needed it, then ran toward the commotion. She followed Hilltop Drive to the highway and crossed Route 74 into the trees to the southwest. Shouting, more air horns, and smoke led her to a house relatively close on the south side of Elk View Drive, perched up high on a hill, nearly half engulfed in bright orange flames already.

Militia members ran back and forth between it and three houses across the street, running buckets of water up and down the big hill rather than follow the winding driveway. Harper scrambled down the hill, heading for a red-walled house. Someone in the chaos handed her a big orange bucket. She carried it inside, waiting in line to fill it from the bathtub. Dennis Prosser moved away from the tub with a full bucket, scooting past her to the door. She held her bucket under the water, but by the time it filled three-quarters of the way, she doubted she'd be able to carry it completely filled, so decided to leave with it mostly full. With a grunt, she hauled it up and stumbled outside, sloshing and splashing after the others.

Trudging straight up the steep hill with the heavy bucket wouldn't work, so she followed the driveway, an easier, albeit longer, path up to the top. By the time she reached the house, flames belched out from the second-floor windows like the breath of dragons. She followed the others heading for the front door. Unprepared for the blast of intense heat, she mostly closed her eyes, held her breath, and dashed in long enough to fling her water at a burning patch of wall a few steps inside before fleeing from the heat.

Back down the hill she went for more water.

Three grueling trips later, the entire upper story glowed with flames. Annapurna, Deacon, and another man she didn't recognize held full buckets, but didn't approach the door. Harper hesitated with them.

"Hang back!" shouted Walter. "It's too dangerous. Buckets aren't gonna do this. Too late. Everyone stay out. That's an order."

Harper backed away until the heat radiating from the house ratcheted down from scary to annoying, and set the bucket on the ground. Since she wouldn't be throwing the water on the fire, she crouched and scooped a few handfuls into her face to cool off.

Walter hurried around to the various militia personnel there. Eventually, he approached Harper. "Hey. This is gonna burn itself out no matter what we do. Just focus on keeping people at a safe distance, okay?"

"Okay. Will do."

He nodded at her and ran over to give the same order to Annapurna.

Harper retreated from the burn even more, then put her back to the house, standing guard in case someone tried—for whatever reason —to go inside. Upon noticing Dennis at the top of the driveway not too far from her, she walked over to him.

"Hell of a thing," muttered Dennis.

"Yeah." She peered over her shoulder at the fully-engulfed house. "I hope no one's in there."

"Nah. Jimmy got out. Said he's the first one to come home from the farm and found a fire in the back. The other three guys he shared the place with hadn't been here yet. Sounds like the circuit breaker or some such. Guess you figured out by now that Jeanette flipped the switch. North part of Evergreen's got power. Either they're running the voltage a little hot, or when the transformers blew up on the poles during the attack, it melted something inside this place."

"Yeah, maybe..." She cringed at the thought. *Crap. Is our house gonna burn, too?* "At least no one got hurt, right?"

"Truth." He patted her on the back.

"Aww, son of a bitch," muttered Cliff.

She gasped and spun, near to screaming with joy at seeing him alive and back from his scavenger run in one piece.

Cliff came tromping around the side of the burning house, an empty water bucket in each hand. He looked more angry than anything else.

It took every ounce of self-control Harper had not to run over and pounce-hug him. *He's okay!* He paused by Walter for a short conversation to complain about them just turning on the master switch before going around to every house and making sure the breakers in each one had been shut off, or at least scheduling it with an announcement asking people to be home to catch crap like this before it burned out of control. Walter mumbled something she couldn't hear over the roaring flames, but it seemed to placate Cliff enough that he nodded and walked over to her and Dennis.

With him in arms' reach, she couldn't resist any more and grabbed him.

"Hey, kiddo. Good to see you, too." Cliff dropped the buckets and returned the embrace. "You okay?"

"Sorry." She let out a huge sigh of relief and ceased clinging to him. "Just bad thoughts. The power came back, Madison actually made a joke, and I thought the universe would punish me for being happy by doing something bad. You were out on a scav..."

"Ahh." He chuckled. "Never did believe much in that woo woo stuff. Thinking about that'll drive ya crazy."

"You're sure no one was in there?" asked Harper.

"Yeah, few of us got here before it went up big. Checked it m'self." Dennis gestured at the inferno. "Shame to lose such a nice place, but no one's hurt."

Harper leaned against Cliff, staring into the blaze and wishing as hard as she could their new home didn't burn like this. Of course, even if it did, it's not as if they'd end up homeless and broke. Anne-Marie Marbury would simply assign them to a new building. "You're gonna check our breaker panel when we get home, right?"

"You bet." Cliff spat to the side.

Other guys he lived with... oh, crap. "Dennis?" Harper grabbed his arm. "Who else lived here?"

"Some single guys. Uhh, Jimmy, Hank, think there's a Rob."

"Logan?" Harper tensed.

"Aww, no. He's all the way down the end of this road where it loops back around. They're assigning people along this street in the order they arrived in town. Them boys is fairly recent."

"Oh, whew." She sagged with relief.

"Wait, you're dating this kid and you don't know where he lives?" Cliff raised an eyebrow.

"Shouldn't you be happy I don't know where he lives? That means I haven't gone to his room unsupervised."

He put on a stern 'Dad face,' but a twitch in his lips from fighting a smile made it amusing rather than scary. "You make a good point."

Timber, perhaps the second story floor, collapsed inside the house with a loud *crash* and a massive belch of sparking flames into the sky, glowing orange snow going upward into dark indigo. She jumped, gasping, and stared in awe at the spectacle.

"Hope they had insurance," muttered Cliff, again spitting to the side.

Dennis shook his head, chuckling. "That ain't right, man."

EVENTUALLY, LITTLE REMAINED OF THE HOUSE BUT A GLOWING PILE OF embers and timber.

By that point, someone had arrived dragging the 'body cart' loaded with hose from the fire station. They'd also brought the necessary tools to open the hydrant all the way down at the end of the road some 400 feet away. The hose crew sprayed the remains of the house until it stopped glowing. Walter sent the four guys who'd been living there to the quartermaster to pick up some additional clothing as they'd lost everything but what they had on.

Harper and Cliff walked home together, arriving after dark—but the inside had plenty of light.

"Feels so strange having working electricity again," said Harper.

Cliff held the door for her, then stepped in, closing it. "That it does. Almost like a dream."

"Is our house going to catch fire?"

He glanced around with an unreadable expression. "If it was going to, it would've already lit up. But I'll check the panel."

"Eep."

Madison, Jonathan, Lorelei, Renee, and Carrie entered via the back door. Evidently, Becca and Mila had already gone home for the night.

"What happened?" yelled Madison. "Can we eat now? I'm starving."

Lorelei looked up at her. "No you're not."

Everyone stared at each other in uncomfortable silence.

"Umm." Madison cringed, guilt all over her face. "Sorry. You're right. I mean I'm really hungry."

"Don't be sad." Lorelei hugged her. "Be happy you're not really starving."

Harper closed her eyes, trying not to think about how close they really all were to literal starvation. Any of a dozen different things could go wrong with the farm and that would be it. She still didn't quite trust the fish from Lake Evergreen, but perhaps the mountains between here and Denver shielded the water from collecting too much fallout.

"Wow, you're like a cop and a firefighter, too?" asked Renee.

"Not really. Buckets didn't help much." Harper rubbed her sore arm. "Some guys evidently raided a fire department for hose and tools, but it took them so long to get there, the house was a lost cause."

"So what happened?" Jonathan leaned on the counter.

"A house caught fire. They think the circuit breaker panel burned when the power came on. It might've been damaged from EMP. But no one got hurt. Just lost a building."

Carrie and Cliff murmured with each other in the living room. She seemed mildly annoyed at him, but he merely smiled at her. She said something to the effect of him being too sweet for his own good, though Harper couldn't eavesdrop too effectively while surrounded by loud tweens.

"So can we eat yet?" asked Lorelei.

Cliff entered the kitchen, sniffing the air. "So what are we cooking tonight?"

"It's a bit late to start a fire, isn't it?" asked Harper before realizing she already smelled ravioli.

He grasped her head gently in both hands, turning it so she stared at the stove—which held a simmering pot. "I think we can save some firewood tonight."

"Oh, duh…" She whistled. "I didn't even think about the stove working."

"Already heated food." Jonathan smiled. "But we waited for you to come back."

"We brought a couple cans since we'd be eating over here tonight." Renee lightly kicked the 'empty can bag' by the counter, which clattered.

Harper patted him on the head. "Nice. You guys could've had dinner. Just save me some, but I appreciate you wanting to wait."

"Hey, we could even keep like deer meat in the fridge for a while now." Jonathan pointed at it.

"Eep." Madison grimaced.

"Or fish."

"Fish doesn't keep that long even in a fridge. And it makes everything else in the fridge smell like fish." Carrie scrunched her nose. "But we do have freezers. Though, I'd like to wait and see how stable the power is before trusting them. Nothing stinks as bad as rotting meat left in a freezer you didn't know conked out."

Harper and Carrie went for the pot of ravioli at the same time. They locked eyes. A sudden sense of deference came out of nowhere, as though the woman had already started to fill in the hole Mom left despite being a bit younger at thirty-four. Mom would've been forty-three this year.

"I can get it if you don't mind, hon," said Carrie.

"Oh, umm. Sure. Thanks." Harper backed off and took her seat.

Carrie portioned out food for everyone.

Madison shot Harper a look under flat eyebrows that could mean resentment at the woman trying to be Mom as easily as it might've been questioning if the woman had intended to come off that way. Harper tried her best to send an 'it's okay' with her eyes. The challenge in her little sister's expression lessened.

For the rest of dinner, Harper wondered what would have happened to them if their parents had died to something like a car accident instead of looters after nuclear war. Would the courts have made Harper be adopted at seventeen, or would she have ended up on her own with Madison? Dad made a mortgage paid off joke soon after the bombardment, so she definitely would've lost the house to a bank.

No way could a seventeen-year-old have earned enough money to pay for a house, at least not with any legal job. So, if she *had* been adopted or forced into foster care, the people would have been doing her a massive favor. Of course, she would have been grateful to them and not resentful that they tried to be her parents.

Harper decided to appreciate Carrie's attempt to become part of their family. She clearly had feelings for Cliff. Perhaps tonight had been a test to see how the kids would take to the idea. So far, the siblings appeared either accepting or oblivious except for Madison who'd already forgotten whatever mood hit her earlier. They couldn't use Lorelei's reaction, since the girl adored everyone. Though, she *did* insist on clinging to Harper at night, so perhaps that meant something.

I used to hate this canned crap. She stared at one of the mass-produced raviolis on her plate. *Once we finish this batch, I'll never see this stuff again.* What had once been cheap, mass-produced laziness now felt like a near delicacy. Harper took her time eating, sectioning each piece into four small bites to make it last as long as possible.

"What are you doing?" asked Madison.

"No one's gonna make this stuff anymore. Once it's gone, we'll never have it again. This is like filet mignon now."

Jonathan's face said 'oh, wow.' Lorelei didn't react at all. Carrie and Renee both appeared saddened at that thought.

"That doesn't mean we'll have no food. Just not this particular form of processed stuff." Cliff ate a whole pillow in one bite.

Jonathan and Madison started talking in fake fancy voices about their ravioli as though they'd gone to a super expensive restaurant. Harper laughed at the silliness so she didn't cry at the truth of their situation. Living in a constant state of dread at what would happen five minutes into the future had to be as unhealthy as the radiation she worried hung all around them.

Smiling felt like a lie, so she kept her head down, hiding her face behind her hair while eating in small, slow bites, savoring the canned pasta as though she'd gone to a thousand-dollar-a-plate restaurant.

PLAYING THE ODDS

After dinner, Harper sat on the couch with *The Secret Garden*, attempting once again to read it. At least, the return of electric light made it less hard on the eyes. The kids sprawled on the rug playing a board game while Cliff sat in his recliner, also reading—only Carrie sat half in his lap. Renee curled up on the right end of the sofa, holding a book, but her head kept nodding forward. She'd probably be asleep in minutes.

Harper's luck with that book held up. She'd barely gotten four pages deeper into it before Grace knocked and poked her head in.

"Hey. Am I interrupting?"

"Nah." Harper replaced the bookmark and set the novel aside. "What's up?"

Grace entered and flopped on the couch at her left. "Bored. Just wanted to hang out. Kinda freaking out over seeing lights on again."

"Yeah, me too." Renee sat up, also setting her book aside and seeming much more awake at the concept of doing something other than reading. "I hope the people who don't have it yet aren't gonna get mad."

"It's only the north part of town at the moment." Harper tried to remember the map in the militia HQ. They haven't connected anything south of Stagecoach Boulevard yet. Jeanette and her people still need to make sure the system they put together can handle stuff."

"Lot of the power lines here and west of 74 are underground," said Cliff. "The wires should be okay. The transformers are the tricky parts."

"Yeah," muttered Harper. "They're more than meets the eye."

Cliff looked around. "Need something to throw."

Harper chuckled.

"I heard they're going to link the school in, combining the panel system there with the rest of it." Grace examined her hands.

"Something wrong with your fingers?" asked Harper.

Grace looked up. "No. It still feels weird having normal nails instead of French tips. And I mean, I *don't* miss it. Mom always demanded I look perfect."

"Ugh. Sorry, that sounds annoying." Renee picked at her nails. "But I'd rather have reliable food than electricity."

"Electricity helps there be reliable food. We can use freezers and fridges again." Cliff peered over his book at the girls. "Assuming, of course, we have luck with hunting... and the panels don't break down in a week."

Harper cringed. "It is kind of a small solar farm even if there's only like a hundred occupied houses connected to it. I guess we should expect it'll crap out at some point."

"People managed to get by without electricity for centuries. If need be, we can do it again." Cliff turned a page. "The world still had some places without it even before the war."

"Oh, guys... Did you hear? Beth is pregnant." Grace fidgeted.

"That's shocking," deadpanned Harper. "I hear them going at it three times a week when I'm walking around on patrol."

Cliff coughed. Carrie whispered something that made him cough louder.

A few minutes of general gossiping about what Beth and Jaden would do occupied them for a little while. The way they talked to each other after Harper caught them together in an unassigned house, she figured they'd stay together. The boy did seem genuinely in love with her.

"I'm kinda worried about that," whispered Renee. "We could like *die* from getting knocked up now. Like back in the 1970s before they had real hospitals."

"Don't you mean the *1870s*?" asked Harper, suppressing a laugh.

"Whatever." Renee rolled her eyes. "That's what I meant."

"The 1970s were dark times indeed." Cliff shook his head. "Disco..."

Carrie laughed.

"That's a hundred year 'whatever.'" Grace made a pinchy gesture. "Quite a bit of difference in medical technology."

Harper looked at her. "How bad is it? You're working with the doctors now, right? What did they say?"

Grace exhaled, lips fluttering. "I'm so overwhelmed with reading stuff that I'm not really paying attention to what they talk about except for when they are deliberately trying to instruct me or bring me in to observe a patient session. But, I think having a baby is still reasonably safe. The biggest problem we'd have here would be certain complications like internal bleeding, sepsis, or like pre-eclampsia. Stuff we don't have the right meds for or the surgical facilities to really deal with."

"So, like, how deadly are babies now?" Renee gnawed on her finger.

"Depends on what kind of weapons they get their hands on," muttered Cliff.

Carrie swatted at him. "That's not funny."

"I dunno really." Grace stood. "You'd have to ask one of the doctors. Things probably aren't going to be any worse than underdeveloped countries before the war. Then again, the US did have a shamefully high maternal mortality rate for a superpower. Be right back, need more water." She walked past the arch to the kitchen.

"So, basically, it's like cowboy times again... just without those ridiculous dresses?" asked Renee. "People still had babies back then and humans didn't die off."

"Yeah," called Grace from the kitchen. "But people had like a dozen kids just so three made it to adulthood."

"It can't be *that* bad." Harper twisted to peer at her over the sofa back. "We still have some medicine left, right?"

Grace returned carrying a full water glass. "We lived through a nuclear strike. We're all gonna get cancer and be dead by forty."

"Your friend is morbid," said Madison.

"It's not that bad." Cliff lowered the book away from his face. "The average age of survivors from Hiroshima was around eighty. I remember reading a study showing they died an average of about four months sooner than citizens in unaffected areas."

Harper blinked at him. "That's kind of a weird factoid to have at the tip of your brain."

"You ever work security?" Cliff's expression remained serious. "You make two friends. Coffee and the 'random article' button on Wikipedia."

Everyone except for the kids laughed. Madison and Lorelei ignored the remark while Jonathan looked up, confused.

"But, yeah, some stuff like that I had to know back in the Army."

"Just kinda weird to think about," said Harper in a low voice, trying to leave the children out of the conversation. "Never really thought about a penis being a literal deadly weapon."

Grace sputtered her water laughing. Renee covered her mouth.

"Mostly…" Harper looked at Grace, dropping her voice even more to a near whisper. "I'm worried about them." She pointed with her foot at the kids.

"They should be fine." Grace smiled. "Unless they're shot or eaten by bears. They're old enough to have gotten their vaccines, the important ones anyway. It's our kids and their kids who are going to be in trouble. One bad part about being back in the 1800s is we're probably going to see a resurgence of diseases that we once considered relics of the past."

Harper cringed. "Not so sure about…" She nodded toward Lorelei before whispering, "That girl's mom didn't care enough to keep her clothed. When the strike happened, she just took off and left her alone. I doubt her mother bothered with vaccines."

Grace frowned. "Aww. How could anyone be so cruel? I just wanna hug her."

Lorelei sprang to her feet and jumped on Grace. "Okay. I like hugs!"

"Your..." Grace paused. "Is she technically your sister or daughter?"

"Somewhere in between." Harper made eye contact with Carrie, still in Cliff's lap. "Kinda daughter-y now."

"Cool. Anyway, she is totally adorbs." Grace hugged the little one. "Ruby at the med center was asking how she's doing."

Harper reached over and ruffled Lorelei's hair. "She's doing much better."

The lights faltered, winked out for a second, and came back on.

"Eep." Madison looked up. "That was scary."

"It's wires, not ghosts." Jonathan made a move on the board game. "Lore, your turn."

Lorelei reluctantly stopped clinging to Grace and scrambled back to the board game.

"I talked to Anne-Marie about making clothes. Apparently, the library here has some books about how people used to do that stuff by hand. I gave myself homework." Renee frowned. "Designing and stitching, no problem. Making actual cloth from fibers? That looks like a serious pain in the butt."

Grace chuckled. "Trade ya."

"Pass." Renee held her hands up. "I thought I wanted to be a nurse for a while, but ugh. I didn't realize how nasty it could get. Doctor stuff is not for me. I can't handle gross."

Flickering lights are scary even without ghosts. Harper stared at the floor lamp by the front window. *We're an inch from losing electricity for good. The nukes might've made it cold enough that the farm fails. Fish from the lake could be irradiated, and random jackasses could show up with guns at any time.*

Evergreen started to feel like a death trap until she remembered sleeping on trash bags in an enclosure behind a fast food place. The whole country had become dangerous. Had she not come here, the Lawless or some other gang might get her. Or starvation. Or stumbling blind into an irradiated area. No, all things considered, she really had found an oasis of safety... at least as much as anywhere could be considered safe anymore.

Here, she could sleep at night without being so scared she woke up every fifteen minutes to look around. But she still couldn't shake the pervasive feeling of fear that snuck into her thoughts whenever she didn't think about anything in particular.

Whether they knew it or not, her two sisters would be pulling duty as stand-in teddy bears tonight.

SURVIVAL

Two days passed in relative quiet. Electricity had gone out on Thursday for a few hours while she'd been patrolling. Something blew up with a bang at the old public works garage Jeanette had turned into the town's power center. Whatever exploded must not have been too big a deal, since they had the juice back on before dark.

Friday warmed a bit and saw another pool visit. Though, this time, Harper had been prepared for Lorelei with a little help from Renee's sewing skills. Her friend scavenged fabric from an adult one-piece into a pair of two-piece suits for Madison and Lorelei. She'd also stitched a bikini for herself out of scrap fabric. The quartermaster's didn't have much in the way of swimsuits, but Harper did find *one* in her size: a way-revealing neon green two-piece that would've made Dad faint and Mom scream 'no way.' She'd never have worn a suit that skimpy in the normal world, but all the other ones there would've fallen straight off her. And despite how much skin she showed, it somehow wound up being less embarrassing than swimming in her underwear, and *far* less embarrassing than skinny-dipping.

That, she might someday do with Logan, alone, off in a woodland stream somewhere with just the two of them. Certainly not in a public pool with kids around.

Lorelei offered no protest to wearing a suit. She evidently didn't prefer skinny-dipping as much as simply didn't want to get her dress and underwear wet. If Harper went too long without washing laundry, and her stuff smelled too bad, Lorelei would simply traipse about in her birthday suit instead of putting on a dress dirty enough to smell from across the room. Fortunately, the squalid conditions in which the child had lived before the war gave her a significantly higher tolerance for filth. What the girl considered too smelly to wear would make Harper gag.

She decided to jump in the water as well, since she wanted to enjoy it before the water became unusably dirty. While she didn't know how much chlorine or whatever remained in the storage garage, it didn't feel likely that the people who knew how to look after a pool would be able to keep it clear for much more than two or three seasons. A few of the hockey players fake cringed away from Harper in a bikini, yelling about being blinded. She flipped them off, smirking, and spent a couple hours trying to have fun with her siblings.

For the briefest moment, she almost stopped thinking about the war and allowed herself to smile.

SATURDAY MORNING, CLIFF LED A SURVIVAL EXPEDITION INTO THE woods west of town, heading toward an area Fred Mitchell—who'd been on sniper detail at the bus barrier—called Snyder Hill. Carrie, Mila, and Becca joined them.

About fifteen minutes of walking later, Cliff pointed at a fallen tree that looked like it had been there for quite some time. "If you see something like this, keep in mind it's a good source of fatwood."

The kids laughed.

"What the heck is fatwood?" asked Harper.

"It's the hardwood core of a dead pine tree—or any hardwood tree really—impregnated with resin. Scrape some shavings of that onto kindling and it makes starting fires much easier. New fatwood is sticky with sap, but it eventually dries out into resin. So long as it's not wet, it doesn't really matter how sticky it is. The stuff will burn quite well."

The kids nodded.

Cliff crouched by the log and pulled it apart with his bare hands, the old, damp wood crumbling easily. He attacked a spot where a thick branch intersected the trunk, using his combat knife to clear away the outer layers until he had a roughly banana-sized hunk of pale, dense wood. "This is still a bit wet from the last rainfall, but once it dries out, it'll be good." He handed it to Jonathan.

The boy looked it over, then passed it to Mila.

Cliff pointed at a plant with broad heart-shaped leaves. "Do any of you know what that is?"

"Poison ivy?" asked Lorelei.

Chuckling, Cliff shook his head. "Nope."

Five small blank faces, and two not-so-small blank faces stared back at him.

"Weeds?" asked Carrie.

"And this is why we're out here." Cliff patted the leaf. "Come, take a closer look so you can recognize it. This is burdock. The taproot is edible. If you catch one with flower buds, those can be eaten before they bloom. Kinda taste like artichokes."

"Blech," said Jonathan.

"Artichokes are good." Madison patted her stomach. "I like them. Much better than meat."

"But plants don't scream when you cook them." Mila grinned.

Everyone stared at her. Madison gasped.

"I'm just teasing. Really." Mila put on an innocent face. "Seriously. Just a joke."

"Thought you were giving up on the creepy thing?" Harper playfully swiped at her hair.

"I am. But that moment was too good to miss." Mila snickered.

Madison continued staring at her.

"Come on, Mads." Mila poked her in the stomach. "I don't really want to make animals scream."

"I like animals, too." Becca bounced on her toes. "But I don't wanna starve. Wolves and lions eat other animals, so it's not 'against nature.' If we *have* to eat meat not to die, it's okay."

Madison sighed, reluctant acceptance in her eyes. "I guess."

"So… the stalks are edible, too. But you have to peel them first. They can even be eaten raw." Cliff stood. "Leaves as well, but they get tougher the older the plant. Of course, if we are eating wild burdock, we're not going to be worrying too much about how it feels to eat. We are in need of food."

The kids all nodded.

Cliff resumed walking into the forest. "Dandelions are another possible food source."

"Eww, really?" asked Becca. "They're weeds."

"Yep." Cliff scratched his beard while looking around. "You know it might not be a bad idea for us to start supplementing our diet with some of these plants on the side. We could use the extra calories, plus it'll get you used to them." He stopped walking. "Aha!"

Everyone jammed to a halt, bumping into each other.

He indicated a low-lying plant with small, waxy, teardrop-shaped leaves and a faintly reddish hue to the stems.

"Is *that* poison ivy?" asked Lorelei.

Cliff chuckled. "It isn't. This is purslane. The leaves are edible raw." He plucked a few, handing them out, also eating one to demonstrate.

Madison tossed it in her mouth without hesitation. "I think I've had this before."

The somewhat sour, salty flavor made Harper salivate, and cover her mouth to keep from dribbling. "It's strong."

Mila and Jonathan tried test nibbles, then ate their leaves. Becca took the longest to try it and made the worst face of the lot.

"That Greek place." Madison crouched and plucked another leaf, which she ate. "They had this stuff in the salad there. Or at least something that tasted like it."

"Could have been purslane," said Cliff. "Some Greek places use it."

"But they're not running around the woods to collect it, right?" asked Becca.

"Nah. Commercial farming. But, that's kinda gone now." He waved for them to follow and kept going.

Cliff wandered in no particular direction for some time, pointing out other plants like chicory, pennycress, and wax currant. He described Oregon grapes, though they didn't see any, then cautioned them not to eat any berries they weren't absolutely sure of identification. Upon spotting some chanterelle mushrooms, he mentioned those could be eaten as well.

"Wild mushrooms can be dangerous. Again, if you're not absolutely sure what you're looking at—especially with mushrooms— better to leave it alone. Avoid any 'shroom that has a skirt or ring on the stalk or any part of it is red in color."

The kids exchanged looks, seeming nervous.

"Don't panic. Remember, I'm showing you this so you can be prepared in case something goes wrong."

"Like nuclear war?" asked Mila.

"Okay, if something goes *more* wrong." Cliff gestured off to one side. "We've got the farm, some animals, lake fish as well. I don't want to promise you we're going to be perfectly fine, because anything can happen. But odds are in our favor that it won't come down to us *needing* to rely on wild growth any time soon. Don't freak out if you don't remember all this stuff right away. It takes time."

Jonathan relaxed visibly, as did Madison.

Harper found herself wishing her phone worked for the first time in months, so she could take pictures of the 'good' plants.

"Is *that* poison ivy?" asked Lorelei.

Everyone turned to look where she pointed.

"No, that's wood sorrel. If you dig it up, you'll find a tuber like a small potato, which you can eat. The leaves are edible as well."

"How do you remember all this?" asked Harper.

"Heh. When you know that certain information can save your life, the brain makes room for it."

While they continued hiking, he rambled about survival training on the way to become an Army Ranger, back when he'd been twenty or so, before Harper had even been born. Upon finding another fallen tree, he crouched and pulled at the bark, exposing a cluster of squirming white insects.

"Grubs," said Cliff. "The larval stage of beetles. These are also a good source of protein."

Becca gagged. Madison clamped a hand over her mouth. Carrie looked about ready to pass out. Harper cringed at the thought.

Lorelei tried to grab one.

Cliff caught her hand. "Not raw, hon. Bugs can easily have parasites and need to be cooked first."

"I'd eat them." She smiled. "I eated bugs a'fore. Used ta catch 'em in my room."

Madison bit her arm to muffle gagging sounds.

"Best way to cook grubs is to skewer them and roast 'em over a fire until the skin goes crispy." Cliff pinched his fingers to his lips like an Italian chef.

"Ugh, I'm gonna hurl," muttered Becca.

Cliff set the hunk of wood back down, covering the grubs. "Look for rotting logs or behind the bark on trees where it's separating already."

Harper clenched her jaw. *I'd have to be* real *damn hungry to eat grubs. Gah.*

"Grasshoppers are good eats, too. Best to pluck the heads off, which will pull their guts out. That helps reduce the chances of there being a parasite or nematode."

Becca gagged again. "Ugh. Please stop."

"It sounds disgusting until you're starving. And I don't just mean 'Dad, can we have dinner I'm starving.' I mean real starving."

Lorelei appeared frightened for a second, then clamp-hugged him.

He rubbed a hand up and down her back. "It's okay. No one's gonna let that happen to you again."

She mumbled something inaudible into his chest.

"So, grasshoppers, crickets, ants, termites, wood lice—which taste like shrimp—are good, too."

"Lice?" Madison shivered, scratching at her hair.

"Not that kind. Umm... what the heck did we call them as kids, oh 'roly polies.'"

"Still eww." Madison stuck out her tongue.

"Okay, okay. C'mon." Cliff backed away from the grub log. "We can save the bugs for an emergency of absolute last resort."

"Please," said Becca.

They walked around in no great hurry for a while, Cliff quizzing everyone on plant identification. Lorelei kept asking if everything she hadn't seen before was poison ivy. Eventually, they happened upon a small stream, where Carrie asked if they could take a break and sit for a while.

The kids removed their shoes and waded into the shin-deep water, squealing at the cold. Harper, Cliff, and Carrie sat on the ground nearby while the kids explored the creek, collecting shiny rocks. Carrie stretched out and leaned against Cliff.

"Any water you find out in the wild should be boiled before you drink it," said Cliff. "Unless you've already gone three days without any water and don't have a way to make fire, it's better to be safe."

Harper kept half her attention on the kids, the other half on the woods around them. The shotgun might not have the range of a combat rifle, but it did tend to make people hesitate. As much as she'd like to think being this close to Evergreen meant safety, she didn't.

The kids whispered amongst themselves about the horribleness of eating bugs, at least until Lorelei piped up.

"I eated a few bugs when I's alone. They tasted like squirmy legs. Hard part was tryin' ta bite 'em afore they crawled outta my mouth."

Jonathan paled. Becca doubled over and retched. Madison grimaced, tongue out.

"Okay, that almost made *me* throw up." Mila held her hands up. "Can we stop talking about eating bugs now?"

Cliff chuckled, then muttered, "Hell of a thing. Starbucks and PlayStation one week, giving serious consideration to slurping down some beetle larva the next."

Harper's stomach gurgled. "I think I'd rather starve."

"Heh. Trust me. When you're at that point, even grubs look good."

Everyone all got the idea to stop talking at once. Harper watched the kids amusing themselves in the stream, taken by how relaxed they appeared. Not one complained about being outside in the woods or missing video games, phones, electronics, or whatever. She couldn't remember ever kicking off her shoes and wading into a random stream… though she did step into the fountain at the mall on a dare once.

"Is this how it used to be before technology?" asked Harper. "Like kids just playing out in the woods?"

"No idea." Cliff flashed a wry smile. "I'm not *that* old. Though, yeah, probably was something like this. Sticks made good toys, but they had some stuff back then I think. Wooden trains, dolls, jacks or some such."

Around a half hour later, Cliff called the kids out of the water. After a delay for feet to dry and bathroom breaks, the hike resumed.

"More plants?" asked Harper.

"Nah. I'm about ready to circle back to town. Just figured I'd make a loop around in hopes of finding a deer or something."

"Can we not?" Madison squinted up at him with the sun in her face. "I really don't want to watch you shoot an animal. Bad enough I have to eat them."

"No one's forcing you to watch."

"You know what I mean." Madison scowled at the ground.

Harper rested a hand on her sister's shoulder. "I'll take her off a bit so she doesn't have to see it."

"But I'll hear the shot. You're not gonna get me far enough away that I don't hear it."

"Plug your ears?" Jonathan made a silly face, fingers in his ears.

"Why does everyone wanna kill animals?" Madison stomped.

Cliff stopped walking and crouched to eye level with her. "We don't want to 'kill animals.' We want to 'not die.' We've had this chat before."

"I know." She stared down. "I'm eating it, aren't I?"

"Hey what's that?" Mila pointed.

"Is it poison ivy?" asked Lorelei.

"No, doofus. It's like a house or something." Mila jumped on the nearest tree and climbed higher. "Yeah. It's a small house."

Cliff gazed in that direction. "Hmm. Yeah. You guys wait here. I'll go take a look."

Harper gathered the kids into the undergrowth and crouched with them.

"Be careful," whispered Carrie. When Cliff turned toward her to respond, she kissed him.

"Ooh," whispered Madison.

"I will." Cliff winked, raised his AR-15, and stalked off toward the unknown building.

Carrie joined Harper and the kids.

Upon spotting a green caterpillar on a tree, Jonathan picked it up, holding it so it walked in an endless loop between his hands.

Minutes later, Cliff called out, "Clear. There's no one here."

Harper stood. Carrie and the children followed her in single file through the trees toward his voice. She soon found a trail worn into the ground that led down a mild slope to a clearing in front of a structure somewhere between a small house and large cabin. Walls of plywood stained and varnished rather than painted framed a boxy structure with a passable attempt at glass windows. About forty yards to the left of the building, a suspicious lump of vegetation resembled a pickup truck. Someone had either hidden it under camo netting, or it had been there for a *long* time.

Harper descended the hill. As she neared the cabin, the smell of damp wood overpowered the earthy scent of the forest. By the time she reached the door, the cloying reek of spoiled meat added to the bouquet.

Since Cliff had entered the place already, she walked right in, holding her breath.

A single large room took up most of the building's space; however, it had two interior doors, one at each corner of the back wall. An open area on the left contained an ancient cloth sofa and a recliner that had seen better days, patches of foam visible where the upholstery had ripped open. On the right, a small round table stood in front of a tiny counter with an electric range and steel sink.

She let the air out of her lungs and risked a slight inhale. The bad meat smell pervaded the room, but not to the degree it made her nauseous. Nothing appeared obviously rotten—stove clean, table clean, sink clean—so she eyed the fridge.

"No one open that freezer," said Harper. "Or that smell's going to get ten times worse."

Madison and Mila headed over to search the cabinets by the kitchenette and started gathering canned goods out onto the floor. The sight of the girls reacting to soup, Spaghetti-Os, and baked beans like kids on Christmas morning rooting around under the tree made Harper choke up.

Jonathan went for the left door while Lorelei amused herself by jumping on the sofa. Harper checked the door on the right, nearer the kitchen—and discovered the most cramped bathroom she'd ever seen. The miniature toilet faced to the right, pointing at the shower stall. It looked uncomfortably small for anyone older than twelve. Most of a roll of TP hung from the ceiling on a loop of wire above the commode. If she sat on it, her legs would be in the shower stall. The itty bitty sink in the near-left corner didn't have enough room to bathe a housecat.

Worse, the bad smell appeared to be coming from that tiny room. Or at least, stronger in there. She cringed away, not daring to lift the toilet lid out of fear of what she'd find under it.

"Wow. They converted a closet into a bathroom."

"Dad," called Jonathan from beyond the other door. "There's like guns and stuff in here."

"Don't touch anything," said Carrie.

Madison hurried over with Cliff to the room Jonathan went into. Harper followed.

A space about half the size of her new bedroom contained an improvised plywood worktable with an odd metal machine that appeared to be hand operated via a lever on the side. Four rifles plus over a dozen handguns of various types hung on pegs on the wall above it and to the left. Two metal shelves on the right held boxes upon boxes of ammunition as well as cans of gunpowder, boxes of primers, and loose bullets in varying calibers.

Oh. That must be a reloading machine.

Cliff whistled. "Nice."

"We shouldn't touch anything." Carrie leaned on the doorjamb. "Someone could still own this stuff."

"Where are they?" asked Jonathan.

"I, uhh, wouldn't worry about it," muttered Cliff.

"Maybe Scott and that other guy lived here?" asked Harper.

"Who?" Carrie peered at her.

"Umm. Two men who shot at us last week."

"Oh." She shrugged. "Maybe. Or they just went out hunting."

Jonathan climbed up to stand on the worktable and lifted a large, black rifle off its pegs. "Whoa. This is like a space gun."

Cliff moved up behind the boy, bracing hand at his back so he didn't fall. "That's a PSG-1. Sniper rifle. Not cheap. Hmm. The guy who lived here had some money. FN-FAL, two AR-15s, two AK47s, .30-06 bolt action, 7mm Remington Magnum. Good grief is that a .454 Casull?" He plucked a huge revolver off its pegs. "Heh. It is. This will ruin someone's day, though it would be better used for hunting bears."

Jonathan set the PSG-1 back where he found it. "We should probably not be in this room when the owner comes back or he'll think we're stealing from him."

"Could be a woman. You don't *know* it's a guy." Harper folded her arms.

"Whoever lived here had a .454." Cliff held up the revolver. "Notice the chamber's got *five* holes? Not saying it's impossible a woman would use this gun, but it wouldn't be my first guess. And the, umm. Never mind."

Harper gave him a 'what?' look, but he cringed and gestured at the kids.

Jonathan jumped down from the worktable and opened the doors of a cabinet beside it. Eight large cardboard boxes sat inside it, one opened. "Whoa. MREs."

Madison screamed, sounding as if she'd gone outside and around behind the house.

"Shit!" Harper spun on her heel and sprinted across the outer room to the door.

"She just found the body," deadpanned Cliff.

Once outside, Harper veered left since the continuing screaming seemed louder in that direction, and went around the corner of the cabin. Madison dashed toward her, jumping into a hug before exploding in a storm of tears.

"What?" Harper aimed the Mossberg at the corner of the building, ready to end who or whatever frightened her sister. "What's wrong?"

Carrie ran up behind her, Cliff walking after, seeming unbothered.

Mila hurried around the far corner from the back of the house where Madison had been. Harper twitched, but held her fire. The girl seemed a little paler than usual, but not visibly upset.

"There's a dead guy on the ground. Madison almost stepped on him. Does that mean we can take the stuff in the house?"

Harper slouched with relief, lowering the Mossberg. *Ugh. That stink isn't bad meat in the freezer.* Cliff walked past her. She slung the Mossberg over her shoulder, freeing up both arms to hold Madison. Having no interest in looking at a dead person, Carrie remained with them, sorta-hugging them together. Jonathan also walked to the far corner.

"Jon, stay back here," said Carrie.

"It's okay. I've seen dead people before." He peered around the corner. "Oh. That's not too bad."

Metal clattered.

Madison quieted, still shivering a bit, but stopped crying. "So disgusting. He's like purple."

"Poor son of a bitch. Talk about unlucky." Cliff came back around the corner into view. "Guy probably fell off the roof and broke his neck. Still holding a screwdriver. Either that or he decided to have a heart attack right when he reached the top of the ladder."

"There's a shovel in the gun room." Jonathan looked at Cliff. "Should we bury him?"

"Yeah. That'd be the right neighborly thing to do wouldn't it." Cliff handed his AR-15 to Carrie. "Hang on to this for a bit? Burying him is the least we can do in trade for that arsenal."

"Okay." Carrie took the rifle. "I have no problem making a body if need be, but stickin' them in the ground is past my tolerance. That smell's already getting to me."

"I'd say you get used to it, but ya really don't." Cliff chuckled and headed back inside, Jonathan scurrying after him.

Curious, Harper crept to the end of the wall and peered around in such a way as to prevent Madison from seeing. The dead man lay on his back, close enough to the wall that both his boot heels rested against it. His face and hands—the only exposed skin on him— appeared greenish black with smears of purple in places. A long, wild beard and decay made it difficult to determine his exact age. Older than Dad, but not elderly. She figured fifties or early sixties. His thick insulated vest over a lighter coat suggested he'd been dead since winter. Small rips in his jeans and gnaw marks on the face and hands hinted at opportunistic small animals.

She swallowed bile and turned away. "Ugh. Poor guy."

Cliff went by carrying a shovel. Jonathan accompanied him, wielding a much smaller collapsible military-green shovel. They stopped about fifty paces from the house in a patch of open dirt.

"This looks good." Cliff jabbed his shovel in the ground, stepped on it, then looked toward Harper and Carrie. "Why don't you guys go inside, gather up anything useful. Food. Clothes. Ammo. Tools. Whatever might come in handy. Pile it up in the middle of the room and we'll figure out what we can take back to town with us."

"I could go get the big cart the militia always uses to move dead people." Mila tossed her hair off her face with a quick sideways nod.

"Don't run off alone." Carrie put an arm around her.

"We're not taking the dead guy to town," called Jonathan.

"Not for him, for the heavy stuff inside." Mila huffed in exasperation. "And, if there are bad guys out here, they'll come from that way." She pointed north, and swept her finger around to the southwest. "Not between here and town. And I know how to hide."

"Ehh, not really enough of an emergency to take the risk." Cliff tossed a shovelful of dirt aside.

"I got from my house to yours in the middle of the night when the shadow men ran around trying to kill me." Mila folded her arms. "I think I can handle going to fetch a pull cart. There's a lot of guns and ammo, and they're heavy."

Harper put a hand on Mila's shoulder, but looked at Cliff. "Are you saying we should take the food first, then come back for the weapons and ammo?"

He leaned on the shovel. "Community is great and all. But those MREs would go a long way to buying peace of mind. You know on airplanes, how they used to say secure your own oxygen mask before helping the kids? Can't help anyone if you're delirious. Thinking those MREs might be our oxygen masks."

Eight months ago, Harper would've been aghast at his suggesting they keep the food in the cabin for themselves. But, she understood his reasoning. Having a cushion of emergency food *would* be nice—especially to safeguard Madison, Jonathan, and Lorelei. "There's nine cases. Do we take them all? What if we hit a rough patch and people are starving? Do we give them out? Could you look people in the eye, watching them get thinner and thinner while knowing we had food hidden away?"

"No. That's not what I mean. I..." He hung his head. "Nine cases of MREs over the entire town will be gone in one or two days. Twelve meals per case, but they're about 1,300 calories each. In desperate times, we can ration them to one a day. They wouldn't be much help if spread thin over the whole town. Not even one meal for everyone there. But, yeah... it would be damn hard to look someone in the eye."

"Looter's Privilege." Harper smiled. "We keep one case for emergencies. One to Mila, one to Becca's family."

"Is Carrie our family yet?" asked Lorelei.

Cliff busied himself digging. "Speaking purely in legal technicalities, she gets her own case."

"Technicalities, huh?" Carrie walked over to him, careful not to look at the body when she passed the corner of the house.

Harper's mood brightened. Invoking Looter's Privilege for an up-front claim on one box of emergency food didn't feel like being crappy to people. "Great. Let's go get the cart."

"I can make it back to town." Mila furrowed her brows. "I'm sneaky."

"You couldn't even move that thing. It's a trailer designed to carry small excavator machines. I can barely pull it." Harper's hands hurt from the memory of dragging the cart to Katherine's house the other day.

"Why don't we use the truck over there?" Becca pointed at the lump of 'vegetation.'

"It's dead." Harper glanced at her.

"You don't know that. Did you even try to turn it on?" Becca started walking toward the camo-covered vehicle.

"No way in hell are the keys inside that thing." Harper pointed at the corpse. "They're probably in his pocket. And the truck is toast."

Becca stopped, cringing. "I don't wanna touch a dead guy."

"We're way out in the middle of nowhere here." Cliff squinted up at the sky. "Possible it could start assuming the fuel's not rotted. Worth trying at least."

"Okay, but I'm not checking his pockets." Harper shuddered.

Even Mila backed away as if hoping not to be asked to do it.

A tug pulled at Harper's belt.

She peered down at Lorelei.

The little platinum-blonde sprite grinned up at her and dangled keys. "Onna table by the couch."

Cliff paused digging. "Go on and give it a try."

"Right…" Harper marched over to the camo netting.

Yeah, this thing is as dead as civilization.

It took her a few minutes to remove the concealment, which she bundled up in a wad and tossed aside to reveal a Chevy pickup that had to be older than her, spray-painted camo, with oversized, knobby tires. She couldn't quite tell if the guy did the paint himself or it might have been an actual Army truck, since the bumper looked heavy duty and had a round metal plate with the number 384 on it.

"Hmm." She opened the door and climbed in.

The interior looked so basic and utilitarian that she decided it *had* been an actual Army truck. Probably super old since it didn't have a CD or even a cassette player. She slid the key in, smirked, and turned the starter. When the low rumble of an idling diesel engine filled the silence, she almost screamed in shock.

"Holy shit!" yelled Harper. "It works!"

Lorelei slid down off the roof to stand on the hood in front of the windshield. She thrust both hands into the air and shouted, "Holy spit works!"

Laughing, Harper cut the engine and jumped out. "C'mon." She plucked Lorelei off the hood and set her on her feet. "Guys! Start grabbing everything useful."

9

ONE NIGHTMARE AT A TIME

Harper lay in bed that night, awake and replaying the afternoon ride over and over in her head.

Driving a truck through untamed woods proved to be both a challenge and an amazingly fun time. Cliff let her take the wheel since she'd only had her license for a little while before the war. As much as she wanted to keep the vehicle, she didn't even ask. A working diesel truck needed to go toward the benefit of the entire town. Though, being on the militia, she might wind up driving it again at some point, or at least riding in it.

They didn't make good time, little faster than walking while weaving around trees, but the truck—which Cliff called a CUCV, or civilian utility cargo vehicle—allowed them to carry all the canned goods, ammo, guns, MREs, toilet paper, some clothes, and a few other miscellaneous items in one shot.

Walter had been saddened to learn of the death of a man he believed to be Arthur Green, something of a local hermit who had been out there for several years. He'd been friendly in town but didn't like people near his home. The guy evidently had a few demons left over from Iraq where he'd served overseas.

No one objected to them claiming Looter's Privilege on a box of

MRE's each, and the militia had been thrilled at the infusion of ammunition and weapons—not to mention a truck ripe for conversion to take biodiesel.

She clung to her sisters, half protecting them, half seeking comfort herself. Too many worries swam around in her head to allow sleep in easily: starvation, radiation, attacks, the Lawless gang, what became of her friends, and lingering survivor's guilt over her parents' deaths.

Eventually, the warmth of a cozy bed and two small bodies cuddled up to her lulled her into a bleak dream of wandering endless fields of rubbled city. Madison, Jonathan, and Lorelei called her name repeatedly from every direction at once, leading her through the ruins.

Madison screamed from right beside her. In her dream, Harper spun to find her sister standing there in a nightgown, mouth wide open, shrieking for no apparent reason. The instant Harper grasped the girl's shoulders, she snapped awake to find Madison screaming for real.

"Maddie?" Harper sat up and pulled her into an embrace. "Shh. It's okay. You're safe."

Madison clung, her screaming fading to soft sobs.

The bedroom door opened. Cliff leaned in, one eye open wide, the other still closed.

"Nightmare," whispered Harper.

Cliff nodded, emitted a zombie-like moan, and backed out, closing the door.

Lorelei didn't react, not even a twitch.

Harper sat there holding Madison for a while, sometimes gently rocking her, sometimes patting her back or squeezing her arm. Eventually, the girl stopped crying and stared into space.

"Wanna talk about it?" whispered Harper.

"I gotta go to the bathroom."

"Okay." Harper relaxed the hug.

Madison stared at her, pleading.

Oh, boy. That must've been a good one. She nodded, eased Lorelei to one side, and slipped out of bed with Madison, who refused to let go of her hand until they closed the bathroom door.

"Don't watch. Just… be here."

"'Kay." Harper turned her back, 'standing guard' at the door.

A moment later, the toilet flushed. Madison walked up beside her. "Sorry for being a scaredy cat."

If I don't pee now, I'll have to go an instant before I fall asleep. Grr. "It's fine. The stuff we've survived, *I* should be having nightmares, too. Sec. Gonna pee."

Madison turned her back to wait.

Once finished, Harper took her sister's hand and walked with her to their bed. Madison curled up at her side, head resting on her shoulder. As if sensing their return in her sleep, Lorelei rolled back into place under Harper's left arm.

"It's totally fine to have bad dreams and freak out," whispered Harper. "We saw… you know."

Madison shivered. "Yeah. Thank you for protecting me. It's really scary now. I'm like constantly afraid and I hate it. I want the world to go back to normal. Is it ever gonna feel safe again? I wanna wake up from this nightmare."

A gurgle slipped out of Harper's throat, her heart nearly breaking at those words. Warm tears fell from her eyes, rolling down the sides of her head to gather in her ears. "I dunno, Termite. I'm doing everything I can to keep you safe, but… I can't say that we'll ever feel safe again like we used to."

"I know." Madison clung tighter.

Harper squeezed her hand. "Hey, at least we don't have to worry about being hit by cars anymore."

"That's not really a good thing. I'm sorry you can't go be a party girl at college."

"Hah. Me? Party?"

Madison emitted a whispery chuckle. "Thanks for keeping me safe. Sorry you had to shoot people. But I'm glad you didn't let them hurt me."

"I'm going to say something sappy."

"Shocking."

Harper smiled despite tears still running from her eyes. "You're the only reason I didn't just give up after Mom and Dad died. I *had* to protect you. And now, I've got Jonathan and Lorelei, as well."

"Are we gonna make it? Starving sounds really bad."

"We're working on it. It's not going to be easy, but there's no way I'm going to give up."

Madison managed a feeble smile. "I promise I won't still be a little wimp when I'm grown up."

"You're not a wimp, Termite. You're the toughest ten-year-old I know."

"I'm not tough. That's Mila. She threw a knife at some guy's eye —twice."

Harper brushed Madison's hair off her face. "Everything we've seen, and you're still able to smile right now... you're as tough as it gets."

"You, too." Madison's lip quivered, but she didn't cry again. "We should go to sleep before Cliff yells at us."

"Good idea." Harper closed her eyes and waited.

Sleep. Yeah right.

10

A BOX OF GHOSTS

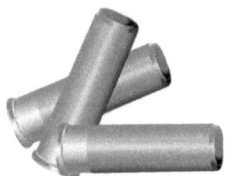

Saturday, June second, 2019 started like any other day after the end of the world.

Harper and Madison both overslept a bit, but it didn't matter since neither of them needed to be anywhere specific that day. By the time she'd had enough of lying awake in bed, hit the bathroom, got dressed except for shoes, and walked out to the kitchen, Cliff had left the house. She emerged from the hall into the dining room area between kitchen and living room and stopped to yawn a few times. Jonathan sat on the sofa, reading a book on plant identification.

"Hey." He twisted around to look at her. "Cliff had to do some militia stuff. He said you don't need to worry about it and he'll be back soon."

"Okay." She trudged over to the kitchen and reached for the cabinet above the sink for some of the box cereal they had left.

A scrap of whitish pink caught her eye to the right: a small nightgown on the floor by the back door.

Not again.

With a sigh, she peered out the window over the sink at the yard, where Lorelei sat in the grass playing with some old Barbie dolls. Neither the six-year-old nor any of the dolls had a scrap of clothing on. Shaking her head, Harper set the cereal on the counter and stepped to the door, leaning outside.

"Lore!"

The girl looked up, smiling.

"C'mere."

Lorelei sprang to her feet and ran over, a Barbie in each hand. "Morning!"

"Why is your nightgown on the floor?"

She swayed side to side. "Daddy said I couldn't go outside wearing it."

"Why are you naked?"

"'Cause I don't have anything on."

"Why are you *outside* naked?"

"'Cause Daddy told me not to go outside with a nightie on."

Harper face-palmed. "Please, go get dressed."

"Okay." She ducked around Harper and zipped down the hall, nearly crashing into Madison in the doorway.

I'd ask why she didn't get dressed before, but she'd say Cliff didn't tell her to. He probably assumed she would change.

Madison walked into the kitchen, doing the T-shirt, jeans, and barefoot thing, too. She pointed over her shoulder with a thumb. "Lore forgot her clothes again."

"Yeah, I noticed." Harper picked up the nightgown, set it on the counter for the time being, and dumped cereal into two bowls.

"It hasn't been *that* long since the nukes. We're not supposed to go tribal already, are we?" Madison swung around to face the hall. "I'll go make sure she doesn't do something silly like just put on a hat and call that dressed."

"We have hats?" Harper raised an eyebrow.

"No, just saying. You know how she is. She'll put on just socks, or just a shirt, or wear her underpants on her head."

"Yeah. But that, I think she does to make us laugh on purpose." Harper carried the bowls to the table and sat, getting started on her dry Corn Pops cereal.

A few minutes later, Lorelei ran by in an off-white dress and went outside again. Madison took her seat and proceeded to eat her breakfast by the handful. The two of them eating filled the silence with munching for a while.

Madison looked up with a quizzical expression. "There are nineteen cows on the farm. Why are we eating cereal dry?"

"Because, the doctors have been protesting raw milk until they figure out a way to pasteurize it. Plus, we didn't have refrigeration before. I don't think they trust that the power's going to stay on yet either. It's been going in and out all the time."

"Yeah." Madison frowned.

"Fuzzy!" yelled Lorelei.

"Uh oh." Harper leapt to her feet, nearly knocking her cereal across the table, and rushed to the door expecting a bear—but found Lorelei waving at a small, brown rabbit. "Ugh." Since a small rabbit didn't pose a threat, she returned to the table and resumed eating.

After finishing her cereal, Madison ran outside to keep Lorelei company. Harper dusted off the bowls and put them away before retrieving the compound bow from the hall closet. Jonathan, evidently having had enough of the plant book for the time being, also ran outside.

When Harper entered the yard holding the bow, the kids relocated around to the front of the house, trying to stay clear of her archery practice. She'd gotten much better at grouping, but didn't want to take any chances a weird bounce or misfire could hurt someone. That would've been horrible enough in the modern world. With the limited medical assistance available, she worried about even the smallest injuries.

As she did every few days, Harper proceeded to practice firing the compound bow, working on rapid aiming as well as grouping. At some point soon, she'd have to go out to Route 74 and set up a long range target, since her backyard only had so much space.

Becca and Mila arrived not quite an hour later, along with another eleven-year-old from the school, Christopher Dominguez. Harper paused her archery practice as the kids ran into the backyard, cutting through on their way to the street behind the house. There, they proceeded to organize into smallish teams to play street soccer.

Harper found it difficult to imagine shooting a moving target with a bow just yet, though more often than not, she landed her four practice arrows inside a four-inch circle. Cliff had rambled on the other day about medieval archers, saying they hadn't usually worried about pinpoint accuracy since they merely lobbed thousands of arrows in the general direction of a huge crowd, hoping to hit someone in a vital spot.

If I need to use this thing for real, it's not going to be an invading army... at least I really effing hope not.

While practicing, she kept her attention on the children to the point her accuracy suffered a little. Not as much as it should have, which quietly impressed her for being able to aim while only one-third focused on the target. Dread that someone could jump out and hurt the kids at any minute haunted her. Nothing specific had her on edge, but between the shadow men and Scott the barista more recently, the notion of Evergreen being as safe as a pre-war suburb shattered, perhaps irreparably.

Shortly before noon, Cliff exited the house via the back door and walked over to her.

"Hand-to-hand time?" Harper lowered the bow.

"Actually... I had a slightly different idea in mind." He stuck his fingers in his mouth, letting off a loud whistle. When the kids all looked, he beckoned them with a wave.

"Are you going to start teaching jiu-jitsu to the kids, too?"

"Nah." He put an arm around her. "Well, maybe. But not today."

Suspiciously, the kids ran by and went inside as if they'd been expecting his summons.

Cliff guided Harper to the door and into the kitchen where the kids, Carrie, Renee, Grace, and Logan stood beside the table, surrounding a plain brown cake. A Post-it note affixed to an ordinary house candle in the middle of the cake bore the number 18. The sight of everyone there smiling at her felt like a hug that came with a knife slicing her belly open for a painful samurai death.

It gutted her to face the first birthday her parents wouldn't be there for. Seeing her friends, siblings and sorta-parents smiling at her prevented her from having a complete emotional breakdown. The clash between sorrow and feeling loved closed her throat off with a giant lump.

"Guys," she rasped.

"Happy birthday, Harp!" Madison beamed at her, clearly having been in on it.

"Please excuse the sticky note. Wasn't much icing left." Carrie ushered her up to the table. "Go on, make a wish."

She looked at her siblings one after the next, and closed her eyes. *Please let them be safe and healthy.* Harper leaned forward and puffed out the candle.

Everyone clapped.

"What 'cha wish for?" chirped Lorelei.

"She can't say, or it won't come true." Madison shook her head.

Carrie handed her a pink book, a blank diary. "Not sure if girls still even do this, but I figured you might be interested."

"Thank you." Harper hugged her, still barely able to talk.

Madison gave her a small faerie music box, knowing she had a thing for faeries. "Happy birthday, Harp."

"Thanks, Termite." She squeezed her.

Jonathan gave her a box of Hostess cupcakes.

"Thank you, kiddo." She hugged him.

Lorelei handed her a white sundress still in the Walmart packaging.

"Aww. Thanks, sweetie."

Renee gave her a bundle of novels, and Grace handed over a pack of black, lacy underthings.

"Oh, umm… wow. Thanks." Harper blushed.

"That's more a present for him," muttered Cliff while wagging his eyebrows at Logan.

Harper wanted the floor to open up and swallow her.

Logan coughed, his cheeks reddening slightly. He pulled a large teddy bear—the size of a three-year-old child—out from behind his back and handed it to her. "When I was roaming the shelves at the QM, I couldn't stop going back to this little guy. Maybe it's silly, but the war took too much innocence out of the world. I hoped I could maybe give you back a little."

Grace and Renee whispered, "Aww" simultaneously. Madison and Lorelei grinned. Jonathan looked off to the side. Carrie wiped a tear. Cliff gave Logan the 'you hurt her and you'll regret it' stare.

"Umm." Harper took the bear, choked up at the gesture. "Thanks."

"What'd you get her?" asked Carrie, eyeing Cliff.

"Oh, just a few random things." He held up a 'one sec' finger and headed to the front door.

Harper, too overcome by the teddy bear, didn't pay much attention to a slight commotion in the living room. She hugged Logan with one arm, the bear clutched in the other, trying her damndest not to give in to tears. *Why did he have to make me think of Mom and Dad?*

"Hope you're not mad at me," whispered Logan.

"No. It's really sweet. Just emotional about everything." She bit her lip, resisting the urge to complain that she had been hoping no one made a big deal of her birthday.

Cliff, Ken Zhang, Fred Mitchell, and Deacon came in lugging two large trunks between the four of them.

Confusion blanked Harper's mood. "What the heck?"

"Did you guys break the one item rule?" asked Renee.

Cliff backed into the kitchen and set his end of the box down. Ken lowered the other.

Fred and Deacon set the other trunk next to it, then approached to wish her happy birthday.

"Used to tell people two more to the big one when they turned eighteen." Deacon patted her on the back, grinning. "If someone hit twenty-one, I'd say 'all downhill from here,' but I ain't gonna say that no more. I'll get back to ya next year when I come up with a new birthday line."

"Heh. Thanks." She hugged the big guy.

"Go on, open 'em." Fred winked.

Harper eyed Cliff. "What did you guys do? That better not be full of like deer meat or something."

"Nah. You're either going to be happy or wanna kill me." Cliff fake cringed.

"Oh, boy." Harper walked up to the box on the left, knelt, and lifted the lid, getting a blast of 'wet fabric' smell.

Inside lay a collection of clothes, books, and random junk. She stared at it, not sure what to make of such a bizarre treasure chest... until she spotted a tiny gold shotgun on the tip of a trophy sticking out from under a green sweater. Hand shaking, she lifted the wool, revealing the award she'd won for shooting when she'd been thirteen. She stared at her name engraved on the small plaque at the bottom, her mind replaying her father going nuts with joy that whole day.

The sweater she moved had been a Christmas gift from Mom two years ago. The contents of the trunk slam-shifted from miscellaneous junk to all the stuff she'd been forced to abandon in her bedroom back home in Lakewood. Some of it had a coating of plaster dust. Framed pictures of her parents with her and Madison at varying ages, more trophies, a fair amount of her clothes, another pair of sneakers, and the small army of stuffed animals that had been on her bed.

Madison squeaked and gawked at Cliff in complete shock.

Too stunned to even breathe, Harper lifted the second trunk's lid. That one contained things from Madison's room. Mostly clothing, dolls, music boxes, some dance awards, and even the ceramic Starbucks mug she always used for hot cocoa. He'd essentially collected what he considered useful (clothing) or highly sentimental.

Madison ran over, pawed at the stuff for a moment, then clamped a hand over her mouth.

"We made an unscheduled stop on that last scav run to, umm, grab you a birthday present." Cliff hooked his thumbs in his pockets.

Harper stared at the framed photo that had been on her dresser: Mom, Dad, her at about fourteen, and Madison at seven. Her parents looked a little strange. It hit her that she'd started to forget exactly what their faces looked like. The entirety of it all—the day in general, everyone being there, the reminder of all that had been lost—proved too much. She collapsed over the trunk, bawling.

"Ahh, shit," muttered Cliff. He took a knee and put an arm around her back. "Sorry. I didn't think—"

She spun into a hug, clinging to him while managing a teary, "Thank you."

"You didn't tell me you were gonna *go there.*" Madison gawked at him. "You said you wanted to know what our old address was so you could avoid the bad guys."

"Wouldn't have been much of a surprise if I told you about it." He chuckled.

"You could've been killed." Harper relaxed the hug so she could look him in the eye. "This stuff is… sentimental, but it's only stuff."

"Ehh, wasn't no problem." Deacon folded his arms. "Them boys didn't give us any trouble we couldn't handle."

"Not a bit." Fred smiled.

"Think they pretty much gave up on the outer burbs for the time being." Ken traced his finger around in midair, perhaps drawing something that made sense only to him. "The Lawless seem to be staying up near the stadium these days. Probably think they got everything of value out of the houses already."

"Wait, you *all* went to our old place?" She blinked at them. "Great. Now I feel super guilty. If anything had happened to you…"

"It didn't. So don't dwell on what-ifs." Deacon patted her on the back again. "Now go on, cut that cake."

Madison ran into a hug with Cliff. Whatever she tried to say came out in a blur of crying.

Once she collected herself, Harper sliced the cake. Carrie held plates out to receive each piece and gave them to everyone in line. Cake in hand, everyone clustered in groups: adults in the kitchen, children on the living room floor, and the four teens on the sofa, squished together.

Carrie disappeared for a few minutes, returning with a fat bottle of champagne. "Dave's firm gave this to him for his fifth work anniversary. We never did get around to opening it. This is a good a time as any to..." *Pop!*

It struck Harper as oddly morbid to think that a bottle of fizzy wine would outlast the man it belonged to. But maybe Carrie wanted to get rid of it because it made her think of him. She didn't appear at all somber or sad when she opened it, and had rarely talked about him much. Harper cut a small bit of cake off her piece with a fork and ate it. It didn't taste exactly like cake she expected, but she couldn't tell if she merely forgot what cake tasted like or if it had been made from improvised ingredients that came close to cake without fully hitting it.

Voices filled the room around her in a meaningless blur. She stared into space, wondering if the guys had seen her parents' bodies in the house. What had the place she'd called home for seventeen years looked like? Her clothes in the trunk smelled damp. She knew a large piece of concrete or something thrown by a nuclear blast punched a hole in the ceiling of her bedroom, half crushing her bed. It had rained numerous times since they fled, so the house had to be a ruin by now. The bed she'd spent her whole life thinking of as a place of security would likely be disgusting now. There'd be moldy, waterlogged carpet all over. At least upstairs.

Even if they *could* go back to Lakewood, the building had to be unlivable. Never mind whatever horribleness came from her parents' bodies sitting there for months. No... she didn't want to go back there ever again. She couldn't bear to see the place in a state like that. Better it remained in her mind as an idealized memory of happier times in a happier world, an alien world with small niceties like law, police, higher education... and hope.

Random bullets happened before the war, too. Just not around where we lived.

Bad enough, the two months they'd spent hiding in the basement after the strike had tainted her memories of home with terror. Even then, 'the upstairs' had ceased being a sanctuary and became dangerous territory. Someone could see them if they left the basement. Going above ground exposed them to possible fallout or other dangers.

Her brain tortured her with imagining what her mother's body might have looked like slumped over the kitchen sink, or Dad flat on his back in the hallway between the dining room and kitchen. She closed her eyes, trying to force the horrible thoughts away and focus on the house as it had been *before.* Laughter. Arguing with Madison. Friends over. Movie night with the family. Holidays. Homework.

"Hey, birthday girl." Carrie tapped her on the arm with a small glass of champagne, snapping her out of her daydream/nightmare. "Here."

"She's spacing out," said Renee. "We've been talking to her for like ten minutes and she's just staring."

"Sorry." Harper smiled and took the glass. "Thanks. Lot on my mind."

"Understandable. Lot of weight in those boxes." Carrie sighed. "Don't let sadness eat you up inside or there won't be anything left. Not saying ignore it, but you can put it on a shelf for now. Enjoy today."

"Okay." Harper sipped the drink, cringing at the fizz going up her nose. "Oof. Gah."

Grace snickered. "Never had this before?"

"Nope."

Carrie gave the kids each a tiny portion, roughly equivalent to a shot glass worth. Jonathan made a face that said he'd be happy to live out the rest of his life without ever touching champagne again. Madison and Lorelei appeared to like it—the carbonation set the little one off giggling. Becca and Mila appeared to share Jonathan's opinion. Christopher got the sneezes from it.

"Toast," called Cliff.

"Ugh." Harper blushed. *Drat. He knows Introvert Prime doesn't do the 'talking in front of people' thing.* She stood, looked around, raised her glass, and said, "Thanks."

"Aww, come on. A real one." Cliff winked.

Her cheeks burned; her hands shook—but not as bad as when she had to address the entire militia. Children, family, and a couple of the militia guys she knew relatively well didn't intimidate her as much as a crowd of strangers.

"I'm still not sure if I should call you Dad or Cliff."

Laughter and chuckling went around the room.

"You've been looking out for us eight months. And I know that's not really a lot of time in the world we all used to live in. But now, things are different. I don't know where I'd be, where Maddie would be, and Jonathan, without you here for us. Going back for that stuff is the most amazing thing anyone's ever done for me. Thank you. And thank you for being Dad." She raised her glass at Cliff.

He wiped a tear. "Aww, I'm just a mall security guard who happened to get stuck with the overnight on the wrong damn day."

"Do we drink yet?" whispered Lorelei.

"Wait for her to drink," whispered Grace.

"Thank you, everyone, for the birthday party." She bowed her head. "I'll be honest. I'm still pretty messed up about my parents and I'd been kinda hoping no one remembered today. I wanted to forget about birthdays because I didn't want to think about how much has changed. Parents lost, friends missing, our whole future taken away and reshaped into something big, dark, and scary."

Everyone—even Lorelei—sat there in total silence, staring at her.

"But..." She raised her head, not quite crying. "I'm glad you guys did the birthday party thing. Sometimes it's easy to miss how much people care. You didn't let me sit in the dark all by myself and dwell on the bad stuff. The future might be a scary bastard, but I'm happy that you're all here to take him on with me."

Harper held her glass up.

Logan tapped his glass to hers. "Good toast. You almost didn't look nervous."

She chuckled.

Deacon whooped. Carrie and Renee pumped their fists in the air while hollering. Fred toasted in silence. Cliff appeared choked up, but managed a smile as he raised his glass.

"Nice!" said Ken.

The kids all cheered.

Jonathan farted.

"Ugh. Really?" Madison stared at him.

"Sorry. Her toast took too long. I couldn't hold it anymore."

A few people sputtered champagne on sudden laughter.

After the toast, the adults hung out in the kitchen talking while the kids ran to the backyard. Logan, Grace, and Renee remained in the living room with Harper, though Renee moved to sit on the floor so the other three didn't squish together as much. Deacon, Ken, and Fred came by to wish her happy birthday again before heading out, citing militia detail.

Renee tilted back the last of her champagne. "Well, it isn't exactly the 'mega-eighteen' we'd been planning but, I'm—"

"Stop." Harper threw a small pillow at her. "This is awesome. Thanks, guys. Really."

"Okay, it wouldn't be a proper birthday..." Cliff walked into the living room. "Without something super cheesy and lame like charades or Pictionary."

"Ugh, shoot me now," muttered Harper. She held her hands up. "Joking. Just joking."

THE REMAINDER OF THE AFTERNOON PASSED IN A BLUR OF LAME PARTY games and lamer jokes.

Tired of charades, Jonathan and the kids went out to the yard. Madison gathered her dolls from the trunk. Prior to the war, she'd paid them little attention, claiming to have outgrown them. However, she appeared overjoyed to have them back. She gave some to Lorelei and told her she could play with any of them whenever she wanted. While Jonathan, Mila, Becca, and Christopher tossed a Frisbee around, Madison and Lorelei played with dolls, though Madison appeared more interested in amusing her little sister than the dolls themselves.

Renee randomly mentioned something idiotic Mr. Collins—a history teacher from their school—did that ended up destroying a photocopier, and that set off a back and forth with Grace as they compared stories of various people doing legendary, stupid, funny, or crazy things at their schools. Harper mostly tuned out of the conversation, not caring to be reminded of people she'd probably never see again.

When it got on toward dinner time, Becca, Mila, and Christopher headed home. Carrie and Cliff cooked up a surprisingly robust meal of venison, potatoes and carrots. That explained his momentary disappearance—to grab meat from the refrigerators at the school building where the town had been storing it.

Later that night, Harper caught a stiff case of the doldrums. She found herself standing in the corner at her own birthday party feeling like an intruder. Ken returned not long after they finished having dinner, bringing with him two one-gallon milk bottles filled with Earl's homebrew beer. He, Cliff, and Carrie talked about something electrical related. The kids played Uno in the living room. Renee and Grace, still on the couch, sipped beer, both having made themselves tipsy. Logan hovered beside her all day, seeming genuinely happy to be there and not at all bored.

Her sense of being an outsider started when she'd glanced at the two big boxes still sitting in the kitchen. Survivor's guilt smashed her mood straight into the gutter. Those two trunks held all that remained of her life before the world went crazy. Perhaps it had been the beer and a half she'd drunk that made her feel as though she had become a ghost floating around someone else's house, watching someone else's party.

When Logan excused himself to hit the bathroom and let the beer out, Harper snuck out the back door into a brisk, chilly night breeze. She sat on the rear porch, head down to her knees, long, red hair draping over her legs almost to the dirt.

Despite consciously wanting to cry over her parents, she couldn't summon any tears.

Her friends had teased her all last summer with their mysterious, grandiose plans for an eighteenth birthday. Whether or not they actually *had* plans or merely messed with her, she didn't know. If she survived the bombardment, Veronica would've been the first of her crew to hit the big one-eight last November, roughly two weeks after Harper fled her home. Her friend Christina would've turned eighteen on May twenty-third, again, if she lived. Andrea in April, on the thirtieth. Darci's eighteenth birthday fell a little over a month from now.

The voice of her pothead friend echoed in her memories, laughing her fool head off while explaining how she'd been a stubborn baby and didn't pop out of her mother until 12:02 a.m. on July fifth, missing the fourth by two minutes.

But, more than lost and possibly dead friends, Harper missed her parents. *I should be in my fifties or older before I had a birthday Mom and Dad wouldn't be there for. Not eighteen. Not goddamned eighteen.* Bad enough she'd chickened out and let Dad get killed, she'd abandoned their bodies to whatever the gang might have done to them. *I'm sorry for just leaving you guys there.*

She imagined her parents telling her she had to run and didn't have a choice.

The porch creaked.

Someone large-ish sat beside her. Too heavy to be Logan. Definitely not Renee or Grace.

"Hey," said Cliff.

Harper lifted her head, gathered her hair off her face, and picked her beer glass up. "Hey."

"I know you've probably been thinking about it all afternoon." He offered a hand. "We buried them in the backyard. In the corner by that tree with the white rocks around the bottom."

She took his hand, flinching at the meaning of his words. "Thanks." She pictured the spot right away, the same tree her father had made a tire swing on when she'd been six. Mom went through a phase a few years ago where she put little white rocks around most of the bushes and stuff. Random memories came and went of her backyard. Dad cooking on a grill for the party he threw when she'd won her first shooting competition. Being eleven and having her friends over to injure themselves on a Slip-N-Slide. A water-powered rocket kit she got for Christmas when she'd been nine. It landed on the neighbor's roof the first time they launched it. Madison, at four, had spotted rabbits around that same tree in the corner of the yard by the fence.

Harper tried to guess where they'd buried the bodies. Side by side most likely… straight in front of the tree, or against the fence to the left or right?

"How… were they…?"

"It didn't look like anyone bothered them after."

"I mean. How bad were…" She shivered, then chugged the last half of her beer in one go.

"You wouldn't have known who they were just by looking at them."

She clenched her jaw, eyes shut. Two tears crept silently down her face.

He put an arm around her.

"Thank you." She leaned against him. "Did you see any Lawless?"

"Yeah. Small group came to check out the van. Nothing we couldn't handle. Four of them, and only one had a working gun."

"You killed them?"

"Yup."

She nodded. *Just baddies in a video game. They don't count as people anymore. I'd shoot them all if I could. Every last stinking one of them.* Killing a hundred Lawless wouldn't bring her parents back, wouldn't change what happened.

Another tear rolled down her face.

Dad would be heartbroken at me wanting *to kill someone.* She leaned against Cliff for a few minutes, letting the rage and sorrow bloom and fade away. He kept an arm around her until she gathered herself enough to once again face the house full of people who'd come to help her remember what happy felt like.

"You okay?"

She squeezed him. "Better than I was. Not sure I'll ever really be 'okay,' but today is helping. Thanks for getting our stuff, and… burying them."

"No problem. Figured that'd be better than a water pistol from Walmart."

Chuckling, Harper playfully punched him on the shoulder. "Yeah, just a little."

He grinned and took a sip of his beer.

The door behind them opened.

"What's up?" asked Logan.

Harper wiped her eyes before standing to go back inside. "Just needed some air. All good now."

HARPER LUGGED THE TRUNK OF HER STUFF DOWN THE HALL TO THE bedroom.

Everyone who didn't live there had gone home for the night. The kids gathered in the living room playing Uno or something. She sat on the floor in her room and stared at the trunk with little desire to open it. Harper had come close to asking a scavenging group to stop at her old house once before, but decided against it. The risk hadn't been worth it... and she didn't want to see her parents' corpses. As much as she'd wanted her things—mostly clothing—now that they sat in front of her, it took her a few minutes to find the nerve to open the lid.

More than simple objects sat inside the trunk. But she couldn't ignore the emotions contained in there forever. Eventually, she gathered her willpower and got to work.

Harper set all three framed photos she had of her parents on the dresser, creating something of a shrine to their memory. The trophies she'd won for shooting, though sentimental, went into the closet. Having them out in sight felt too much like bragging. She'd only displayed them in her old room for Dad's benefit. Handling them made her think about him, how proud he'd always been of her... and how he had to moderate the comments on her YouTube videos. Aside from the usual creeps saying inappropriate sexual stuff, she got an alarming number of awful comments from people who made it sound like her father allowing her to touch firearms had been worse than giving her hard drugs or pimping her out.

Every article of clothing she pulled out of the trunk set off a cascade of memories, either of the moment she bought or received each item, or a strong memory associated with wearing it, like her junior prom dress. Standing there being poked and fussed over by the woman at the shop had been *so* annoying. At least the junior year prom had been fun. She knelt there a while feeling sad that she'd never go to senior prom. Then again, she couldn't claim any strong feelings for Micah. They probably would've gone together, but she doubted any relationship with him would've lasted much more than another year into college.

One green sweater with a panda on it reminded her of Mom's birthday two years ago when Aunt Caroline tripped and spilled an entire glass of white wine all over Harper, and that panda.

I think everyone has an Aunt Caroline. It's like a law of the universe.

A construction-paper fairy that Madison made for her years ago went atop the dresser as well as a bunch of her fairy-themed collectibles, all of which mostly came from her mother or sister on various birthdays or Christmas. Her books, also smelling of wet dog, wound up stacked in the corner since the room had no shelves. At least the paper hadn't gone moldy. She hung her old dresses in the closet and packed the non-hangable clothes away in a big trash bag to await laundry day. All of it still smelled funny: wet wood, mold, a hint of dead person.

Harper shivered at knowing *who* the dead smell came from. No way could she wear any of this stuff before washing it. Getting her things back didn't feel as much like reassembling her life as she'd hoped it would. In truth, it made her homesick to see the stuff displaced from their usual surroundings in her old bedroom. However, she still treasured it.

After taking a few minutes to let her emotions settle upon emptying the trunk, she hauled it back out to the kitchen and grabbed the handle on the box of Madison's stuff.

We're almost out of space. Maybe we should keep this whole trunk in the room as like a toy chest for the girls. Yeah... that'll work. The other trunk can go in Jon's room.

She dragged it to the bedroom, positioned it under the window, and spent a while unpacking her little sister's things, making a pile of dolls in the other corner. Madison's clothes also went into a trash bag to await washing since they, too had a hint of odd smell, though nowhere near as bad as Harper's. Then again, her sister's room didn't have a giant hole in the ceiling. Maybe the door had even been closed to keep out the smell of death.

Once she'd finished unpacking everything but the dolls and a few other toys, she plucked one small picture of her parents from the dresser, curled up on the bed, and stared at the faces she'd almost forgotten.

11

TOO NORMAL

F lickering light changed the bathroom into a scene from a cheap horror movie.

Harper stood naked in the tub, staring at the faucet knobs. A yawn forced its way out. No one in Evergreen had any real idea of accurate time. Even with power, radios didn't do much without broadcast stations to pick up. Every frequency had played only the same blank hissing. Based on the stove clock, an hour and forty minutes had passed since sundown.

She had a pretty good feeling the time wasn't 3:32 p.m.

Having electric light again nudged bedtime back from sunset a little, but not by as much as she once desired. Why stay up late and use electricity on unnecessary light when she could just go to sleep earlier and wake at sunrise? A life divorced from a clock had been weird and alien at first, but after eight months, syncing up with the sun had become almost a reflex, as if some long-buried genetic instincts had resurfaced.

Back in touch with nature, I guess. Well, here goes nothing.

She opened the hot water knob and took a step back to spare her legs the spatter of icy water. In a moment, actual hot water came out of the spigot. She hastily added cold to get the temperature to a comfortable point, then flicked the lever to redirect the flow to the showerhead.

Ten seconds after standing under a working shower, Harper leaned against the tiles and succumbed to a silent sobbing spell. This felt too normal. People shouldn't be standing in a bathroom having an ordinary shower after civilization fell to pieces. They should be living in tents, dancing around the fire at night, swimming naked in the rivers and catching salmon with their teeth. A lapse to total primitivism would have been easier to cope with, a clearly different world that bore no resemblance whatsoever to the life she'd known. That would have made it easy to distance herself from her old life as a weird fantasy that never really happened. Having the half-dead ghosts of modern civilization all around teased her with a life she could never go back to. Showering made the nuclear war feel like a bad dream she couldn't escape from.

Moment after moment replayed in her head. Rushing to shower before school, hurrying to get ready for a shooting competition at stupid-o'clock on a Saturday morning. Madison sneaking into the bathroom while she showered to flush the toilet, hoping it would make her scream from cold water so she'd finish faster and surrender the room.

Burdened under the weight of grief, Harper picked up soap and a washcloth and cleaned herself. Bathing once a week or once every two weeks had become the norm. Using up limited firewood and the chore of having to boil water by the buckets for a bath had been the primary reason for such infrequent washing. She didn't really even notice the smell anymore by the end of week two most times. While power held up, and for as long as the house's hot water heater remained operational, she might be able to clean up every three-ish days.

Squirting shampoo into her hand triggered an out-of-nowhere fit of pure rage, mostly directed at whoever started the war. Something as ordinary and mundane as washing her hair with real shampoo felt like a luxury. She couldn't just go to the store whenever she wanted and have her pick of a hundred different hair products. When the supplies she had ran out, they'd be gone. *Maybe* they'd scavenge more, but at some point definitely within her lifetime—on the sooner side of later—there wouldn't be any more shampoo. Or toothpaste. Or soap… at least, mass-produced soap. Hopefully, the library had information about making homemade soap. She had no idea what went into the process, if it required chemicals they couldn't make anymore or even what they made it from. Soap had always been just soap, there whenever she needed it. But they'd had it in the 1800s, so someone should be able to make it.

The bathroom door opened, then closed again. Harper grinned out of reflex, expecting it to be Madison coming to freeze-flush her so she'd hurry up and relinquish the bathroom. Someone small rustled about for a few seconds. Lorelei pulled the shower curtain aside and hopped in the tub with her. The instant the child stepped into the water, dark grime rolled down her body, pooling around her feet before trailing into the drain.

"Baf time!" She gasped, scrunching her shoulders up against her neck. "Eee!"

Harper pushed the shower curtain closed. "What are you squealing about?"

"It's raining in the tub!" Lorelei squinted up at the water. "Why?"

"Because I'm taking a shower. When people get a little older, they do this instead because it's faster."

"I like bafs more." She grabbed her toy boat from the corner and made it swim around in the air. "I can't play wif boats in the rain."

"Yeah, that's kinda difficult. Boats don't like to fly." Harper laughed and hugged her. *I really needed a dose of cute. This kid is going to keep me sane.*

She resumed showering while Lorelei played. Once Harper finished, she shifted the water back to the normal spigot and flipped the stopper to run a bath.

"Yay!" Lorelei sat and thrust her arms into the air. "Baf!"

Pretty sure I was like eight or nine before I took baths alone. She sighed in her head. *Guess I'm Mom now.* Harper stepped out of the tub and dried off a bit before wrapping herself in a towel, kneeling beside the tub, and helping Lorelei wash.

12

ALL THAT'S LEFT

The bathroom door opened.

Madison poked her head in, wearing a towel from armpit to shins. "Hey. You didn't tell me you were running a bath. Didn't see the fire."

"Electric's in a good mood today. Hasn't cut out at all, so I rolled the dice with the hot water heater. Worked. Once I get Lore cleaned up, you could shower by yourself like normal if you want… at least until the power grid quits for the last time and we're back to buckets."

Madison stepped in, closing the door behind her. A faint glint of her old personality flickered across her eyes, but rather than run back out to wait, she ended up looking forlorn after a few seconds. "You know how families used to be a lot closer before technology? Like, the whole last year before it happened, we barely talked except to argue about the bathroom."

"Yeah." Harper poured shampoo into her hand and worked a lather up in Lorelei's hair. "Sorry."

"It wasn't your fault." Madison dug her toes into the bathmat. "I don't miss running in the door from school and running right back out in ten minutes to go to dance class or gymnastics or soccer or Girl Scouts and stuff." She scratched at her arm. "I mean, I wish the war didn't happen 'cause lots and lots of people died, but maybe it's not so bad going back in time. Feels like we're a family."

She still doesn't want to be alone. Kinda weird bathing together but, if it lets her feel safe... "Not sure if we went back in time or what. This isn't exactly the 1800s. We have some electricity, some tech left. Not really sure what we've got."

Madison crept closer. "We've just got each other."

"Oh dammit." Harper hugged her, soapy hands and all. "Stop making me cry. If you wanna hop in, hop in. Whatever makes you happy, Termite. I mean it. Shower on your own once Lore is done, or we can keep doing the Frontier thing if you want."

Madison stared at her, blank-faced.

"What's wrong?"

She fidgeted. "A shower would feel too much like nothing happened. I don't wanna cry anymore either. I don't think I'm ready for normal yet."

"Yeah, I know how you feel."

Lorelei made boat-engine noises while moving the little plastic toy around in the water.

Madison let her towel drop and climbed into the tub, easing herself down behind Lorelei. "Wash my hair?"

"Sure. Sec."

While Harper finished teaching Lorelei how to take a bath, Madison washed herself. Eventually, Harper squirted another capful of shampoo into her hand and started on her sister's jet-black hair, which had grown halfway down her back.

"Your hair's getting kinda long."

"Yeah. Is it okay if I keep it?"

"It's your hair, Termite. Do whatever you want with it."

"Mom liked it long. I'm gonna keep it long. But not so long I sit on it. That's annoying."

Harper teared up again while working soapy fingers through Madison's hair, overcome with fierce protectiveness. It didn't matter who or what might potentially threaten her, she'd happily kill or even die to keep her kid sister safe. She *had* already killed to protect her.

She'd do it again without hesitation. That she hadn't felt anything about doing it worried her to a point. Whenever she accidentally stepped on a bug, it made her guilty. If she saw a cat kill a mouse, she felt bad for the mouse.

But watching the Lawless go down in a spray of buckshot and blood didn't trigger any guilt whatsoever. On some level, she wanted to find more so she could do it again. *That might be a problem. No... I'm not addicted to killing. I'm just pissed at them for taking Mom and Dad away, and trying to hurt Maddie. I'm not a killer, only doing what needs to be done.*

"You're crying again, aren't you?" whispered Madison.

"Just a little."

"Did I do something wrong?"

"No. Not at all." Harper patted her on the head. "These are happy tears because you're okay."

"I'm okay, too." Lorelei twisted to look up at her.

"Yep." Harper booped her on the nose.

Madison lifted one leg out of the water and ran the washcloth over her foot. "There's been entirely too much crying in this house today. Your birthday's supposed to be happy. Can we be happy tomorrow?"

Harper exhaled hard. "Yeah. You know what. Yes. Tomorrow, we'll be happy."

13

FARM DAY

Monday morning started with a rare treat: pancakes. Unfortunately, they had to make do without syrup. Still, having a warm—and filling—breakfast kept the kids happy. Not used to such a heavy meal so early, Harper had to drag herself through the motions of making sure her siblings got ready for school and walking them out the door.

Madison tugged on her arm. "Miss Olson said we're going to be learning on the farm all day today."

"Yeah." Jonathan rubbed his stomach. "School's gonna end this week for the summer, so they're just having us go to the farm today and tomorrow."

"At least there's no tests." Madison grinned.

He shrugged. "I didn't mind tests. But I don't miss them, either."

"Which farm are you guys supposed to go to? The big one or the old golf course?" asked Harper.

"Umm. The corn one." Madison scratched her head. "I think that's the golf course."

"Yeah." Jonathan nodded. "That sounds right."

The old golf course stood between where they lived and the school, so stopping by there on the way to check didn't require any real detour aside from taking the slow route. Harper led the kids along the weaving streets directly north from the house instead of going west to Route 74 for the shortcut of a straight line. After weaving around residential streets south of the former country club, they reached a long, narrow corn field growing from where a golf course had once been. The farmers left a strip of open ground to the right of the corn not quite as wide as a car, which made for easier passage than plowing in among the stalks.

Harper led the kids along the edge of the field to the middle of the farm area. Violet Olsen, the teacher who started Evergreen's postwar school, stood with a cluster of kids, tweens and younger, near one of the sheds the farmers put up to hold tools and supplies. Madison, Jonathan, and Lorelei fell in with the students while she approached the teacher.

"Hey."

"Hey yourself." Violet patted her on the arm. "Good morning."

"On the farm all day today?"

"Yeah." Violet looked over a clipboard, marking the kids as present. "Typical end of the school year winding down. Not having to deal with standardized testing really saves quite a bit of time. Figure it helps the whole town if everyone learns the basics of not starving."

Harper kicked aside a brief feeling of annoyance at fate taking away her high school graduation. Diplomas didn't mean a thing anymore. "Yeah. Good plan."

"Welcome to stick around if you like." Violet grinned. "Just waiting on a couple more stragglers."

"Sure, why not?" Harper turned in place, looking out over the cornfields. "This is basically right in the middle of my patrol area."

Madison and Lorelei cheered.

Robin Wheatley and her friend Jax Davis, a pair of seven-year-olds, arrived with Mrs. Wheatley. The boy waved to Harper as they passed to join the others. Not long after them, a slender dark-skinned woman carried little Emmy over, clearly her adoptive parent. Harper struggled to remember the woman's name, but she'd only talked to her once or twice while on patrol. If pressed, she'd call her Therese. The eight-year-old sniffled as if she'd recently finished sobbing hard.

Therese set Emmy on her feet by the class and hugged her. "Just a nightmare, sweetie. Bad dreams can't hurt you. Have fun learning, okay?"

Emmy mumbled something incomprehensible.

Madison approached the younger girl. "I had a nightmare, too. It was scary, but just dreams."

"'Kay." Emmy ground the tip of her sneaker into the dirt.

Therese walked up to Harper. "Hey, are you gonna be here?"

"Yeah."

"Would you mind keeping an eye on Em? She had a bad one last night. The 'sky fire.'"

Harper puffed a strand of hair off her face. *That poor girl sees the nuclear flash every damn night in her dreams.* "Yeah. I'll be here as long as the kids are. This is in the middle of my patrol area anyway so it's not even like I'm wandering far off route."

"Awesome. Thanks." Therese fist-bumped her, spent a minute or two reassuring Emmy that she'd be okay, then headed back off down the former fairway toward her home... more likely to whatever job took up her day.

With all the students assembled, Violet led the class down a long row of cornstalks toward three men and a woman, all in their older forties, standing in a group by the military pickup truck Harper had recovered the other day. Evidently, the farmers had been using it to move stuff around. Bags of topsoil likely taken from a garden supply store filled the bed. They'd parked it beside an old sand trap, though nothing had been done to reclaim that small piece of ground for growth. Probably too much work removing all that sand compared to the size of the area.

At the approach of the kids, the four farmers introduced themselves as Alex, Dan, Lawrence, and Edith, then started talking about how to grow corn and summarizing what the kids would be seeing and doing over the next few hours. Dan had a heavy Spanish accent which caused some of the kids to ask him to repeat himself several times.

Soon after the explanation of the day began, someone in the distance to the north shouted, "Hey! What the heck are you doing?"

The sharp *crack* of a gunshot followed. Men and teen boys screamed. A young man's voice Harper kinda recognized yelled, "Parker!" More gunfire went off here and there along with a deep, unfamiliar male voice shouting a bunch of curses.

Children dove to the ground where they stood except for Emmy and Mila. Emmy froze statue still and burst into silent tears. Mila dropped into a crouch. Jonathan leapt up and dragged Emmy to the ground beside him.

Another two gunshots followed. A man wailed in agony.

"Truck! Go! Get down!" Harper grabbed her air horn and sounded one long blast, a 911 code as if the whole town might not have heard the gunfire.

Violet grabbed Emmy—who made no attempt to go anywhere—and dragged her to hide behind the old Army pickup. The other kids scrambled in a half-crawl, some going under the truck, some hiding behind it. Mila jumped down into the sand trap since it put her lower than ground level. That inspired Madison, Jonathan, and a few other kids to crawl out from under the truck and dive into the pit as well. Harper ran to hunker down beside the right front tire. She couldn't see anyone through the cornstalks except for a handful of farm workers running like hell to the south.

Another long air horn blast sounded farther north within the farm.

That's gotta be Marcie or Sadie.

Men and women shouted mostly from the northeast, the area where the farm came closest to the 'edge' of the town's territory. Many of the voices sounded unfamiliar, shouting in between gunshots.

Harper hovered close to the tire, Mossberg poised. Bullets whistled by, snapping at cornstalks. Here and there, someone shouted in pain or surprise.

A child under the truck began crying—for two seconds before someone covered their mouth.

"Shh!" rasped a boy. "Remember the practice drills. If they can hear you, they can kill you."

Emmy started tearily singing a lockdown song.

"Shh!" whispered the same boy. "There's no locks here. Stay quiet."

Multiple children whimpered.

An acknowledgement air horn chirp came from the south.

Harper tightened her grip on the shotgun. Fleeting memories of active shooter drills at her old school replayed in her head. Her heart beat faster; remembered terror at being a potential helpless victim worsened the fear of finding herself in the middle of an actual gunfight with as-yet-unseen enemies.

A bullet hit the pickup truck roof with a *clank*.

She jumped, but managed not to scream. For an instant, she felt like a chicken for sitting there and wanted to run into the corn to help deal with whoever attacked the town. *I'm not hiding. I've got like eleven children hiding here. I can't leave them defenseless. And Madison...* She grumbled to herself for feeling a smidge of favoritism. In the past months, she'd come to love Jonathan and Lorelei like family, too. Though, she felt as if she'd sworn an oath to her dead parents to protect Madison. She'd known Madison for her entire life, all ten years of it. As guilty as it made her feel, she couldn't deny the connection to her blood sister ran a little deeper. She'd absolutely kill or die to protect all three of them. The only real difference being that if anything happened to Madison, it would hurt more.

Sudden worry for her siblings made her pop up to peek over the truck bed, but the soil bags blocked her view of the kids hiding at the near side of the sand trap. An unfamiliar man with a rifle emerged from the wall of wavering green cornstalks lining the far end of the sand trap, pausing to observe the kids. He spotted Harper a half-second later, went wide-eyed, and tried to aim his weapon at her.

Blam.

The Mossberg going off made all the kids scream at once and blotted out the sound of the man's rifle firing. Topsoil sprayed her face the same instant the front of his throat exploded into a crimson ruin. He collapsed over sideways, dead, his rifle falling barrel-first down into the sandpit. Harper shifted her gaze left to where his bullet ripped a hole in a bag not quite a foot away from her cheek.

One of the kids shushed the others, though she couldn't tell who.

Rapid shooting came from the right. Harper spun to aim into the cornstalks on the far side of the grassy strip, sinking down in a squat with her back against the passenger door. *Shit. What' the hell's happening? That guy didn't have a blue sash. It's not the Lawless. Who's attacking us? Why?*

Two of the former Colorado Springs hockey players, now farm workers, ran by screaming f-bombs. One boy had blood spattered on his arm, but it looked like he'd merely been standing near someone else who got hit.

A young-thirtysomething blond man, Ryan Herman from the militia, sprinted out of the corn stalks about twenty feet away from of her position on her left, his 9mm pistol raised behind him, firing at someone deeper in the field. Blood ran down his left arm from a shoulder wound. He squeezed off four shots. An anguished gargle came from the distance along with the thump of a body hitting the ground.

Another unfamiliar man crept out of the corn three paces behind Ryan, AK47 raised. Harper aimed and fired, an almost automatic reflex to a pop up target from thousands of range hours. Buckshot peppered the attacker's chest and face with small holes, but he clenched down on the trigger, pouring a burst of automatic fire into Ryan's back from six feet away; blood fountained out from his chest. He convulsed on his feet and crumpled to the ground.

"Ryan!" shouted Harper.

She stared in horror at him, certain he'd died instantly.

All the kids screamed.

Harper spun to her right. Upon seeing an armed man advancing toward the truck from behind, she shrieked a war cry and jumped to her feet, trying to draw his attention away from the children. Before either she or he could fire a shot, muzzle flare erupted from the corn on the left and the man collapsed dead. Sadie Walker started to emerge from the greenery, giving Harper a 'gotcha covered' nod, but another gunshot from the right knocked her to the ground. She curled up in a ball, moaning.

Harper pivoted to aim at the source of the shot, hesitating only out of worry it might be someone on the militia who shot Sadie without checking targets. An indistinct figure among the cornstalks moved a little closer, raising his rifle to put another bullet into Sadie. Harper fired twice at the shooter as fast as she could click the trigger. The *thump* of a body hitting the ground followed.

That has to be a bad guy. Friendly fire wouldn't have tried to finish her off.

"Sadie!" shouted Harper.

The woman groaned in pain, then wheezed something unintelligible, like she couldn't breathe.

Harper started to run to her, but skidded to a stop as soon as she passed the tailgate of the pickup—due to a pistol against the side of her head. Somehow, she managed not to wet herself.

"Drop the gun, kid," said a man.

She glanced down at her weapon, unable to make her hands open. Her conscious mind tried to obey the command, but something inside her refused to surrender Dad's Mossberg, even with a gun pressed to her head. If she dropped it, she'd probably die *after* being raped or abused for as long as she survived. If she didn't drop it, death would be quick. Giving up the gun would be abandoning Madison, abandoning all the kids to whatever these men would do to them.

Her grip tightened. "What do you want?"

Random gunfire continued from seemingly everywhere.

The man abruptly twisted to his right, pulling the gun away from her skin. A dull *thunk* preceded him howling in pain and stumbling back. She spun on him, jamming the shotgun barrel into his face, right beneath his nose. She locked stares with a man in his later thirties who looked like he used to live in the suburbs. He still had the polo shirt, though his light brown hair and unshaved face said 'homeless' more than 'middle manager.' A leaf knife stuck out of his head, an inch away from his eye, closer to his ear.

"You goddamn pig," whispered Harper.

"Wait," rasped the man. "No."

Harper narrowed her eyes, but held her fire. Something about him seemed genuine.

"I... no. I just didn't wanna have to shoot a kid. Wasn't gonna do anything to ya. Wanted you to drop it so you didn't shoot me. All I wanna do is get out of here."

Mila stood waist-deep in the sand trap, scowling at the man, another leaf knife in her hand, poised to throw.

"Toss the gun and get down," said Harper.

The man chucked a medium-sized silver handgun away and lowered himself to kneel, hands up. Once he flattened out on his chest, she pressed a knee to his back. With reasonable gentleness, she removed the leaf knife embedded in his skull.

He grunted.

"Sadie?" called Harper.

"I'm okay," wheezed Sadie. "Vest took it. Damn this hurts. Gotta be a busted rib."

Jonathan scrambled out of the sand trap and scooped the handgun up. He crouched behind the truck and pointed the weapon at the man who surrendered. Harper flicked the knife into the grass near enough to Mila for her to recover it, then ran to Sophie while bullets hissed by in the air, though she couldn't tell if someone fired at her or the shots passed between two other people.

Sadie lay curled on her side, an olive drab armor vest on over her flannel shirt and jeans. From the ground, she fired her M-16 into the corn twice. Her second shot made a man scream, but another, more distant gunshot silenced him.

Harper gripped Sadie's arm and dragged her to the sand trap. She groaned and gasped the whole way, but seemed to appreciate the help. Once the woman crawled into the hole, Harper stooped to check the children—saw no injuries among them—and ducked down by the rear tire for cover.

"Relax, kid. I didn't come here to hurt anyone, especially kids. We just wanted food. I used to be a dentist. When they started shooting, I just wanted to get the hell out of here."

"That's ironic," said Mila in an eerily calm tone while examining the bloody leaf knife. "A little girl made a dentist scream."

"Just don't move, okay." Jonathan's voice wavered with nervousness.

Roy Ellis from the militia shouted, "Left side."

"Got him!" yelled Dennis.

A rapid series of gunshots went off a fair distance away beyond the sand trap.

"Mila, get down," whispered Jonathan.

"Okay," said the girl.

"I peed myself," whispered Emmy.

"Eww," muttered an unknown child.

"Everyone just stay down and stay still." Harper scanned her field of view for threats. Instinct kept trying to pull her gaze upward for flying clay pigeons, but she forced herself to focus on the constantly moving greenery. Shadows between leaves created the illusion of people moving around. Twice, she nearly fired at plants.

Rapid footfalls from the front of the truck got her attention. She swung the shotgun left toward where she expected to see someone run into view, but held her fire when Kirk, the hockey player who'd taunted Logan about being Mexican, came running toward her, pale as a ghost. Half of his face and most of his left arm had a coating of blood, though he didn't appear wounded.

When the boy came within roughly forty meters of the truck, a blood-spattered man leapt out of the green wall on the right, tackling him from behind. Harper tried to get a bead on him, but didn't trust buckshot at that range not to hit Kirk, too. The man started to put his handgun to the back of Kirk's head; before Harper could jump up to run closer, another man leapt out of the corn and crashed into the attacker, knocking him off Kirk. The two men rolled in the grass, but the attacker ended up on top. Kirk sprang to his feet. He seemed about to run off for a second, looking back and forth, but charged at the struggling pair instead, getting in the way of Harper's shot.

The handgun went off.

Kirk dove on the man, knocking him away. They struggled on the ground, fighting over the weapon. Harper tried to get a clear shot, but couldn't. She ran a few steps closer, but wary of a threat to the kids—especially with the 'dentist' there—she stopped.

The man threw Kirk to the side, but the boy didn't let go, dragging the older man with him to the ground again. That time, Kirk ended up on top, wrenched the gun out of the man's grip, and hammered him in the face repeatedly until he ceased fighting back.

When the man lost consciousness, Kirk looked up at Harper. Despite all the blood spattered on him, he didn't appear wounded beyond a few scrapes and bruises. The look he gave her struck dread straight into her heart. He held eye contact for only a second before tossing the handgun aside and jumping on the person who saved him, holding pressure on a bullet wound.

She didn't have to look. Deep in her bones, she knew who'd been shot.

"Logan!" screamed Harper.

Only the whimpering of terrified children kept her glued in place. She wanted to run to him, but would never forgive herself if something happened to one of the kids. Not since she'd first ventured into the ash-covered streets of Lakewood eight months ago had her hands trembled that much.

"Hang on, man," said Kirk. "You're gonna be okay."

Logan groaned.

Harper squeezed the shotgun so tight she expected to break it. *He's still alive.*

The man Kirk beat senseless emitted a moan.

She ran halfway closer and shot him in the chest twice. "Bastard."

"Gah! Hell!" shouted Kirk, close enough to the body that blood spray hit him.

At that distance, she had a reasonable view of Logan in the tall grass. He'd been hit high and left on the chest. Kirk placed both hands over the wound, applying pressure. She sounded another 911 tone with the air horn.

"No shit!" yelled Marcie from the left.

"Medic!" shouted Harper, her voice cracking with desperation.

The deep *boom* of a shotgun went off twice a good ways north, slower. Pump-action, not semi-automatic like Dad's.

Harper backed up and crouched by the tire, shaking from the clash between wanting to run to Logan and needing to protect the children.

"Don't try it," whispered Mila.

"Easy, kid. Just an itch. I don't have a weapon in my ear," replied the dentist.

"Clear," shouted Roy, from far northeast.

"Clear here," called Dennis, to the west.

"Hostiles down," shouted Marcie, east.

Time seemed to stand still. As soon as Roy, Marcie, Ken Zhang, and Dennis emerged from the corn, hurrying toward Harper's position, she bolted from the tire and ran to kneel beside Logan.

He still breathed, but had become delirious, half conscious. She swung the Mossberg over her shoulder on its strap and grabbed his right hand in both of hers. *No... no... I knew something was gonna happen with him. I never should've even thought about dating anyone.* Tears welled up in her eyes. Logan squeezed her hand back.

The four militia people stopped by Ryan's body. Marcie stooped to check on him.

"Sons of bitches," muttered Dennis. Blood streamed down the side of his head from a grazing wound to his left ear.

"Roy!" shouted Harper, her voice heavy with grief. "Here!"

Roy and Dennis jogged over.

"Aww hell," said Roy. He took a knee on Logan's right, examining the injury site without moving Kirk's hands. "Keep pressure on that."

Kirk nodded.

"You hit?" asked Dennis.

"No..." Harper pointed at the sand trap. "Sadie's hurt. Didn't go through her vest. Got one guy alive. He didn't wanna shoot me 'cause he thought I'm a kid. Surrendered pretty easy. Said he's a dentist."

Roy patted Kirk on the shoulder. "Sit tight. Hold that down." He stood. "Everyone else, come on. Give me a hand." He jogged over to the truck. "Kids, get out from under there."

The four militia climbed in the bed after Roy and proceeded to unload the topsoil bags by heaving them to the ground. A few children crawled out from under the CUCV into the sand pit.

Harper slid her arms under Logan's back and tried to lift him, grunting.

Logan groaned.

"What are you doing?" asked Kirk.

She looked up at him. "Bringing him to the truck. We don't have time."

"Don't. He's got a bullet in his lung. We have to move him carefully. Gonna take a couple people to lift him, not just one. You'll hurt him."

"But..." She forced herself to stop tugging at him, then stared at the truck-unloading. *Hurry up!*

Once Roy, Dennis, Marcie, and Ken cleared enough space for a body, they hurried back to Logan and did their best to gently lift him.

Harper jogged alongside while the militia carried him to the truck and eased him into the bed. Just as she started to climb in, Madison bolted out of the sand trap and clamp-hugged her.

Dennis chucked a pair of handcuffs to Marcie, who restrained the dentist, then pulled a rag out of his pocket and held it to his minor head wound.

"Guess Veronica ran for cover," said Dennis, looking at Harper. "Okay, go on. I'll watch the kids."

Harper shoved Madison up into the truck and jumped in. She sat by Logan's head and kept holding his hand. Lorelei and Jonathan scrambled up behind her.

"Like hell I did." Veronica emerged from the cornstalks holding an AK-47, bleeding from a cut on her right arm and a small-caliber bullet wound in her left shin. "I ain't gonna leave my kids."

"You're shot." Dennis jogged over to her. "And sorry. Didn't see you."

"Got one guy back there. Never fired one of these things before… took me a few tries." Violet offered the rifle to Dennis. "Here. You're probably a lot better with this."

He slung it over one shoulder, then patted the tailgate twice. "Go! Get him to the med center."

Roy started the engine.

Veronica crouched to peer under. "All clear."

"Sokay," rasped Logan. "Stay… kids."

"Dennis is watching them. I'm here." Harper's tears fell onto his shoulder.

"Don't die," said Madison.

"Yeah." Lorelei sniffled. "I don't like dying."

Jonathan wiped tears and attached himself to Harper's left arm.

Kirk, still keeping his hands on the wound, also appeared to be crying.

Roy pulled out into a turn, driving as straight as the cornfields allowed to the southwest on the fastest path to Route 74, which led straight to the med center.

"Come on, Logan. Just a little bit more." Harper gave his hand a squeeze. "Stay awake."

Logan didn't squeeze back.

DEAD INSIDE

Numb to the world around her, Harper stared into space, vaguely aware of the greyish-blue walls of the med center's waiting room. Madison curled up on the chair to her right, leaning against her. Jonathan sat on her left, holding her hand. Lorelei cuddled in her lap, a serious expression on her face for the first time since Harper had met her.

Every few minutes, however, the little one attempted a test smile to try cheering her up.

According to the wall clock, a little over an hour had passed since both doctors had rushed Logan into their operating room... which had probably once been either a dentist's procedure room or a conference area.

The other militia headed out right away to deal with the mess on the farm, except for Roy, who donated blood. Everyone in town had been tested for type in case of such an eventuality. Harper wanted to help, but her A+ blood couldn't be given to Logan who had O+. Walter Holman and Annapurna both showed up to donate as well.

Roy stuck around after the blood draw, putting his paramedic training to use along with Al Gonzalez. They triaged Violet's leg wound as well as six farm workers who'd been caught in the crossfire, though except for the two who died, no one had been injured as seriously as Logan.

Grace examined Sadie, who evidently had a broken rib that didn't require immediate attention, then tended to Violet's relatively minor injuries.

Each tick of the mechanical wall clock felt like bricks dropping to the floor.

Harper had no idea if it showed the correct time—presently six after one in the afternoon. Dr. Hale's voice replayed in a loop saying 'he's still alive' when they'd first carried him in before shouting for Dr. Khan in a tone that worried her. That neither doctor had emerged from the operating room yet both comforted and terrified Harper. They hadn't come out to say he'd died... but they also hadn't saved him yet.

I should have risked the shot when he jumped on Kirk. God dammit. I hesitated again. She closed her eyes, squeezing out the tears that had been lingering at her eyelids. *I didn't want to shoot Kirk. Not hesitation... caution. I can't be reckless. It would've been ten times worse if I murdered Kirk by accident.*

Rage burst inside her head, uncontained fury at the man who'd shot Logan and at the universe for allowing it. Her anger worsened at not having an outlet. The man who did it already died by her hand, but she didn't know why he'd tried to kill them, or who he'd been. Had Evergreen suffered an attack by an organized group? Could there be more?

As if the universe heard her question, Darnell walked in the front door.

Lorelei put on a serious face again and tried to mush Harper's lips into a smile with her fingers.

"Lore, it's okay." Madison pawed at the girl. "Harp's not gonna be happy for a while."

Darnell sat in the row of seats facing her. "How are you holding up?"

"I'm not." With both her hands occupied by other siblings, Harper bowed her head against Lorelei's. "I'm kinda in a state of nothing...

waiting."

"Your dad's leading a team out to track where the bastards came from. That's why he's not here. He's the best we got for that sort of thing."

His absence hadn't even occurred to her until Darnell mentioned it, but the reason for it satisfied her more than enough not to be upset at him for leaving her alone as the adult in the room. She would have been out there with him if she had the first clue how to track anyone. An urge to follow the trail back to their camp or settlement and wipe out every last one of them gripped her.

"What's their plan?" asked Harper in a dead voice.

"Not sure yet. Recon I think. If there are hundreds of them, we're obviously not gonna start anything and focus on defense." Darnell ran a hand up over his afro, leaning back in the seat, every aspect of his presence radiating exhaustion.

Motion caught Harper's eye on the floor to the left, a small black beetle wandering across the white tiles. The sight of it drew the venom from her anger, replacing it with a sense of mourning—for herself. She *hated* what the war had done to her, the person it changed her into. A girl who tried to catch insects live inside the house and release them outside had twice *wanted* to kill people indiscriminately… but she'd still have a harder time bringing herself to step on that bug than shoot the Lawless for murdering her parents, or exterminate whoever attacked them, shot Logan, terrorized her siblings, and killed Ryan Herman.

She hadn't known the thirty-one-year-old well. Thinking of him brought only the notion of him being 'the high-strung guy.' Nervous like a human version of one of those tiny dogs that constantly trembled. The most time she'd spent with him had been the scavenging run when the team met Deacon. But they'd gone through a gunfight together, saw combat. Men that young shouldn't be dying. Worse, it could have been any of them in his place: her, Sadie, Marcie, hell, even the children hiding under the truck or in the sand trap might've caught a stray bullet.

And Mila. Freakin' Mila hit the guy with a knife. He could've shot her for that. She grimaced. *She totally aimed for his eye and he turned at the last second.*

"How bad was it out there?" whispered Harper. "How many were there?"

Darnell wiped a hand down his face. "A damn mess."

Ruby, the doctors' assistant, brought a cup of water for him. "You look dehydrated. Better drink something."

"Thank you." He took the cup and drained it in one long series of gulps.

"Can I have water, please?" asked Lorelei.

"Of course, dear." Ruby patted her on the head before walking off.

"Eleven of them dead and one prisoner," said Darnell. "We lost Ryan, and two farmers. That one boy was like your age."

An away game with his high school hockey team ended with him being shot in the face for tending corn.

"Why...?"

Darnell scratched at his head. "A couple of the other people workin' on the farm said the boy Parker—the one who died—caught a couple of them stealing corn. They shot him as soon as he shouted at them. Kid didn't even have a weapon on him."

Ruby returned and handed Lorelei a cup of water.

"Thank you!" Lorelei flashed a huge grin.

The child's contagious happiness needled at Harper, crawling under her skin and making her feel more miserable for being sad.

"Most of the corn isn't even mature yet." She squeezed Madison into Lorelei defensively. "They shot him for corn... Ryan and Logan died for goddamned corn..."

"He's not dead," whispered Madison. "The doctors are still working."

Harper closed her eyes. *If he dies, I'm never going near another boy. I'm a jinx. I can't take this a third time. This is so, so messed up. I hate what's happened to the world. I should be dealing with finals, graduating high school, having the last big summer break before starting college. I should* not *be worrying if my freakin' boyfriend is gonna survive being shot.* She opened her eyes, memories a surprise shooter drill from her school haunting her with the screams of her classmates who didn't realize the danger was simulated. A girl, Bethany, she knew but didn't consider a close friend spent a whole year terrified that any single day she went to school, she'd never see her family again.

Almost everyone in her class had been on edge. But... none of them expected nuclear war. Perhaps those drills really *had* helped prepare kids for the world they'd inherit as adults. *We spent years trained to think we could be randomly shot at any time.*

"Maybe things haven't really changed that much," muttered Harper.

"Come again?" asked Darnell.

Harper looked up. "I'm feeling morbid. Making a dark joke. My class used to worry all the time about being shot one day out of the blue."

"Mine, too," said Madison in a small voice.

"Ugh." Harper leaned back and took a big breath. "I'm letting myself fall into a hole. Plenty of people used to live in places where they might be shot at any time *before* the war, not the nice, safe suburban bubble I grew up in. Really need to stop feeling sorry for myself."

"Hey, there's no shame in being upset. We had a shitty morning." Darnell got up. "Need more water."

"No one did that, but Emmy peed herself," said Lorelei.

Jonathan snickered.

"What did they do with the 'dentist'?" Harper let go of Madison long enough to shift Lorelei's weight so circulation resumed in her right leg.

"They took him down to the old sheriff's office, but after that mask guy, I don't know if they're going to be too interested in keeping anyone prisoner."

"Are they gonna kill him?" Jonathan gasped.

Darnell shrugged with a 'who knows?' expression. "Not my call. Dude seemed reasonably normal what little I saw of him. Guess it comes down to how good he can talk to Ned."

"He could'a shot Harp and didn't." Madison clung a little tighter.

Harper thought back to that moment when he'd ordered her to drop the shotgun. She couldn't do it, expecting he meant to kidnap her for sick purposes. Had her brain stalled on the idea of choosing death over whatever that man would do to her, or did she simply refuse to relinquish Dad's shotgun?

"He didn't shoot anyone," said Jonathan. "His gun had a full magazine."

"That doesn't necessarily mean anything. He could have reloaded." Darnell walked back over, sipping water. "But, he didn't really seem violent."

Harper glared at the wall. "Violent enough to participate in a raid. First a damn barista now a dentist? What makes people do that shit?"

"Mom's gonna yell at you for swearing." Madison peered up at her for a second, then re-snuggled. "I mean her ghost. I'm not nuts again."

"That's so messed up." Harper chuckled while crying. "Mom *would* nag me for swearing but she wouldn't have a problem with me shooting bad guys."

The creak of a door down the hall nearly made her scream.

Lorelei gurgled in response to Harper squeezing her like a giant platinum-blonde teddy bear.

Al Gonzalez backed out of the operating room, pulling a gurney with Logan on it. Grace walked alongside, crying. Harper's heart leapt into her throat at the sight of tears on her friend's cheeks—but the squeak of anguish building in her lungs didn't grow into a wail before she realized the girl pushed an IV stand. Dr. Khan steered the foot end of the gurney from the rear. Tegan emerged last from the room, weary, blood-spattered, and exhausted. She turned to her right and walked out into the waiting room.

Harper jumped to her feet, clutching Lorelei to her chest like a dangling doll. *IV is good. They don't give dead people needles. Tegan looks tired, not grim.*

"Ngh," grunted Lorelei, squirming.

"How..." whispered Harper.

"Harp, you're squishing Lore." Madison tugged on her arm.

Tegan looked her in the eye. "Logan's doing as well as can be expected given the circumstances."

Harper loosened her grip on the six-year-old, allowing her to slip down to stand. The girl overacted taking a huge breath. "How is he?"

"We removed the bullet and did everything we could to repair the damage. Dr. Khan was able to effectively improvise an intercostal drain. Logan suffered a hemopneumothorax, basically air and blood invading the pleural space around the lung."

"That sounds really scary. Is he okay?" Harper shivered with anxiety.

"Well, if we were in a normal hospital with normal supplies and procedures, I'd say yes, absolutely. His unconsciousness was primarily due to blood loss, which we've resolved with a transfusion. However, his net blood volume is still low. Right now, the worst risk for him is infection. I am optimistic that he will most likely recover, but I can't make any concrete promises given the conditions we're working with. We had to improvise a vacuum bottle for the drain. He's going to be resting here for a while, though."

"Can I see him?"

"He's asleep, so don't expect him to be too conversational." Tegan took her hand and gave it a squeeze. "But I think it would do you good to see that he's still here."

Harper swallowed.

"I'll stay with the kids," said Darnell. "G'won."

"Okay. Thanks. I just have to see he's okay, then maybe I can get them home and not completely break down." Harper nodded to Tegan.

The doctor led her down the hall to the big room with patient beds. She couldn't even guess what it had been used for prior to the war. Sadie occupied the third bed in from the door, a sheet covering her to the armpits, though a nasty bit of bruising peeked up over the fabric on her right side. Violet rested across the aisle from her, shin wrapped up in bandages.

Roy lay on the bed to Sadie's left, still fully dressed in all his pre-war police gear, sacked out. Between the gunfight, donating blood, and scrambling around on paramedic duty, he'd crashed hard. Five men and one teen boy, another former hockey player, occupied other beds in various stages of consciousness. Dr. Khan and Al Gonzalez lifted one of the farmers—a man in his late forties—onto the same gurney they'd wheeled Logan in on. Evidently, he'd been the next most seriously injured and needed surgery as well.

The last bed in the corner held Logan. Grace stood beside it, fiddling around with a plastic hose connecting a small empty tank to his side.

Harper ran over, sneakers squeaking on the tile floor.

"Harper!" Grace caught her in a hug and started crying again. "I'm so sorry!"

"He's alive?" whispered Harper.

"Yeah."

Tegan looked Logan over, then gave Harper a curt nod. "He needs rest. Take a bit to convince yourself that he's okay, then at least for today, let him have quiet, okay?"

"Okay." Harper wiped tears on the back of her arm. "Thanks."

"He woke up in the OR," whispered Grace. "Said your name and passed out again."

Logan woke up in surgery!? Wait, he asked for me? She pressed a hand to her chest. "Woke…"

"The doctors aren't trained anesthesiologists and we don't have all the right stuff. What they used, they kind of under-dosed to be safe." Grace rested her head on Harper's shoulder and whispered, "I dunno if I can do this… be a doctor, or whatever passes for one anymore. It's *so* much harder when it's someone you know."

"You did awesome. He's alive because of you." Harper nearly crushed her with a hug. "I dunno what the hell is wrong with me."

"Oh, come on." Grace sniffled. "Stop being the tough girl. You know damn well what's wrong. I see the way you look at him when he's not looking at you."

Harper stared at Logan lying unconscious in the bed, the whole left side of his chest wrapped in bandages. That Taylor Swift song they'd danced to started playing in her head again, her memories filled with his big smile. She'd become *far* too upset at his being hurt to continue telling herself she hadn't fallen for him. Whatever doubts she may have had about who Logan Ruiz was evaporated when she watched him jump on a man about to kill Kirk, a boy who'd teased him all throughout high school for being Mexican.

Fear kept her paralyzed. If she admitted she'd fallen in love with him, she'd surely lose him. If she kept telling herself she still needed time to feel things out, still hadn't really grown attached to him, it wouldn't hurt as much *when* something bad happened. But... she'd almost lost him and it hurt far more than she'd been ready for.

"I... You're right." Harper released her grip around Grace and approached the right side of the bed. "Was it that obvious?"

"Not really that much honestly, at least until your birthday. Pretty sure he's not going to go from nice guy to dangerous overnight."

"No." Harper gingerly took Logan's limp hand. "I didn't even really know Tyler. Not like we did anything. I thought he was the only person my age left alive in the world. I didn't want to make that same mistake again. I'd been so petrified of losing another person I cared about, I tried not to let anyone else in."

Grace moved up beside her, hand on her shoulder. "I can understand that. Fate's a bitch. Why couldn't it have been Zach instead of Logan?"

"No." Harper shook her head. "He's a total bag of dicks, but I wouldn't wish him hurt or dead, even in trade for Logan's life. And besides, Zach would have just kept running and let Kirk die."

"True."

"I've been stupid. Oh, what's that quote? I don't want to die before I've lived?" She looked up at Grace. "I've been half dead ever since the war, ever since my parents died. It felt somehow wrong to allow myself to be happy after so many people lost their lives. Like, how dare I laugh and have a good time in a world like this? But... you're right."

"I am?" Grace blinked.

Harper looked back at Logan. "If we give up on living, then whoever nuked us wins. My parents wouldn't want me to just quit.

Wandering around in a permanent state of guilt for still being alive when so many aren't isn't really living. I shouldn't give up. The war took everything I knew away from me, and stole half of my sister. Maddie's not the same person. None of us are. I don't want to let the war kill me inside, too."

Grace sniffled. "Dr. Hale says I'm learning stuff real fast. I've always been kinda smart. Maybe you're right. I shouldn't quit because I got squeamish today. Just worried about making a mistake because it's someone I know and I'm freaking out."

"Logan?" Harper leaned over him and whispered, "Hope you can somehow hear me. Sorry for being afraid. I didn't want to admit it to myself, but I think I might be falling for you. C'mon and wake up so I can kiss you, okay? Don't give up."

"Aww," whispered Grace.

"Miss Hughes?" called Dr. Khan. "Need you in here."

"Eep. I gotta go." Grace gave her a quick arm squeeze before running off.

"Tegan wants me to let you rest and the kids need to go home. I'll come back tomorrow, 'kay? Please keep fighting."

Harper stood at Logan's bedside for a few more minutes holding his hand, watching his chest rise and fall with each breath. The plastic tube coming out of his side dribbled with a dark reddish-brown fluid that accumulated in the plastic bottle at the end. He showed no sign of having heard her at all.

After another few minutes, she kissed the back of his hand, rested his arm on the bed at his side, and forced herself to leave him to his rest. Tears wanted to start a few steps into the hallway outside, but she held them back. *Logan's not dead yet.* If I walk out there crying, the kids are going to lose it. She stood still for a moment, gathering her composure and trying to remember how to hope.

As soon as she felt in control of herself, she resumed walking to the waiting area.

Madison and Jonathan looked up at her with expressions that asked 'how's he doing?' Lorelei flashed an overacted cheesy smile that somehow slipped under Harper's armor and made her chuckle.

"He's okay. But sleeping. C'mon. Let's go home." Harper picked her Mossberg off the chair and slung it over her shoulder before taking Lorelei by the hand.

"Cool!" Jonathan leapt to his feet, hugged her, then headed for the door.

Madison squeezed Harper's other hand. "He's gonna get better, right?"

"The doctor thinks so, yeah." Harper started for the door.

"That's good," whispered Madison. "I think he's kinda cool."

Yeah, Termite. So do I.

15

FISH DINNER

A whole grilled trout sat on a plate in front of Harper, staring up at her with an expression of open-mouthed shock.

She hadn't yet touched it. So far, the only conversation to drift across the table had been Renee asking Harper if she was okay about six times and Cliff cautioning the kids to be wary of bones. He'd cooked the fish out back on the cinder block grill because he said it would taste better, and also because the power grid had crapped out again.

Madison didn't appear to have an issue with eating fish. It remained unclear if her vegetarian nature allowed an exemption for lake trout or if general hunger and desire to survive suppressed it. Jonathan looked like a little surgeon, taking his fish apart with precision, searching for bones before eating each bite. Lorelei, as usual, represented an extreme. She picked her fish up with her bare hands and savaged it brown bear style.

"The fish came out wonderful," said Carrie in a low tone. "You did a great job."

Cliff glanced at her. "Just hit it with black pepper and salt, and whatever that red stuff is."

"Cayenne," muttered Harper. "Least... it smells like it."

"Are you gonna eat that trout or just try to communicate with it telepathically all night?" asked Cliff.

Harper almost smiled. "I'm worried about Logan."

Lorelei looked up, her fish draped sideways from her teeth. She play snarled and shook her head like a dog mangling a rabbit it caught.

That made her smile. "Okay, okay." She stabbed her fork into the trout. "Sorry, pal. You're already dead. Don't look at me like that."

Lorelei giggled.

"Why weren't we fishing before when food was running out?" Harper stuffed a forkful of fish in her mouth, and coughed. "Yep, cayenne."

Cliff flipped his trout over and started on the other side. "Ned thought the lake was full of radioactivity. He got it in his head that water picked up a crapton of fallout. He's *still* paranoid about the rain."

"So there's no radiation in the lake?" asked Carrie.

"Well... I'm no nuclear expert, but we did have some training on the aftereffects of an attack. Fallout distributes byproducts of a fission blast, primarily strontium-90, which is a pretty nasty radio-carcinogen. Wide open areas like the lake can soak up a bunch of fallout, and fish tend to absorb all the toxins in their environment. Remember that whole mercury thing? Considering the number of weapons that went off around here, it's almost guaranteed we've soaked up some strontium among other things. No way to avoid it. Question really is how bad? The training had studies from surveys they did back in the Fifties and Sixties from above-ground nuke tests, measuring levels of strontium-90 in baby teeth of children born both before and after."

Everyone got quiet.

Harper peered down at the fish. "Is this fish glowing?"

"The Army didn't pick up alarming levels in the lake." Cliff tossed another piece of fish in his mouth. "So it should be reasonably safe. A somewhat elevated risk of cancer is already our reality. I don't think eating this fish is going to substantially change that. Beats starving."

The floor lamp by the front window came on.

"Power's back," said Carrie in a pleasant voice.

Lorelei resumed gnawing on her trout. Jonathan and Madison also continued eating.

"True." Harper took another bite, which finally allowed hunger to slip past her worry. She attacked her fish with sincere interest.

"Some things never change." Cliff chuckled. "Place I lived before it hit the fan, I lost power a couple times a week. Every damn time it rained, out it went. Or some idiot hit a utility pole. Or something fell apart somewhere."

"That sounds annoying." Carrie cringed. "Did you complain?"

"Sure. A few times. Never helped."

A little past the halfway point of her fish, Harper needed water to put out the cayenne powder fire in her mouth. It made her think of Dad calling her a 'spice wimp.' Surprisingly, she didn't cry at the memory, merely sighed. *Yeah. I am.*

AFTER DINNER, HARPER CLEANED THE DISHES SINCE CLIFF HAD COOKED. Madison helped without being asked to, something she used to do back home only when Harper or Mom had been either sick or highly upset. They exchanged a knowing glance; Her sister wanted to help her feel better and Madison understood she got the message.

Jonathan ran over once he noticed Madison helping out with dishes. He grabbed a cloth and wiped down the table. Lorelei decided to help by 'neatening' the chairs. Renee stood beside Harper, also helping with the dishes and talking about what happened on the farm that morning.

Cliff and Carrie sat together on the couch, talking too low to hear from the kitchen.

Once cleanup finished, Harper hopped in the recliner Cliff usually occupied. *Wow. He must really like Carrie if he relocated to the couch.*

He noticed the surprise on her face and pointed at her. "Don't get used to it. That's still my throne. Just needed a bit more room tonight."

Carrie smiled and leaned against him.

Harper once again picked up *The Secret Garden*. So far, every time she touched that book, something pulled her away within fifteen minutes… or she'd been so worried, she couldn't focus on it. While she *did* worry quite a lot about Logan, the idea of reading to lose herself in another reality proved tempting enough that she found the ability to concentrate.

Renee came down the hall from the bathroom. She paused at the arch where the line between dining room and living room blurred, evaluated the seating positions, then sat on the arm of the recliner by Harper, trying to read the book as well.

"Sorry. Rude of me to read while you're over."

"I'd suggest we play Magic, but all my cards kinda melted." Renee made a goofy face.

Cliff didn't grab my cards. Harper didn't really care that much. She had a couple decks, hadn't been anywhere near into the game as much as Renee and Andrea. "What the heck did girls our age do before phones, movies, and video games?"

"Got married at eighteen and had kids continuously until fifty," muttered Cliff.

Carrie swatted at him. "You're so bad."

Renee rolled her eyes. "I meant like for fun or to pass time."

"Probably read, went for walks, talked. Maybe knitted? That sort of thing." He grimaced. "Wasn't alive back then and I never read Jane Austen."

The kids arranged themselves on the living room floor, Lorelei and Madison playing with dolls. Jonathan crawled half into the TV cabinet. Harper peered over her book at his rear end sticking out from the space beneath the flat panel, wondering if he'd regressed to toddlerdom and wanted to crawl into a tiny hiding place.

"Jon? What are you doing?"

"We found a PlayStation in a house today. Wanna see if it works."

"Oh." She smirked, not that anyone saw it past the book. *It's probably dead… but hang on, the TV here works. Maybe Evergreen didn't get as much of a blast as Lakewood did from EMP.* She resumed reading.

A few minutes later, the once-familiar musical chime of a PlayStation starting up came from the TV.

"Holy crap it's alive!" chirped Madison.

Jonathan scrambled out of the cabinet, sat on the rug, and scrolled the menu.

"Guess video games are an addiction." Cliff nudged Jonathan in the back with his foot. "Not even nuclear war cures it."

The boy laughed.

"Wow…" Harper blinked. *Don't wanna get his hopes up. The next time the power goes out, it could be gone forever.*

Various pings and beeps came from the screen.

"Aww," said Jonathan. "Stupid."

"What's wrong?" asked Carrie. "Is the machine not working?"

"Just these games. They won't start because there's no internet connection."

"Uhh, there's no internet," said Cliff.

Jonathan twisted to stare at him. "I know that. But these games won't start playing without an internet connection."

"Are they multiplayer?" asked Renee.

"No. They just want an internet connection because." He frowned.

"I guess the game companies never imagined the internet would be gone." Renee rolled her eyes. "Seriously. Who'd have ever thought it would just stop existing. Still feels weird not having a cell phone. Do you think the net is permanently lost?"

Cliff scratched at his beard. "Not like the internet sat on a single big machine somewhere that fried. You had thousands of computers all over the world. Some probably got vaporized. Some shorted by EMP. Bigger problem is that millions of wires and cables disintegrated or melted, and there's no electricity going to the server farms. It's unlikely that every single data center was destroyed. *Maybe* someone could bring the internet back once something like a national power grid existed again, but I think society has more pressing problems than fixing online gaming."

"People are worried about not dying." Madison made her doll pour 'tea' for Lorelei's doll. "No one has time for cat pictures and political arguments."

"Hah." Cliff laughed. "Yeah, just a bit late for politics."

Jonathan clicked on another game, which appeared to work: *Mortal Kombat*. "The internet did a lot more than just games. Communication, information, research for school."

"Ooh." Renee hopped off the chair and sat by Jonathan, taking the second controller.

"Schools are kinda gone, too," said Madison. "They're teaching us how to grow potatoes and about weather and making stuff, not like poems or multiplication or stuff."

"History?" Cliff raised an eyebrow.

"A little, not much."

"Odd to think about how much history we're going to lose because of this war." He glanced at Harper. "Your grandchildren might not even know there ever was such a thing as the United States. Or that the Civil War happened. Or the Holocaust. Or the Titanic, any of that stuff. They really did hit the reset button."

"That's pretty scary. I can't even imagine people not knowing any of that stuff." Harper scrunched her toes into the rug. "If society even survives, 200 years from now, they're just going to wind up nuking each other again."

Cliff put on a fake-evil smile. "How do we know it hasn't happened already? Maybe you're right. What if our civilization was the rebuild after the first nuclear war? Or the fifth?"

"That's messed up." Harper whistled.

"Can't be." Jonathan paused the game and looked up at Cliff. "They would've detected radiation from prior attacks, right?"

"Depends on how long ago it happened. If a theoretical ancient civilization obliterated itself to the point we ended up in the Dark Ages, traces of radioactivity would be long gone by the modern world. And, whatever radioactivity happened to be there would've been considered normal background radiation because no one would ever consider it possible that an advanced civilization predated ours. Didn't they find a modern watch in some old tomb somewhere?"

"What?" asked Carrie. "Now you're freaking me out."

"Umm." Cliff scrunched his face in thought. "I read something about a Swiss ring watch found in an old Chinese tomb that had supposedly been sealed for 400 years."

"What the heck is a ring watch?" asked Madison.

Cliff tapped his finger. "Tiny little watch embedded in a ring."

"That sounds like a hoax." Carrie laughed.

"Could be. Probably is. But who knows?" He winked. "We could be stuck in some kind of endless cycle of civilization growing out of nothing then nuking itself and starting all over."

"Or you're just playing with our heads." Harper turned her attention back to the book.

Madison soon joined in on the video game action, playing versus mode with Jonathan. Renee being around still felt more like having her best friend over. She hadn't completely shifted into another member of the family. Though, if Carrie and Cliff ever got married— or whatever passed for married anymore—that might legally make Renee another sister. Still, reading while she had a friend over seemed rude. So Harper also moved to sit on the floor and got in on the video gaming.

This could be the last time in my life I'll ever get to touch a working video game. Might as well play. Books will be around longer than I am. Having a functioning PlayStation felt surreal, like the very concept of video games no longer belonged in her world. *If I ever have a kid, they're not even going to know what video games even were.*

Everyone took turns mashing each other's digital faces in for a few hours. Eventually, it became late enough that Cliff shooed the kids to bed. Renee hung out for a few minutes talking, then gave her a goodnight hug before leaving to go next door to her bedroom in Carrie's house.

Harper stuffed the controllers into the cabinet and shut the PlayStation and TV off.

"You don't need to go to sleep now, ya know," said Cliff.

"Yeah. But. It's dark and I've gotten used to going to bed when it's dark. Besides. *If* I can sleep, that's time I won't be awake to worry about Logan."

He leaned forward, elbows on his knees. "Need to talk about it?"

Carrie did the same, giving her a concerned look. "Are you all right, hon?"

"All right is a wide term. I'm okay in some ways, not okay in others." She shrugged. "Not much I can do about it. Did you find the bastards? Any idea why they attacked us?"

"Lost the trail on the highway. Real bitch to track people on paved roads. But that dentist you detained told us his group had been roaming around for a while, caught wind of the old rumors about Evergreen being a safe place. They hadn't realized how organized we'd gotten, thought it would be easy to slip in and steal some food. That dentist said they hadn't planned on attacking us, merely grabbing whatever produce they could get their hands on and taking off. But that Parker kid spotted them chucking corn ears in a big garbage can and shouted."

"And they shot him." Harper bowed her head.

"Something like that. Alan, that's the dentist, said the guy in charge of that little group initially tried to order them to take off, but they went blood crazed. According to him, he wouldn't ordinarily have associated with men so violent, but he stayed with them for protection. As soon as he saw them kill Parker, he decided to part ways with that group. He worried they would shoot him for trying to leave. So, he kept his head down and attempted to sneak off, but ran into you."

"Who were they?" Harper folded her arms, teetering on the edge of regretting not blowing that guy's head off and feeling guilty as hell for wanting to kill a guy who *might* have been innocent. "Why didn't they just *ask* for food? Why did they have to steal it?"

"Who knows?" Cliff shook his head. "Maybe they got too used to taking whatever they needed from whoever they had to take it from. Long enough time living rough, especially in combat conditions, tends to do weird things to a man's sense of what's right."

"He didn't want to shoot me because he thought I was a kid."

Cliff laughed. "You *are* a kid."

"I'm eighteen."

"Still a kid." He tossed a sofa pillow at her. "At least to me."

Harper got up and moved to sit on the couch between Cliff and Carrie. "You guys are starting to kinda feel like parents. I'm scared that Logan's not gonna make it. I think I'm in love with him and I can't handle the idea of losing him already." She buried her face in both hands, staring between her fingers at the dark window beside the floor lamp.

They both put arms around her.

"Did I mess up not shooting that guy when he jumped on Kirk?"

"Range?" asked Cliff.

"Between thirty and forty yards."

"Damn iffy shot with buck. If you had a battle rifle or slug rounds, yeah you should've taken the shot. Buckshot? You did the right thing." He squeezed her shoulder.

"He'll be fine, hon." Carrie pulled her close. "Stay positive."

"Easy to say. Harder to do." She swept her hair back off her face and took a deep breath. "But I'll try."

Lorelei walked around the couch in her nightgown. She approached Harper and opened her mouth wide to show off her brushed teeth.

"Good job!" Harper tickled her, setting of squeals of laughter. "I guess I'm gonna try and sleep. No real reason to stay awake after dark since I don't have studying to do, there's no phones, cable TV, or internet."

"You say that like it's a bad thing." Cliff grinned.

"Heh. Is it?"

He rubbed his chin. "Nah, not really. I kinda miss my late night movies."

"I have a bunch of DVDs," said Carrie, eyebrows up.

"And that's my cue." Harper headed for the hallway. "Good night."

16

WE'RE ALL GREEN

O nce she'd escorted her siblings to school the next morning, Harper went straight to the med center. Her need to check on Logan pushed her up to a jog for most of the way there. Old habits made her stop at the counter in the waiting room.

Ruby looked up from her book. "Oh, morning, Harper. What can I help you with?"

"Can I see Logan?"

"Sure, go on back."

"Thanks." Harper smiled and hurried past her into the hall, wondering if the woman would've cared if she had simply gone in without asking.

Sadie, plus three of the injured farmers remained in beds, one of them out cold. Harper ran to Logan's side. He had either fallen asleep again or not yet regained consciousness.

"Good morning," said Sadie with a bit of wheeze in her voice. "Thanks for dragging my butt to cover."

Harper sighed at Logan, disappointed at finding him unconscious but relieved to see him alive and not visibly sick—beyond the tube sticking out of him. She patted his hand, then walked over to Sadie. "I hope you feel better than you sound."

"Don't make me laugh, please." Sadie clutched her side with a grimace. "Doctor Hale thinks I have two cracked ribs. Hurts a whole lot, but it's not life threatening. I'm going to be off duty for about six weeks though."

"Ugh. Sorry." She cringed. The thirty-year-old was one of the former sheriff's deputies. Having one of the more experienced militia people 'on the bench' could be a problem. "Better a cracked rib than dead."

"No kidding."

Harper hooked her thumbs in her jean pockets. "Lucky thing you had a Kevlar vest on."

"I have a SAPI vest. If I had Kevlar on, I'd be dead or in real bad shape. That guy nailed me with an AK at fairly close range. That would've punched right through Kevlar."

"Oh. Well, whatever it was. I'm glad you have it." Harper fidgeted at her side. "They have any more of those?"

"I wish." Sadie shot a dark look off to the side, seeming angry. "We only had so many, and a bunch of them went missing right after the strike. Probably taken by the deputies who disappeared. If we still had them, the bastards wouldn't have killed Ryan."

Harper bowed her head. "That's sorta my fault. I shot the guy as fast as I could, but he like fired his gun even after he died." She pantomimed someone clenching up. "But if I didn't shoot, he would've killed Ryan, anyway. Do you think I should have aimed for his leg or something?"

"If you didn't kill him right away, he could've still shot Ryan—or you. Don't take any blame for what happened there. You put the bastard down *before* he could fire. No way to predict that would've happened."

"Do you mean that or are you just trying to make me feel better?"

"I mean it." Sadie wiped a tear and sorta-smiled. "If you did anything different, he could've killed you *and* Ryan."

Oh no... She liked him.

The mood between them shifted from 'sorry you got hurt' to 'I'm so sorry you lost him'. Sadie picked up on the different emotional energy, and they shared a moment of quiet pain.

Harper pictured shooting the man in the knee, making him spin to miss Ryan, but also shooting her as soon as he hit the ground. Perhaps she should've tried the Hollywood thing and shot at his rifle. No, too easy to miss a shot like that while under the pressure of a life-and-death firefight. Much easier to make trick shots on a range—targets don't shoot back. She couldn't afford to take stupid chances when her life depended on not missing.

"Your boy over there was up a bit this morning. Ate a little breakfast, but Dr. Khan gave him something for the pain that put him right back out."

"He didn't give you a shot, too? You're like sweating your ass off."

Sadie twirled a hand around in a form of shrug that didn't require using her shoulders. "I'm only in pain if I move. As long as I sit still and stop breathing, I'm fine. Other people need it more. This isn't so bad compared to labor."

"Whoa. You have a kid?" Harper blinked.

"Not exactly. I was seventeen at the time. Gave my son up for adoption. They didn't even tell me where he ended up. Noah would be thirteen now... if he survived the nukes."

"Oh, my god..." Harper covered her mouth with both hands. "I'm so sorry."

"Even if he didn't make it, those thirteen years would have been way better than what I could've given him, except maybe for the last four." Sadie gestured toward Logan. "Go on. Ya came here to see your boy. I'm okay."

Harper squeezed Sadie's hand. "Let me know if I can do anything."

"Will do."

She returned to Logan's bedside. An empty bowl on the little table nearby still smelled of scrambled eggs. Not wanting to disturb him, she quietly pulled up a chair, sat, and held his hand.

"Hey," she whispered. "I'm here."

The wall clock in the patient room hadn't been set right, showing the time at twenty past seven. It had to be at least an hour early or eleven hours fast depending on how she looked at it. She rambled in a whisper, telling him about Jonathan finding a PlayStation and other things the children did since he'd been hurt.

"So, you know how I was worrying about soap? The library *does* have some books on it. Renee said one of the women who used to live in Evergreen before the war used to make her own soap as a hobby. But, she can't order lye and olive oil online anymore. Jim, the farm coordinator? He said we can make our own lye by leeching it out of wood ash with water. So, Mayor Ned's considering a rule that everyone has to save any of the white ash from fires for soap making. Any fat from hunting, too. Guess it'll be a little longer before we all start to stink."

She kept talking about random stuff, trying to distract herself. Merely sitting there in silence holding his hand would drive her nuts with worry. At ten of eight, the squeak of approaching sneakers made her look up at Kirk walking in, his plain T-shirt and jeans liberally smeared with farm dirt.

The eighteen-year-old stopped by the foot of the bed. "Hey. How is he?"

"What are you doing here? Come to gloat over the Mexican?" Harper cringed. Heat rushed to her cheeks. "Sorry. I... that just came out. You stopped that guy from killing Logan. I—"

"It's okay. I'm the one who should be apologizing. That stuff... just crap everyone said back in school. I dunno, maybe some of the guys really did have a problem with Mexicans, but I didn't. You know how you sometimes just laugh at stuff that isn't funny or say stuff you don't really wanna say to fit in with your friends?"

She looked away from him, back at Logan. "Not really. I didn't hang out with friends who wanted me to say things like that."

"Okay, not friends then. The hockey crew. You know how dudes can get."

"Yeah." She frowned. "I do."

"Logan saved my ass even after all that shit I said. He could've kept running, but he took a damn bullet for *me*. Before, I never really thought much about cracking jokes about Mexicans since all the guys did it."

Harper glanced at him again. "That stuff wasn't a joke to Logan."

"Yeah. You're right." Kirk clasped his hands in front of himself. "I'm sorry, and I know it's cheap to say that, but I am."

"I believe you." She eased back on the hostility in her voice. "After Logan tackled that bastard, you could've run off, but you didn't. You stopped the guy from shooting him again. I didn't have a clean shot. Double-aught buck at thirty yards would've hit you guys, too. If you didn't jump on the bastard, he would've killed Logan before I got close enough."

"I didn't really think about it. In like a second, I realized he saved my ass, and he was about to die for doing it." Kirk ran a hand up over his hair. "Is he gonna make it?"

"Unless he gets a bad infection, yeah."

Kirk relaxed a bit, and finally found the nerve to look her in the eye. "My granddad got sent to Vietnam when he was seventeen. Every Thanksgiving or Christmas dinner, he'd have a little too much beer and start talking about the war. One thing he said was something like 'in the shit, everyone's the same color—green.'"

Harper blinked.

"I never thought I'd ever *really* understand what he meant, but yeah. The old man was a bit racist. Used to tell all sorts of race jokes. I don't think he'd ever like hurt anyone or even say anything bad to their faces, but he was always condescending whenever he talked about them. Like he thought he was better than anyone who wasn't white. But, now I get it. When people are trying to kill you, it doesn't matter what your friends look like on the outside."

She squeezed Logan's hand. "I'm sure he'd forgive you for saying that crap since you sound sincere. So… you should know that in case he doesn't wake up." Harper's voice hitched in her throat. Sudden emotion came out of nowhere, punching her in the gut hard enough to bring instant tears.

"Hey…" Kirk hurried around the end of the bed and grasped her shoulder. "Lo's gonna wake up. You never saw him on the ice, but he's tenacious. When we had a bad game, the lower the score, the harder he played. And yeah, he kinda made some of us varsity guys look bad."

"Thanks." She held her breath a moment to gather her composure. "I'm trying hard to stay optimistic and it's not easy. Hearing that helps."

Kirk leaned against the bed and told her a few stories about hockey games where Logan had refused to accept the team was going to lose no matter what they did. Once, his enthusiasm turned a losing game into a tie, but it usually only changed a total drubbing into a one or two point loss.

Tegan walked in a little after 8:30 a.m. according to the clock, probably closer to 9:30 a.m. in reality. She stopped by Sadie to chat for a few minutes while Kirk and Harper waited in silence. Eventually, the doctor made her way around to the other injured people, Logan being her last stop.

"Is it bad that he's not awake?" asked Harper in a brittle voice. "He's gonna be okay, right?"

"I think so, yes. Bear in mind that neither myself nor Dr. Khan are surgeons primarily, though I have seen an unfortunate share of teenagers with bullet wounds." Tegan frowned and set about changing the dressing around the drain.

"Sorry."

"Nothing you need to apologize for. We traded one crazy world for another. Instead of maladjusted entitled young men lashing out because a girl said no, now people shoot each other over food."

Harper scowled at the floor, thinking of her parents. "Or just because they can."

"Anyway, things look pretty good here." Tegan examined the area where the plastic tube went into Logan's skin. "We don't have a lot of antibiotics left, but he should be okay."

"How bad is it?" Harper looked up, but averted her gaze from Logan's wound. "The antibiotic situation, I mean."

Tegan cleaned the area with an alcohol wipe. "It depends on what happens and how many people wind up needing them. My guess is we'll have maybe another year or so before we're basically dealing with Civil War era medicine. But don't freak out *too* bad. It's not like everyone will drop dead all at once." She opened a packet of clean gauze and re-dressed the drain site.

A year... if they get that biodiesel working, we should scavenge from farther away, like Boulder. She bit her lip, wondering if other people would beat them to any medicines, or if any of it would still be good after so long without electricity. The last time they raided a hospital pharmacy, Tegan tossed quite a bit of stuff due to lack of refrigeration. *If they ask me to go, I will. Is it selfish of me to hope they don't ask me? Maddie would flip out.*

"Is he going to be asleep all day?" asked Harper.

"A few more hours at least. He's going to be in quite a bit of pain for the next few days, so Dr. Khan and I are trying to keep him as comfortable as possible. Once we're able to remove the drain, he should be able to go home in about a week. However, he'll need to avoid all strenuous activity for at least two months."

She took a few deep breaths, searching for calm. "How long until you can take the drain out?"

Tegan crouched to check the bottle on the floor at the other end of the drain tube. "It won't be today." She pointed at pen markings on the side of the plastic approximating a ruled scale. "Once the drainage is less than 200cc over a day, we'll be safe to remove the tube. Hopefully, sooner, as the longer it stays in, the greater the risk of infection." She stood and patted Kirk on the arm. "Keeping pressure on that wound helped lessen the amount his lung deflated. Quite possibly saved his life, too. Did you have first aid training?"

Kirk fidgeted. "No. Just saw a bunch of war movies. Felt like the right thing to do."

"Well, it worked." Tegan smiled. "All right. I'll be in the other room if you need anything. Feel free to stay as long as you like."

"Okay, thanks. I will. At least until the kids get out of school." Harper returned to her seat and again grasped Logan's hand. "They're not going to the farm again today. Wonder why."

"Yeah..." Kirk grimaced. "Speaking of the farm. I should get back. Sorry again about all that crap I said."

Harper pulled her hair off her face so she could see him clearly. "It's okay. And thank you."

He gave her a guilty look, hooked his thumbs in his pockets, and trudged out down the hall.

Best she figured, the kids would leave school in about three hours. Unless someone sounded a 911 tone, she'd sit right there holding Logan's hand for two-and-a-half of them.

17

THAT TIME OF THE APOCALYPSE

D reamland decided to be particularly strange for Harper that night.

She'd found herself back in the normal world sitting in class at her old high school, only everyone stared at her like she'd walked into school naked. She hadn't. But they kept staring at her. Eventually, she'd caught whispers. They knew she'd killed people, and they all seemed horrified. One girl got up and moved away from her, then another. She soon sat in a chair at the center of the classroom with a ring of three empty desks around her. No one wanted to be near a killer.

Then the zombies showed up.

Harper awoke more confused than frightened. Early morning sun teased at the curtains on the window, perhaps ten minutes away from full light. Madison and Lorelei remained asleep beside her. She stared at the ceiling, certain the first part of the dream came from her guilt at having to shoot people. Her having to fight her way past throngs of undead—and Dad's Mossberg somehow fitting in her old backpack—didn't make any sense. She couldn't tell if her brain had tried to scare her with a nightmare and failed… or took a turn for the weird.

A few seconds after she awoke, a burning cramp flared up in her abdomen. She grabbed her stomach and clenched her teeth, fighting the urge to cry out so as not to wake her little sisters. When the worst of it passed, she gingerly scooted to the foot end of the bed and stood. Another cramp nearly took her to the floor, along with a warm trickle creeping down her leg.

She speed-stumbled to the bathroom, doing her best to contain the blood with her hand. After shoving the door closed with her foot, she sat on the toilet and bent forward over her knees, shuddering and gasping in waves of pain.

What's wrong with me? It's never hurt like this before. Did I get cancer already?

One minute blurred into the next. Crippling pain and dull aching traded places back and forth. Harper went from thoughts of going on a murder spree to feeling as though it would be kinder to just shoot everyone she loved now rather than make them suffer a withering but inescapable death over the next year or so before everyone starved or thugs killed them.

At that thought, she burst into tears, runaway emotions careening down a rollercoaster of hormones she could no more understand than control. Harper almost sobbed into her hands, but stopped herself before mushing her bloody palm into her face. More blood stained the front of her nightie and streaked down her left leg.

It had come out of nowhere this time. She'd been so stressed out over Logan, the attack on the farm, worrying about the kids, frustrated at how to discipline Lorelei while being too much of a softie to be strict with a kid who'd had such a rotten life that her 'friend' snuck up on her without warning. She had some supplies that she'd nicked from the Walmart scavenge, but hadn't thought to wear a pad yet due to losing track of time in the recent chaos.

She clenched her fists in sudden anger at the people who'd attacked the farm, blood oozing between her fingers, dripping onto her foot. Harper fumed for a few minutes, furious at those men. Frustration at not being able to do anything more to punish them made her rage. Another droplet of blood fell on top of her right foot. Harper stared at it, bright red on her snowy skin. Rage disintegrated in an instant. She uncurled her fingers, staring at her bloody hand as if she'd murdered someone with a knife for the first time.

Another wave of hard cramps sent a lightning bolt of pain across her lower back and brought on a rush of nausea that almost pushed her to vomit. She groaned at building pressure in her stomach, gripped with a sudden fear that her inside bits prepared to burst like a water balloon. A second later, it felt more like she had a small alien inside her trying to claw its way out. Sipping air in small gasps, she closed her eyes and tried her hardest to mentally command the pain away.

Minutes later, dread that she might've leaked all over their shared bed set off another wave of guilty tears as though she'd suffocated the girls in their sleep.

The door creaked open. Too lost to abnormal crying, Harper didn't even look up until a tiny scream shattered the silence.

Lorelei, one hand still on the doorknob, gawked at her, looking terrified and heartbroken. Before Harper could even open her mouth, the six-year-old bolted down the hall screaming, "Dad! Dad! Harp's been shot!"

She burst into laughter, tears still running from her eyes. Another wave of abdominal pain dragged her back to grimacing silence.

Cliff appeared in the doorway, catching himself on the doorjamb to stop before bursting all the way into the room. He looked at her, her hand, her leg, the expression probably on her face. Understanding dawned in his eyes.

"Girl issues," muttered Harper.

"Ahh." He turned sideways, averting his eyes. "Anything you need me to do?"

"Maybe grab me some clean clothes so I don't have to streak across the hall when I'm done in the shower."

"No problem. Anything else?"

She growled in pain. "Nah."

"Hey, you know… why don't you just chill today? Take a *you* day. I'll mind the rugrats."

That sounds awesome, but... I gotta protect—oh hell with it. I've been running at 110% for months. "'Kay."

"Be right back." He pulled the door shut behind him. "Pee outside unless you can hold it for like an hour."

"Okay," said Jonathan.

Harper sat on the toilet, her left—non-bloody—hand pressed against her abdomen, and wished a thousand deaths and painful tortures on whatever entity designed female anatomy. Having Cliff look at her while only half covered by her gossamer nightie and dealing with 'girl stuff' should have mortified her. She barely had the energy to care, as blasé as Lorelei streaking the pool. Then again, her hormones had strangled the conductor of her emotional train and drove it off the tracks into a lake—of magma.

Two soft knocks came from the door. Cliff walked in, head turned away to give her some privacy. He set a bundle of T-shirt, jeans, and undies on the sink. "There."

"Thanks."

"You got it." He started to leave.

"Dad?"

He paused. "Yeah?"

"It's never hurt this bad before. Do I have like uterus cancer?"

"Uhh… I'm not exactly an authority on girl stuff *or* cancer, but it takes a lot longer than eight months. People who develop cancer as a result of radiation exposure usually go a couple decades before symptoms show up. You wanna go to the doc?"

"Maybe. Right now, standing up hurts too much."

"Okay. I'll stick close. Holler if you need anything." Cliff patted the doorjamb twice and ducked out, closing the door behind him.

Harper sat there for a little while until disgust overpowered pain and the lingering feeling of apathy. She flushed, then grabbed the edge of the sink cabinet for help standing, peeled her nightie off, and stepped into the tub.

Within seconds of her turning the water on, the door opened. Madison and Lorelei darted in and raced each other to the toilet with much grabbing and wrestling. Apparently, neither one of them wanted to water the fence in the backyard like the boy had. Despite their arguing making her headache worse, the normalness of it surprisingly made her feel better. Everyone being so overly nice to each other created a constant sense of gloom, as though even the children knew they were all going to die soon. The girls fighting over who got to pee first made it seem as though they'd gotten past the dread, that they had some hope.

Madison won.

Lorelei stuck her head past the shower curtain, behind her. "Dad says you didn't get shot."

"I didn't." Harper leaned her face into the warm spray, thanking the powers of the universe that the electricity had worked all night, saving her from a blast of icicles.

"Where'd all the blood come from?"

"She stubbed a toe," said Madison.

"Nuh-uh," chimed Lorelei. "Stub toes don' bleed."

"It's just something that happens to us," muttered Harper. "We start bleeding every four weeks or so. Don't be afraid of it. But, you're too little to worry about it yet. I'll explain eventually."

Lorelei stuck her hand in the shower, smiling. "I bleed sometimes too."

"What?" Harper twisted to stare at her in shock. *No way does a six-year-old...*

"Whenever Mommy got mad and hit me inna nose," said the girl without losing any bit of her smile. "She'd get mad at me if I put blood on the rug. An' hit me more."

Madison gasped. "Bitch."

Lorelei backed out of the shower and hopped on the toilet as soon as Madison got up. "Mommy's friends used to call her that a lot. They called her other stuff, too, but I'm not 'llowed to say those words or I get hit for it."

"Oh, Lore." Harper choked up, near to sobbing again due to her damn out of control emotions. "That woman will never hurt you again."

A Madison-shaped blur hovered close on the other side of the shower curtain and whispered, "Hope she's dead."

To Harper, that felt a bit extreme, though she did wish the woman experienced some sort of karmic payback for the way she'd treated Lorelei. She couldn't desire her dead over it though. "We can't fix problems by killing everyone."

"I know," muttered Madison. "Hey, are you okay?"

"Yeah just... you know. Monthly issue." *Mom already had 'the talk' with her. I'm going to have to play mom and explain life to Lorelei someday.*

"Right. I'll stay out of your hair today. If ice cream still existed, I'd go get you a big bowl." Madison sighed, collected Lorelei by the hand, and left the bathroom.

Harper grabbed the soap, staring at the store-bought bar like some precious relic of an ancient civilization. Her mind went off on a tangent with a *Tomb Raider* type daydream of her swinging on jungle vines and running away from an Incan deathtrap to claim one bar of jade green soap.

Today is going to absolutely suck.

CURLED UP IN A BALL, HARPER STARED AT THE WALL OF HER BEDROOM, arms wrapped around her pillow, hugging it to her chest. The intensity of the cramping had lessened somewhat, likely as a result of her not moving much since exiting the shower. Evidently, her uterus had decided to abandon its escape attempt and stopped trying to rip itself out of her and run off into the wasteland.

Children's voices echoed from the backyard for the first hour or so. Soon after Becca and Mila came over, the kids decided to go exploring empty houses and wandered off too far away to hear anymore. Despite Cliff offering to watch them today, Harper felt compelled to keep an eye on them, but the thought of moving hurt. Hopefully, he would either go with them or round them up before they got into trouble.

Her white T-shirt and jeans looked—and smelled—in need of

being washed, but she couldn't care less about that at the moment. If she had access to any drug that would make her sleep for two days to escape the second nuclear war going on inside her abdomen, she'd take two.

Fortunately, she'd gotten out of bed in time to spare the mattress a new stain, but the rug caught some. Madison had done what she could to scrub at it before going out to play. Carrie brought her breakfast, and sat for a while talking. She didn't seem to think anything overly alarming went on, saying 'sometimes, they're worse than others.'

The pain and wild emotions left Harper unusually surly, wanting to be alone. Carrie understood, sharing a brief story about an epic fight she'd had with her former husband one time the cramping got her in a particularly vile mood.

Doing nothing but laying there wishing that the agony would go away made for a slow, boring day. She thought about reading *The Secret Garden*, but that would require getting up to grab the book. So she sat there. Any activity other than holding still would piss off the little monster inside. For a couple hours or so, she felt normal, only slightly achy. Out of nowhere, she randomly started crying again, somehow associating the total silence in the backyard with all the children having been killed in another raid by unknown attackers.

They're all going to die anyway. Why am I even bothering?

The door opened enough to admit a head.

Harper tried to say 'go away,' but only moaned.

"Harper?" asked Tegan. "Heard you're having a fun day."

Oh... Dr. Hale. She forced the urge to snap at people down deep and lifted her head out of the pillow she'd koala-bear-hugged. "A bit, yeah."

"Cliff was a little worried about you. Asked me to stop by in case you wanted to talk." She stepped in. "Is it okay?"

"Sure. I apologize in advance if I say something bad."

Tegan pushed the door closed, then walked over to the bed. "He said you described it as unusually strong?"

"Yeah. It's never hurt like this before. Or come out of nowhere like that. Usually, I'm ready for it, but this morning, I just exploded. And, I think something's wrong. I'm having ridicu-mood swings. The littlest things get me crying or so angry I scare myself."

"It might not be anything to be overly concerned about. High levels of stress during menses can cause depression, crying fits, and even make the cramping worse."

Harper laughed, grimacing at the ache in her guts. "Yeah... stress. Having just a little of that lately."

"How do you feel now?" asked Tegan.

She twirled a hand in the air. "Not too bad. Just seriously considering going on a shotgun rampage and clearing the Lawless out of Lakewood. Only thing stopping me is it hurts to walk."

Tegan performed a cursory exam, including gentle prodding of the abdomen while asking questions about how that felt. "You seem to be in good health. I don't feel any swelling or unusual inflammation. You are most likely only having a bumpy road this cycle. Here, I brought a couple of Midol tablets that will help with the pain."

"Wow, I can't believe you actually had Midol."

Tegan smiled. "While it's basically a pain reliever, it tends to be the last one to go. The ibuprofen and Aleve go fast. Men don't want to use that stuff for some reason."

When her mother had 'the talk' with her at twelve, she'd used that exact phrase. *Sometimes, it's a bumpy road.* Harper lost herself to uncontrolled crying again, heartsick for her dead mother as if the woman had only died a minute ago.

Tegan sat on the edge of the bed and comforted her until the abnormal emotional storm faded.

"I hate this. Everything makes me sad. My mom said the same thing about the road can be bumpy. I miss her so much. Thought I'd kinda dealt with it but I can't stop crying today."

"Grief isn't cut and dried. It runs off and hides sometimes, then jumps out and bites you when you least expect it to. You're under a lot of stress, and on top of your present condition... it's rough."

Harper sniffled, trying to fight off the unnatural sadness. "I gotta be Mom for Maddie and Lorelei. I gotta be GI Jane now, too, and I hate having to do that." She let out a long, shuddering sigh, struggling to gather her composure. "I hate that I've had to kill people, and I hate it more that I know I'll have to do it again and I'm not gonna wimp out. Why do people have to be shitty?"

"There have always been people like that. That hasn't changed, but now, there's no legal system left to stand between them and the rest of us. And desperation can bring out the worst in people."

"Yeah." She pushed herself up to sit and talked about Scott the barista and the dentist, Alan. Two once-ordinary guys who she came within a hair's breadth of killing.

"I spoke to Dr. Butler. He's really a dentist. Either that or he's spent six thousand hours reading Wikipedia." Tegan chuckled. "Didn't seem like a bad guy to me. Says he didn't hurt anyone. If he can convince Ned of that, they might let him stay."

Harper raked her toes at the carpet. "Guess it would be stupid to kick someone with skills like that out into the wasteland."

"You don't want him to stay?" asked Tegan.

"I dunno. He makes me think about the farm attack… and Logan." Sensing an imminent swerve from the emotion rollercoaster, Harper clamped her eyes shut and concentrated on not giving in to weird, random feelings. "He's okay, right?"

"He's doing well. Sadie told him he slept through your last visit, so he only wanted some painkillers today."

She perked up. "He's awake?"

Tegan nodded.

Harper dragged herself upright, clenching her jaw to weather the protests of her sore plumbing. "I'm gonna go visit him."

"That will do you both some good, though you might want to put some shoes on first."

"Yeah. And take these." She gazed at the Midol tablets in her hand. "You little guys are going to keep me from committing murder today."

18

FLEETING

Walking down Hilltop to Route 74 didn't hurt as much as Harper thought it would.

Tegan accompanied her since she needed to return to the med center anyway. Near total silence—the absence of children's voices—suggested Cliff took them on another woodland hike or they'd gone quite a ways off to rummage houses and buildings.

She found Logan sitting up in bed when she arrived at the patients' room. Sadie had evidently gotten the green light to go rest at home. Only two of the injured farmers remained, the other four also missing.

"Hey," rasped Logan, his voice weak. "Good to see you."

It took a great deal of self-control for Harper not to jump on him with a hug. She hurried around to his right side—away from the drain and bandages—and took his hand in both of hers. "Logan…"

"Yeah. That's my name." He flashed a goofy smile… and proceeded to ramble about how much he disliked strawberry-flavored ice cream, milkshakes, and candy. "I mean, I don't know why anyone would ever make chemical strawberry flavor. It's so rancid."

"Umm…"

He blinked at her. "Oh. I think I'm a little high. Dr. Hale gave me morphine. It came in a needle. They never bothered me, but Luisa always screamed at the doctor's office when she needed shots. She hated needles. Dr. Hale gave me a needle of morphine. I never minded getting shots."

"Wow. You are like super high." Harper giggled.

Logan spent a few minutes wondering aloud about where the word 'needle' came from, and why people called them that. Then, he rambled about his little sister always messing with his stuff, mostly electronics. He laughed about the time she put her music on his phone or Mp3 player, used his computer all the time, and so on. She sat there, grinning like an idiot listening to him, not minding at all whatever random turns his conversation took.

Since seventh grade, she'd considered roughly six boys to be 'boyfriends.' Granted, the first three had been little more than an innocent trip to the mall or movies, only hand-holding changing them from 'friend' to 'boyfriend.' Once in high school, she'd tried the kissing thing, but she'd never done anything more intimate than that. Not like her friend Darci.

That girl had been the first of her group of friends to 'go all the way,' though whether it happened during sophomore or junior year remained a matter of mystery. She freely admitted to having given a BJ or five earlier than that, though considering how often the girl got high, it might have been fuzzy memory or even exaggeration to seem like the 'cool rebel.' Christina and Andrea had both lost their virginity as well, Andrea over the summer before senior year and Christina a week before the nukes fell.

Her friends considered Renee the most prudish, having been relatively vocal about her intention to wait either for marriage or until she'd graduated college before doing it. The only real difference between her opinion and Harper's had been that Renee talked about it. Though, Harper never planned on specifically waiting until she'd gotten married. She only wanted to wait until she found a boy she *loved*, not merely dated because her whole crew had boyfriends and she'd found someone she could tolerate being around.

But the more she listened to Logan ramble and thought about how he'd nearly been killed saving the life of a boy who'd spent three years hurling racist abuse at him, the more she feared she would die before ever knowing what love felt like. Too many books and movies had given her this strange expectation for what falling in love would be. Ever since she'd 'noticed' boys, she'd been expecting love would be an overwhelming, sudden realization of knowing she'd found the 'right' boy and there'd be fireworks in the sky, music from nowhere, maybe some doves flying by in the background… not constant gnawing doubt and guilt about her feelings being genuine. Not the dread that the instant she admitted she felt differently about Logan than any other boy, he'd go away.

"… puck went flying over the plexi and nailed the old guy right in the forehead." Logan snickered. "I shouldn't be laughing about that, but he'd been screaming at Zach the whole game, calling him a pansy or preppie boy. I think it's when the codger told Zach he probably still breast-fed from his mom, he hit him with the puck. Claimed it was an accident."

Harper grimaced. *Now there's a mental image I never want to see.* "Hey, Logan? Can we change the subject off hockey?"

"Sure. Sorry. I'm on morphine. Whatever you want to talk about. Hey, why do you have a shotgun?"

"Because."

"Oh, the war." He wiped his face. "Right. Thought I dreamed that."

"So, umm. I made you a promise the other day when you were sleeping." She bit her lip, squeezing his hand. "You're still pretty high, so maybe I'll need to repeat it again once the drugs wear off. But, umm…" Heat rushed to her cheeks. "If you still want to kiss me when you can sit up…"

Logan made a goofy grin at her. She couldn't help but think he looked like a small boy who'd gotten something he really wanted for his birthday.

The space inside her heart that once held all she loved had become like a room in an abandoned house full of cobwebs and disrepair. Her parents' bodies, decayed to the point she only recognized them by the clothes they'd died in, lay sprawled on a faded rug in front of a cold fireplace, Madison cowering in the corner, afraid of her own shadow. The ghosts of her friends milled around, staring at faded paintings of her former home, friends' houses, and other places she used to adore. Renee stood by the only door out as though she'd just stepped into that inner sanctum, coughing at the dust and waving a hand back and forth in front of her face.

Geez, Harp. You need to clean the hell up in here.

If she let Logan into that room, he could burn it down... but he might also start repairing it.

Oh, hell with it.

Harper stood, leaned over his bed, and kissed him. He somewhat clumsily reached up and brushed a hand over her hair, cradling the back of her head while they made out for a few minutes as gingerly as possible. Her emotional rollercoaster flew around a loop and shot straight off the tracks. In the span of two minutes, she went from not wanting to ever leave his side, to feeling like her life would end without him, to knowing for a fact that he'd be dead in days, to just wanting to curl up and forget the whole world existed.

Each time his lips touched hers or their tongues met, he pulled her back from the precipice of hopelessness, terrifying and exciting her in equal parts as to what these new, uncharted emotions might mean. When she started considering doing more than simply kissing him, she forced herself to lean back, not wanting to hurt him.

"I shouldn't take advantage of you." She smiled, breathing a little hard. "You're high."

Logan pulled his fingers through her hair. "Yeah, I am. You're stronger than morphine."

"Umm..." Stomach butterflies and menstrual-induced nausea did not play well together. She gurgled.

"Yeah, I know that was kinda cheesy but I don't care. It's true." Logan let his arm flop back to the mattress. "I wish you'd have told me all it would take to get you to kiss me was being shot. I'd have done it myself months ago."

Harper laugh-cried. She sank to sit in the chair she'd pulled up beside the bed. He'd meant it as a stupid joke, but his comment made her question whether her feelings came from pity. After a moment of squeezing his hand and staring into his eyes, she let that worry go. She didn't have a trace of resentment. A relationship started out of pity would be forever tinged with resentment and doubt, none of which she experienced now. "Don't joke about that. No shooting yourself."

"Promise." He closed his eyes in a blink so slow he might've fallen asleep.

"Kirk was here. He apologized."

"Yeah. He came back already. We talked for a while. It's all good with him, now. He's a different person when he's not in Zach's shadow."

Harper frowned. "Zach resigned from the militia. Haven't seen him in a while. Not sure what he's doing other than *not* farming. Probably still thinks it's beneath him or something."

"He expected to have a cushy ride at some Ivy League school and end up working the stock market or some corporate boardroom." Logan shrugged. "Pretty much *everything* left is going to be beneath his expectations. Kirk told me Zach's apprenticing with the plumbers now."

"I can't think of a better person to deal with everyone's shit." She smirked.

Logan started laughing, which got her laughing.

He abruptly stopped with a pained grimace. "Ouch."

"Sorry."

"No problem." He raised an eyebrow. "How about another dose of painkiller?"

With a mischievous grin, she stretched up over the bed again, and kissed him.

19

THE FIRST TIME

Word arrived from Walter Holman later that night, soon
after dinner, that he needed to meet with her in regard
to the dentist situation and the attack on the cornfield.
Despite the notice not feeling like she'd been called to the principal's
office, she expected trouble sleeping... but a day of battling her
monthly enemy had worn her out.

The next morning after walking the kids out to the farm—the
main farm, not the old golf course—Harper hurried back down the
road to the militia HQ. She wanted to return to the farm as fast as
possible. The kids all seemed worried about another possible attack,
and wanted her around. That, almost as much as a nuclear war
happening for real, threw her for a loop. Sure, people might have gone
to her for emotional support when they needed a hug... but physical
protection? Harper Cody? The girl who quietly faded into the
background at school whenever two guys so much as shouted at each
other in the hall?

The world really has 'gone to plaid' as Dad would say.

Walter got up from behind his desk when she walked in, shook her
hand, then gestured at one of the chairs before sitting again.
"Morning, Harper. Cliff mentioned you were a bit under the weather

yesterday. Hope you're feeling better."

"Bit sore still, but much better than yesterday. Thanks."

"Good to hear. So as you may know, we're still trying to figure out what to do with our dentist friend. I'd like to hear your version of what happened with him the other day."

Harper raked her hair off her face and took a calming breath. "I'd taken cover by the truck. The kids got down in the sand pit, so I decided to hold that position and guard them. Couldn't see too much with all the corn, and I didn't want to charge off into a gunfight and leave the children on their own."

"Sounds like a good idea." Walter nodded.

She explained the man on the far side of the sand trap trying to shoot her, then seeing the other one sneak up on Ryan. "Sadie shot a guy heading for my position from behind, but another guy shot her. I shot him, then tried to run to her. The dentist was hiding behind the truck and he jumped out, putting a gun to my head as soon as I passed him. Told me to drop my gun. I figured he was going to kidnap me."

"What happened then?"

"I froze. But not like terrified froze. Dropping the gun could've been worse than death. Since he didn't kill me right away, I thought I could maybe talk to him. But Mila distracted him with a knife. Would've put his eye out if he didn't see it coming and flinch. When he jumped back, I got the shotgun around on him, was gonna blow his head off—again, 'cause I thought he wanted to rape me—but he yelled like 'no, wait.' The dude looked genuinely terrified, so I held my fire."

"What made you think he wanted to assault you like that?" Walter tapped a pen on a notepad.

"His not simply shooting me right away and wanting me to surrender. That's it. The guy watched me shoot one of his friends. I figured why else wouldn't he just blow my brains out? But, he dropped his gun right away when I told him to. Said he didn't want to kidnap me, just didn't want to shoot a kid. The guy seemed to be trying to get away from the fight. He claimed he didn't hurt anyone, and I heard his gun was full... no bullets used. "

"Yeah, that's the same thing he's telling us. They didn't really have a settlement, just a roving group moving from place to place in search of supplies. According to him, they underestimated how organized we were and hadn't planned on meeting any significant resistance. Guy used to be a dentist. Do you believe it?"

"Dr. Hale seems to think he really is." Harper fidgeted at a strand of her hair draped over her chest. "Wonder how he joined a group of raiders."

Walter leaned back in his chair, tapping his pen against his hand instead of the pad. "That is the big question. Mr. Butler—possibly Dr. Butler—says he got caught up in the 'otherworldly' nature of the aftermath and figured being with a rough group would provide protection. I suppose it's plausible that witnessing destruction of this magnitude can cause people to do strange things. Dr. Hale seems to believe he'd be stable in more normal surroundings. The man is requesting to stay here as a citizen and we are considering that request. I have two questions for you."

"Okay." She sat up a little straighter.

"Did you see him act aggressively toward anyone or cause injury? And, do you have any objection to him staying here?"

She blinked. "Really? If I said yes, you'd kick him out?"

"More than likely. But there are multiple things to consider. Your opinion does, however, weigh heavily considering your direct interaction with him."

"Wow..." She exhaled hard, uncomfortable with having that much power over someone else's fate. "I believed him when he said he didn't want to hurt me. And, I didn't see him shoot anyone or even hit them. The guy didn't even curse at Mila for sticking a knife in his skull. But... people always accused me of being too nice."

Walter chuckled. "There's no such thing as being too nice. The world needs more of that. So, how are you holding up after that? Things are apparently more, erm... *active* than we expected."

She let all the air out of her lungs in the bastard offspring of a huff and a sigh. "I really hate having to shoot people. Maybe that's why I camped by the truck instead of running around looking for bad guys... but those cornstalks. Someone probably would've gotten the drop on me if I ran around like an idiot. Besides, I couldn't leave the kids there. And, well, as far as having to shoot people goes, I've already crossed that bridge. If I need to do it to protect someone, so be it. I'm broken already. Better it's me than Madison, Jonathan, or Lorelei... or anyone who hasn't ended up taking a life." Harper bowed her head. "As long as I'm alive, I'll never forget that I chickened out and got my dad killed. I won't make that mistake again—but I hope I never have to pull the trigger on anyone again."

"I was thirty-four the first time I took a man's life." Walter leaned forward, crossing his arms on the desk. "I'd been a patrol officer. Pulled over this ghettoed-out Honda Civic with enough gold on it to make Mr. T jealous. Spoiler, rims, spinners on the rims, license plate frames, gold trim on the windows even. Total bling-mobile. Guy had been doing eighty miles an hour in a thirty-five zone. I'm expecting a couple of young thugs, right? I get to the window, it's this forty-something white dude with an upside-down cross tattooed on his cheek. Soon as we made eye contact, dude raises a gun at me. I barely dodged away as he shot. Ran around the car while pulling my weapon. We traded bullets over the roof and he went down. Whole thing took mere seconds. I can't explain how in the hell he managed to miss me with all eight shots. Swore a few of them came close enough I felt the breeze on my ears."

"Holy shit," whispered Harper.

Walter leaned his chin in his hand, one finger at his temple. "Found out later that the guy had escaped from a county jail in New Mexico while awaiting a transfer to the US Marshals Service. He'd been sentenced to life without parole on federal arson and murder charges and evidently decided he would do anything and everything except spending the rest of his days in Lewisburg Penitentiary."

"Kinda stupid of him to speed like that, right?"

"Yeah. I figure the son of a bitch either wanted to commit suicide by cop rather than go away forever or he wanted to kill as many cops as possible on his way up to Canada. He pulled right over, didn't try to evade at all. And he had the gun right in his lap, ready and waiting." Walter sighed. "Sometimes, I still have nightmares about that day. Still see his damn dead eyes staring at me over the roof of that car. That man looked at me the way you might look at a cockroach before stepping on it."

She shivered. "Creepy. I'm glad you're okay."

"Heh. Me too. I can't imagine being in that situation at your age. If you ever want to talk about the nightmares, I'm always here."

"Thanks. Maybe if I stop having nightmares about my parents being killed, I'll have time for one about shooting people."

"Harper, are you okay?"

"Yeah. I think Da—Cliff's sense of dark humor is rubbing off on me." She scratched at her eyebrow. "Though I think maybe I *did* have a bad dream about killing. Saw myself back in school before the war and everyone was looking at me weird, avoiding me because I killed people. Not really a scary dream, but I suppose I feel guilty about it. Just too freaked out about other stuff to dwell on it."

"That's possible. You know Dr. Hale is becoming quite the therapist."

"I've talked to her." Harper glanced down at her lap, picking dirt off her jeans. "She thinks I'm compartmentalizing what I've had to do by thinking of the Lawless as nameless, faceless bad guys from a video game. I'm not taking lives away from people with hopes, dreams, and futures… just knocking down hostile creatures that kinda look like people."

Walter chuckled. "Considering the state the world's in, that may well be a truer statement than you realize. Oh, one last thing before you go. I'm sure you're aware that the school will be suspending classes for a couple months like good ol' pre-war summer break. I'd like you to keep on the schedule you've been following so far. Patrol the residential district south of the school until, say two or three in the afternoon, then go watch the kids. Yeah, it's lighter than the old nine-to-five, but we figure that being on call 24/7 is the tradeoff for the sweet work hours."

"No problem, boss." She grasped the armrests of the chair and looked around. "So, the dentist? He's going to be staying?"

"I'm thinking probably, yeah. We don't have any dentists here at the moment, and his background would make it easier for Dr. Khan and Dr. Hale to cross-train him with standard medicine. Probably keep an eye on him for a while, but based on your feedback and what I got from Dr. Hale, I'm going to recommend to Ned we welcome him into town. Really does seem like the guy's a bit of a chicken who decided to stay with a rough group for protection."

"That's cool, I guess. Still don't know why they didn't simply ask to move in if they needed food that bad that they'd just shoot Parker in the face."

Walter shook his head. "You called them 'raiders' before. That about sums it up. Why trade or barter when you can simply take what you want?"

"So stupid... so senseless."

"Yeah..." Walter tossed his pen onto the desk. "Just like the whole damned war."

20

THE NAKED TRUTH

Harper returned to the main farm and found the class dispersed around in small groups.

Some kids tended chickens, others walked among tomato plants learning how to identify ripe ones and care for the plants. Alas, none of the tomatoes appeared close to ready yet. The oldest kids attending school, the thirteen-to-sixteen-year-olds, worked with Jim Rollins, the farm manager, helping put together a greenhouse. Someone had erected a framework of thin pipes in the general shape of a long building. The students, Jim, and three other adults presently lugged around giant rolls of industrial plastic wrap, making the walls and roof.

While working, Jim explained that they expected all the ash, dirt, and other sediment kicked up into the atmosphere by all the nuclear explosions would cause a few degree drop in temperature that would shorten the growing season. To combat this, they intended to construct as many greenhouses as they could and pack them with potatoes.

"Dinner time might get boring, but we're gonna survive." Jim waved to Harper. "Mornin'. You running a bit late... oh, no... Never mind. You're not a student."

"Hi." She returned the wave. "Nope. Think this will work?"

"Has a reasonable chance of it, yeah. Plenty of grow huts use plastic sheeting. Might take ten to twenty years for the cooling effect of the blasts to settle down. This is the best insurance we can have against a shorter growth season. Next year, we're gonna get various things started in these huts early, then move them out to the fields when the weather warms. Gonna keep at least two filled to capacity with spuds."

"Didn't the Irish starve because they relied exclusively on potatoes?" Harper tilted her head.

Jim chuckled. "Nope. Technically, they starved because they *ran out* of potatoes."

She didn't know whether to sigh or laugh, so she sorta did both. "Right."

"Keep your head down, kiddo." Jim returned to his 'class.'

"Yeah… I will." Harper turned in place, staring out over rows upon rows of greenery. Carrots, potatoes, tomatoes, cucumbers, even lettuce. *Why'd they bother planting lettuce? It's got no nutritional value.* She squinted. *Oh, wait. Maybe that's cabbage?*

Madison and Jonathan stood with a group of tweens listening to an older man talk about how to care for cows. Not wanting to interrupt, she walked up behind them long enough to give her siblings back pats and let them know she had returned to the farm.

A few minutes of patrolling later, she found the youngest kids, nine and smaller, clustered by the chicken coops listening to a woman she vaguely remembered as being named Donna instructing them on how to tend to the birds. Lorelei stood at the back of the group, but appeared to be more interested in her surroundings than the information on chicken-rearing. For no particular reason, she started pulling her dress off.

Dammit. What am I supposed to do with this kid?

Harper ran over and grabbed her before she could disrobe.

"Hi!" chirped Lorelei, grinning up at her.

I can't yell at a face that happy. Harper crouched to eye level. "What are you doing?"

"Learnin' 'bout chickens."

"I mean…" She lowered her voice. "Why were you about to take your dress off?"

"'Cause I didn't wan' anyone ta get shotted."

The *boom* of an imaginary train crash went off inside Harper's brain at the two completely disconnected concepts. "What?"

Lorelei stared up at her, all innocence.

Harper face-palmed and sighed. *Not her fault. Blame that bitch of a mother.* "You need to keep your clothes on when you're outside, okay? What does taking your clothes off have to do with people being shot?"

"I got scared bein' onna farm and wanted people not to get shotted." She swished side to side.

"Okay, I'm going to regret asking this, but what makes you think taking your dress off will help?"

Lorelei grinned. "Mommy's friend Bucky said girls always get what they want, if alls they gotta do is take their clothes off."

The farmer, Donna perhaps, stopped speaking and just stared at her.

Harper about fainted. She collected herself and swallowed the lump in her throat. "Did he say that to you? Did he, umm… make you do things?"

"No." Lorelei shook her head. "Just talkin' to no one. He was mad 'bout somethin'. I don't think he likes kids. He always pretended I wasn't there at all."

Harper relaxed, beyond relieved. "Bucky… umm. Lied. He said something mean. He was probably angry and just ranting."

"Mean?" Lorelei kept swishing side to side, her huge smile fading to a look of curiosity. "Sometimes, he'd hit Mommy, and when she took her clothes off, he'd stop hitting her. It worked."

Oh, gawd. I wish I had one of those little thingees that can erase memories like that movie. "Yes. Mean. That's not a nice thing to say about girls at all." Harper took Lorelei's hand. "Excuse me." She pulled the child away from the class far enough not to be overheard by little ears. "Do you keep wanting stuff to happen? Is that why you keep 'forgetting' your dress?"

"Uh huh. First, I wanted food. When Tyler got sick and had to go away, I wanted you to be my new mommy... and you did. An' then, I wanted Dad to be my dad, and he did. An' then, I wanted Maddie and Jon to like me." She scrunched her face in thought. "When we went to the pool, I just wanted my clothes to stay dry." She grinned. "An' they did!"

The words 'wanted you to be my new mommy' stabbed Harper right in the feels. She gathered Lorelei in a fierce hug and rocked her. The girl squealed in delight, squeezing her back with all she had.

"Lore, I need you to do me a really big favor, okay?"

"Okay."

"Stay dressed when you're outside. Taking your clothes off doesn't make wishes come true. It makes you cold and you'll get sick. I don't want you to get sick, okay? What Bucky said was a mean lie. Do you understand?"

"Uh huh." She stared at her for a long few minutes, the most serious expression ever on her angelic face. "If my wish didn't work, why did you wanna keep me and be my mommy?"

"Because." Harper brushed a hand over the girl's cheek, smiling at her. "You needed me and as soon as I saw you, I knew I had to take care of you."

"You wanted to? The wish didn't make you?"

"Nope." Harper shook her head. "No magic. I wanted to."

Lorelei leapt back into a hug, sniffling. "You're really not gonna throw me away?"

Tears rolled down Harper's face. "No, never."

The group of sub-ten-year-olds all watched them in silence. A few teared up. Donna looked about ready to cry as well.

Harper and Lorelei clung to each other for a moment, then the girl leaned back with a worried gasp.

"What's wrong?" asked Harper.

Lorelei twisted to peer out over the farm. "If Bucky lied an' takin' my dress off don't make my wishes happen, we could be shotted at."

"I'm not going to let anyone *shoot* you. The militia is here, too. And this farm isn't full of corn. We can see all the way to the other side. If bad people show up, we can stop them."

"Okay." Lorelei returned to her usual calm, smiling self in an instant. "Miss Donna's teaching us about chickens."

"You should listen to her then." Harper grinned, then led her back into the class group.

Lorelei eagerly rejoined her peers. Donna stared at Harper, who gave her a thumbs-up and tried to project the message 'all back to normal' with an expression. Once the woman resumed teaching about chickens, Harper sighed at the ground. *These kids are all traumatized. They ought to be watching cartoons or playing video games or having fun... not worrying about random bad guys showing up to shoot them.*

Again, she thought about all the drills at her old school. Kids had already been terrified of random people showing up with guns. For a brief moment, Harper felt as if humanity deserved to be nuked, but pushed that thought out of her head. Nothing could ever possibly justify what happened. Seeing a group of grubby five-to-nine-year-olds in dingy clothes all being so quiet and serious while Donna explained egg collection broke her heart. And of all those kids damaged by whatever they'd seen during the nuclear strike and its aftermath, she couldn't help but feel even worse for Lorelei.

Despite *not* wanting to think about it, Harper kept dwelling on what sorts of awful things that girl had witnessed before the war. Her mother had clearly been a drug addict of some kind, probably with a string of physically abusive men in her life. She'd no doubt watched her mother use her body to get what she wanted, and tried to emulate that without a true understanding of why her mother undressed. Harper thanked the universe that the girl remained innocent. Except for a near miss with starving on the street, the apocalypse had *improved* Lorelei's life.

Killing that bitch of a mother she had is wrong, but I might just punch her in the nose if I ever see her.

STAYING POSITIVE

After the 'school day' ended and the kids left the farm, Harper took them home to change before going to the pool. Nice weather, unusually warm for early June following nuclear war, prompted all three kids to plead with her about going swimming. Harper again decided to join them in the water.

She left the Mossberg at home, bringing her .45 handgun, which she could conceal in a towel... or leave with Sadie on lifeguard duty.

Oh, crap. She's too hurt to do that. Would they have closed the pool without a lifeguard? Oh, who am I kidding? It's not like anyone's following safety codes anymore.

Her worries about dealing with disappointed kids faded when they found Roy Ellis at the pool standing guard in swim trunks. She paused to chat with him for a few minutes. The former cop with paramedic training had evidently also qualified as a lifeguard back in his college days. Harper left her .45 with him, then found a nearby lounge chair that she used to store her T-shirt and jeans after taking them off, exposing her skimpy bathing suit underneath.

"Gah! I'm blind!" screamed Renee. "Retinas melting."

Grace, standing beside her, burst out laughing.

Harper turned, smirking. Her friend, a short distance away,

crossed her arms in front of her face as if standing in the path of a solar death beam. "Very funny. You're on the pale side, too yanno."

Grace continued to snicker.

Madison pulled her dress off, revealing her dark blue swimsuit.

"Eep. You're both reflective!" Renee cracked up. "You two should go stand at the solar farm, you'd double the power output."

"Harp?" Madison looked up at her. "Will I get in trouble for giving her the finger?"

"Nope."

Both Harper and Madison gave Renee the bird, which only made her laugh more.

"Seriously, though, you guys should be careful. Don't get too much sun." Renee checked the cloth bag she'd taken to carrying around. "I did score a tube of sunblock from the QM. If you're gonna be outside a lot for the militia, you might start needing a hat or something to keep the sun off your face."

"Maybe..." Harper shrugged. "I've never been much of a hat person."

After the sun cream made the rounds, Harper joined her siblings, friends, a bunch of other kids, and several townspeople in the pool. Swimming filled her head with memories of going to Christina's house. Mr. Menendez had been a VP or something for a big company. They had a nice in-ground pool. Ever since Harper met Christina in like fifth grade, they'd spent lots of time in that water during the summer months.

Distracted by daydreams of pool parties, barbecues, or hanging out at Christina's place, Harper didn't notice the volleyball coming until after it bounced off her face. She blinked, stunned, not sure what happened until Madison's laughter snapped her out of the fog. No one attempted any sort of organized water polo, just swatted the ball around at random trying to keep it from hitting the water for as long as possible. Harper joined in, allowing herself a little levity... but not too much.

If she surrendered completely to having fun, she knew something bad would happen in retaliation. She felt guilty enough for swimming in a pool after nuclear war and trying to pretend that any semblance of normality still existed in the world. At least seeing Madison, Jonathan, and Lorelei happy prevented her from giving in to grief and sadness over Christina. She had no idea if her friend remained alive or not. Fair bet her house in Lakewood was off limits, possibly destroyed, probably ruined. No one would ever have fun at that pool again.

Eventually, she'd had enough stretching for the volleyball and drifted away to relax. She didn't *swim* around so much as stand shoulder deep in water or float. Sore muscles from the vicious cramping that hit her the other day kept her stiff and uninterested in moving all that much. The water proved to be a little too cold to fully enjoy, but the unusual warmth of the day made it tolerable. Realizing she continually looked around at the distant cornstalks for threats and kept one eye on her weapon bundled in a towel beside Roy reminded her that her life had become the exact opposite of normal. That truth hung over her head like a black cloud.

The world had changed.

She had changed.

Harper Cody shouldn't be worrying about the fastest path to a lethal weapon or the best place to hide when bullets started flying. She probably shouldn't even be in a bathing suit at all. Except for lame spy movies, a skimpy bikini with no shoes didn't make for good apparel in a firefight. Then again, she had already killed a man while wearing a nightie, but he'd invaded her home in the middle of the night trying to abduct Mila who'd gone there to hide. Then again, according to Renee, showing that much skin would let Harper blind any would-be attackers.

Eventually, she noticed Lorelei's lips going blue, so she pulled the little one out of the water. After collecting her weapon from Roy, she sat on one of the lounge chairs to dry off. The girl chattered happily about how much fun she had in the water, and that she liked chickens. Then asked if chickens would want to go swimming, too. Harper laughed. At random, Lorelei started talking about the dolls Madison gave her. Apparently, two of them had become angry with the third for taking too many vitamins and always sleeping. They wanted her to stop taking vitamins.

"Well," said Harper. "She should stop taking so many vitamins if they make her sleep."

Lorelei nodded. "Yeah. Mommy used to take vitamins all the time, too. I told her ta stop, but she didn't. Priscilla's gonna stop. She likes her friends more than she likes her vitamins."

Oh, crap.

"Mommy liked her vitamins." Lorelei looked down.

Harper pictured the woman injecting heroin or popping pills, and the girl walking in on her... some lame excuse about vitamins being taken as truth by an innocent mind. "I'm sorry."

"You don't gotta be sorry."

"Lore?" Harper brushed a hand over the girl's head. "Those weren't vitamins. She had bad stuff that made her do bad things, like not pay attention to you. She didn't like that stuff more than she liked you... she couldn't help it."

"I know they's not vitamins. Vitamins are eaten and they taste like cherries. They're not inna needles." She shook off the gloom and grinned. "I'm happy you're my mommy now."

Harper wrapped the girl in a towel. "Me, too."

LATER THAT AFTERNOON, HARPER SWUNG BY THE QUARTERMASTER'S while Carrie watched the kids. She picked up their weekly food allotment, which contained a fair amount of vegetables now that the farm had started producing some stuff, as well as a fresh loaf of Bobby's bread. The clerk, Patricia Rivera, gossiped with her for a bit about Beth and Jaden's upcoming baby as well as asking if Cliff and Carrie were a thing.

How the heck does she know that?

Pretty much everyone in Evergreen knew that telling Patricia anything basically amounted to the post-nuclear equivalent of a public Facebook post.

Harper decided to err on the side of caution. "They're friends. I mean, Cliff's basically my Dad. Not like he's going to tell me about his love life."

"Oh, that's true. Well, I hope for your sake it works out. A kid needs two parents. Even if you're not really a kid anymore. So, how's it feel being a legal adult?"

"It feels like Wednesday."

Patricia chuckled. "Yeah, you poor dear. Had to grow up fast. Oh, is it true they're going to let the guy who shot that Parker boy stay in town?"

"No. Wherever you're getting your rumors from, you need to ask for a refund." Harper whistled. "The guy's a dentist. He didn't actually shoot anyone. Just… wound up in that gang for protection I guess." In hopes that the rumor system in Evergreen might stop people from randomly attacking the guy, she stepped aside out of the way of other people collecting their food, and spent a while clarifying exactly what happened, and that she believed the guy wasn't any danger.

Eventually, she headed home, packed away the food, and got started on a 'Madison-approved' meatless dinner: two cans of red beans, potatoes, carrots, peppers, onions, zucchini, a can of chicken broth, some water, and a box of butterfly pasta. She added the last of the paprika and garlic salt… perhaps the last of either she'd ever see in her lifetime, and sighed at the empty bottles.

"Someday, stupid little things aren't going to make me sad anymore. Who'd have ever thought the world would run out of crap like paprika? All the stuff we just got from stores…"

She became acutely aware of the sanitary pad she'd put on after returning from the pool, mostly because the number sixty-two burned into her memory: all she had left. Things slowed down enough that she'd probably stop wearing it tomorrow and keep her fingers crossed next month's 'attack of the blood monster' would give her a little more warning. She couldn't afford to waste them, and dreaded the idea of pressing one into extended service no matter how nasty it felt to wear the same pad until it actually absorbed something.

Regardless, her meager stash of pads and tampons would be long gone before her sisters competed for resources. What the heck would any of them do then? Spend four-to-six days constantly on the toilet? *Women had to do* something *back in the old days, but what?*

"And I'm not really thinking about this while cooking, am I?" She sighed. "I'd give my left ovary for some real Starbucks."

The siblings, plus Mila, Becca, and Christopher, came running down the street. They invaded the backyard and proceeded to kick a ball around. Every time the *thump* of a foot on rubber happened, she looked up at the kitchen window over the sink and cringed. *If they break a window, it's going to stay broken forever.*

Possessed by the spirit of Mom, Harper leaned out the patio door. "Guys, be careful, okay? If you put that ball through a window, there's no way to fix it anymore."

The kids all looked at her, pondered this, then nodded.

Cliff returned home soon after and followed his nose to the kitchen. "Hey, that smells real good. What is it?"

"Just veggies and beans with some pasta."

"Ahh. Can't wait to dig in."

"Anything going on?"

He took off his web belt, which held extra magazines for his AR-15 plus a handgun as well as some small tools, and hung it on a peg in the kitchen. "Deacon and Anna are going to take the van to that Army survivors' camp in Eldorado Springs tomorrow."

"Oh?" She turned to look at him. "What for?"

"Ned worked out a deal with them. We're gonna bring them a bunch of vegetables and fish in trade for wire and electrical supplies."

She folded her arms. "The army has Humvees, right? Couldn't they pick it up?"

"They already dropped off the wire and such. Why do you think we have power?" He smiled. "Took the farm a bit to produce. We needed the power to make ice to pack the fish in so they survived the trip."

"If they're on ice, aren't they dead already?"

"I meant survived as in not rotting to the point they can't be eaten."

"Oh."

He approached the stove and lifted the lid to give it a sniff. "Nice. So, how did your day go?"

"Not bad. Umm... Maybe I should tell you about this now while the kids are out of earshot."

"If the next words out of your mouth are 'I'm pregnant,' I make no promises about handling that well."

She laughed. "No. That's not at all what I'm going to say. I think I found out why Lore's always streaking around."

"It's more than just her mother neglecting her?" He shot her a grim look. "Please don't tell me it's something dark."

"Not dark, just sad. Apparently, her mother had a boyfriend who she overheard say something about 'all a girl has to do to get what she wants is take her clothes off.' Lore was 'making wishes,' trying to get whatever she wanted."

"Oh, brother." Cliff rubbed the bridge of his nose.

Harper kicked the toe of her sneaker at the floor while explaining all the 'wishes' the girl had made. "Guess I'm a teen mother after all. My parents would be *so* disappointed."

Cliff gave her side eye. "That's humor, right?"

"Yeah." She smiled. "They'd be totally proud of me for taking care of her."

"So, I take it you've dealt with that particular issue?"

"Hopefully." On a whim, she added a couple shakes of black pepper to the pot, then talked about the rest of the day. When she got to visiting the pool, she again thought of Christina's place, and consequently, her friends. "Hey, Dad? Do you think Deacon or Anna might be willing to look around the camp for my friends?"

"I don't see why they wouldn't. Suppose it depends on exactly how bad of a shit show it is down there." He paused, making an odd face.

"What?"

Cliff scratched his beard. "I'm trying to figure out if Eldorado Springs is an 'up there' or a 'down there.' It's lower on account of not being in the mountains, but it's also north of us."

"Hmm. I'd say up there even if it is at a lower elevation. What time are they leaving?"

"Probably fairly early, but not *too* early. It'll take time to load up the van."

She checked the food and found the pasta ready to go. "Okay. I'm gonna try to ask them in the morning. Food's ready."

"Awesome. I'll get the kids."

"Hey, Dad?"

He paused with a hand on the patio door, looking at her.

"What did women do for, umm… sanitary needs before they invented pads and tampons?"

"Don't know. Don't wanna know." Cliff cringed.

"Why are guys always freaked out by that? You're an Army Ranger and you're flinching at girl talk?"

"That, my dear, is one of the fundamental laws of the universe. We have our steak and football, you have pads and, umm… Tupperware parties."

Harper smirked. "You better be making a crappy joke."

He laughed. "Of course. If I'm Dad now, that means I need to be fast with the stupid jokes all the time, right?"

She sighed at the ceiling, but ended up grinning.

AFTER DINNER, SHE AND RENEE HEADED TO THE MEDICAL CENTER TO visit Logan.

She nearly jumped out of her sneakers with joy upon seeing the drain tube removed. They sat around for a while talking about random stuff until the topic of near misses came up. Renee got clingy with Harper over being saved from the Lawless before she'd been forced to murder someone or been molested.

"Total luck," whispered Harper. "I'm really glad I found you, too… and that idiot Zach didn't kill you. I don't even want to think about the odds. If Tegan didn't suggest going for meds on that day, and we didn't go to that hospital…"

"It's almost like the universe knew you wanted your friends back." Renee shivered.

"Damn." Logan whistled. "It's amazing you got away from those guys without them touching you. What'd you do, kill a couple?"

Renee shook her head. "No. I lied about my age. Told them I was only fourteen. Guess they haven't gone totally savage yet."

"Nice." He cocked an eyebrow at Harper. "Why do you call Dr. Hale, Tegan?"

"Because she wanted me to. Maybe she thought I looked broken or something and needed a human touch."

Renee play-punched her in the shoulder. "You did kinda look broken, but you're starting to seem a little more like you."

"Heh, thanks."

They talked on, following random topics for about an hour, not realizing how loud they were before Tegan walked in and gently shooed them out of the med center for the night. Harper said good night to Logan with a careful hug, then headed down the hall, but paused, waiting for Tegan to finish checking on him as well as the two other men still recovering. Eventually, she headed into the corridor. At seeing Harper just standing there, her tired expression shifted to concern.

"You're worried about Logan? Drain came out nice and easy. No sign of infection. We cleaned him up and stitched the site. Another week or so and he should be able to walk around."

"Awesome." Harper lowered her voice. "Hey. Awkward question?"

"All right. If it's about birth control, we don't have any. Otherwise, do you want to go into a room somewhere?"

"No, it's not that. I've got like three boxes of pads left. What are we supposed to do when they're gone? What did women in the 1800s do?"

"Oh." Tegan chuckled. "Well… that depends I suppose on where they lived. You have to remember that the world was quite a bit different in those days. Women of childbearing age often had multiple children, some in a near constant state of pregnancy. That interrupts the cycle, as does lactation. Having five or six kids spaced fairly close made for quite a few years that bleeding wasn't even an issue for them. But, some women used wool or rags… or just bled on their clothes. Remember though, the dresses they used to wear back then weighed like twenty pounds."

Harper chuckled. "Ick. Rags? That'll soak right through."

"Wear skirts or dresses until things slow down. I think in Ancient Rome they used to wrap cloth or lint around wooden slugs and use them like tampons."

"Ouch. No thanks." She cringed. "My luck, I'd get a splinter up there and die of an infection. So… rags. Great."

"You should check with Liz. I know they cleaned out at least three Walmarts' worth of feminine products plus every supermarket we could reach. No way we've run out of them all by now. But it won't last forever. At some point, things are going to get pretty medieval. Or at least pretty Old West."

"It's already the Old West. I'm honestly surprised no one has pulled a gun over a poker game at Earl's brewery."

Tegan laughed. "Can't gamble when there's no such thing as money."

"Oh. Right. Duh. Night… and sorry for getting a little loud in there."

"It's all right. More than two teenagers in one place generally requires hearing protection. You can't help it."

Chuckling, Harper waved and headed out into the near-pitch-black night. It took a second or six for her eyes to adjust from the electric lighting inside the med center enough to see the road. No blinking lights from aircraft went by overhead, nor did any of the city's streetlamps work anymore. Jeanette had disconnected them to save power for homes, the med center, and the quartermaster's. They'd hacked together a giant battery cluster from pretty much any large batteries they could scavenge. Deacon had done most of the work on the wiring that tied them all together into a single power system. Still, they had no real source of replacement parts without risking long-range scavenging trips using unreliable vehicles—and no guarantee parts would exist at all.

She'd have to accept the likely reality that Evergreen having electrical power might be a short-lived last hurrah of civilization.

One, two, maybe as long as five years from now, the town would go dark and stay that way.

Harper stared at the endless black of the sky. *It's so damn quiet. As if I needed another reminder the world is broken.* "No. That's the wrong way to think. I gotta stay positive if we're going to survive this. All the noise pollution is gone. It's tranquil." *Hopefully, the fallout won't get us.*

She clutched the Mossberg's strap tight and made her way home.

22

ELDORADO SPRINGS

Thursday morning, Harper rushed the kids through breakfast and out the door for their last day of school. Rather than another farm day, the teachers wanted them at the school for a recap of the stuff they'd learned so far. No doubt, the kids would appreciate the feeling of safety that came with being inside.

She hurried back down Route 74 to the quartermaster's building. Sure enough, the white van Rafael resurrected sat parked near the door. Annapurna and Deacon helped load boxes in the back, as well as a bunch of Styrofoam coolers that smelled strongly of fish.

"Umm, guys?" Harper grabbed the next box of fish and carried it out to the van. "Any chance you could do me a favor while you're at the Army place?"

"What'd you have in mind?" Deacon took the box she carried and loaded it.

"Can you ask their records guy if any of my friends are there? I'd really like to know if they made it out alive."

"Aww." Annapurna put an arm around her after handing Deacon another case of fish. "We can ask. Who are they?"

"Christina, Andrea, Darci, and Veronica."

"What do they look like? Last names?" Annapurna walked back into the quartermaster's building.

Harper followed. "Umm. Darci's kinda thin. Black hair, blue eyes. Looks permanently stoned. Kinda punk. Veronica's black. She's athletic and—"

"Why don't you just come with us?" Deacon grabbed two boxes at once and started back outside.

Harper picked up the last Styrofoam cooler, biting her lip. Leaving Evergreen still worried her, mostly over what it would do to Madison if anything happened to her. She had to stay alive to protect her siblings. But, her *need* to know what happened to her friends turned out to be a worthy opponent for her nerves. "How long a ride is it?"

Annapurna grabbed a white plastiboard box with Postal Service markings full of cabbages. "Before the war, it would've been about fifty minutes depending on traffic. There's no traffic at all now, but we don't know what shape the roads are in. The Army said it's a decent run straight up Route 93. Skirts past Golden, avoids Denver entirely. It probably won't take us too much more than an hour each way."

Dammit. I hope I don't regret this. "Can you guys give me like twenty minutes? I need to check with Walter if it's okay and then—wait. An hour? We should be back before the kids are out of school. Okay, five minutes. Just need to ask Walter if it's okay. Is that cool?"

"Sure." Deacon nodded. "Wouldn't mind having that cannon of yours along for the ride."

Harper emitted a nervous laugh. *I really shouldn't roll the dice with my life like this. Anything could happen. But what if the guys are alive and okay at that camp? Not knowing is eating me up inside. Screw it.* "Okay. Be right back."

She handed the cooler of fish to Deacon, then ran across Route 74 and down a bit to the office building that had become city hall. Walter and Anne-Marie stood sipping coffee in the same room with the big town map where she, Cliff, Madison, Jonathan, and Summer Vasquez had been interviewed six months ago. They paused their conversation to look over at her.

"Good morning, Harper." Anne-Marie smiled. "Is everything okay? You look… urgent."

Walter raised his mug in greeting.

"Sorry. The trip to Eldorado Springs… Is it okay if I go with them? There's a chance that my friends might have been evacuated there and I have to know if they made it."

"Are you sure?" Walter walked up to her. "It's not a particularly dangerous trip, but you've got that sister of yours to think about."

She looked at him. "Have you been letting me slide on scavenging runs for Maddie?"

"Well… You ever see *Saving Private Ryan?*"

"Yeah."

"You two lost your folks, maybe your friends. It's possible I've been trying to schedule you on the less risky scavenging trips for Madison's sake. She's already lost her parents. It's got nothing to do with thinking of you as a kid, or weak. Just, well, I'm an old sap and I don't wanna leave that sister of yours all alone."

"I…" She sighed. "I'm both a little insulted and a lot relieved."

"But, you've been on some supposedly routine trips that became decidedly un-routine. The route's mostly open highway. Not going into any cities or places where bad actors could hide. They're also not planning to stay at the camp for too long, so if you go looking around, you'll need to do it quick."

Harper stood tall. "I understand and won't add a delay. Heard some rumors that it's not really all that great a place to be, so if my friends are there, I'd like the chance to get them out. Is it okay if I bring them back?"

"How many are we talking about?" asked Anne-Marie.

"Four at most. Girls my age."

Anne-Marie gave her a nod. "I have no problems with that. Another four teens wouldn't throw off the food calculations."

"Awesome." She bowed her head. "I know it's really unlikely that all four of them will be there."

Walter gripped her shoulder. "Listen up, Harper. You keep yourself safe. Don't do anything nuts. And you get back here to your family. That's an order." His serious expression faded to a smile.

"Understood, sir." She froze. "Am I supposed to salute you or hug you?"

"You're not enlisted, so either one works."

Laughing, she hugged him, then rushed out, sprinting home to grab shotgun shells. She usually only carried an extra twenty or so in her hip bag for patrols, but wanted to bring more on any sort of trip away from town in case something went wrong. As fast as she could move, she dashed to her bedroom closet, opened the box, and transferred several handfuls, not bothering to count.

After zipping it, she hurried back outside and sprinted down Hilltop Drive. Fortunately, the van waited for her. As soon as she climbed in the side door, Rafael started the engine. It struggled a bit to catch, but not so much that he seemed worried. Deacon filled the passenger seat. Annapurna sat on the floor between the two front seats, facing the cargo area. The van didn't have a lot of room left, but Harper managed to squeeze herself in the space between the sliding side door and the Postal Service boxes of veggies.

The smell of fish and produce filled her sinuses.

Annapurna gave her a little smile, somewhere between appreciating her nerve and being grateful to have another gun on the trip. With her AR-15 and dark blue police jumpsuit, she totally looked like a SWAT officer. Deacon also ended up joining the militia, though helped Jeanette on the side with electronics work. He carried one of the M4s taken from the earlier attack. Another AR-15 rested in an improvised sling under the dashboard to Rafael's left.

She couldn't see much of the road ahead from her spot on the floor, though the side window at least offered a view of the sky.

Dad? Mom? If you're out there in any sort of way, please tell me if I'm being stupid.

A few minutes into the ride and for no particular reason, she found herself humming the song *Mad World*. It made her think of her friend Darci, who'd been obsessed with it after a goth girl on one of those singing talent shows covered it.

Yeah... the world really has gone mad.

Deacon and Rafael discussed the route while the big guy fought with a paper map.

"Now I know why people made damn iPhones." Deacon seemed frustrated enough to shred the map because it wouldn't open right. "These shits is a pain in the ass."

Rafael laughed.

He shook the paper, finally locating the stubborn fold and opening it flat. "Think we'll be making this run often? Trading with the Army?"

"Not sure. There won't be any usable gasoline for much longer. This thing still runs off unleaded. I had to spike it with some pure ethanol from Earl's to get it to work. Honestly, I'm surprised the thing is still running on this gunk. Gas usually degrades in about six months. Damn good chance this is the van's last ride."

"Are we gonna get stranded out there?" Annapurna tilted her head back to look at Rafael.

"This gas is at least eight months old, probably closer to nine since I'm sure whoever owned this van didn't fill it up the day of the strike. Hear all that knocking and shit? Course, if we get stuck at the camp, they can give us a ride back." Rafael grinned back at her. "If we wind up trading with the Army on any sort of routine basis, it's gonna be horses and carts like something out of medieval times... unless we get the biodiesel working, or start brewing ethanol."

"Hope this thing doesn't take a dump on the way there." Deacon gestured at the cargo area. "Be an awful waste of food."

Harper eyed the boxes. *I guess we're not doing too bad if we can trade away this much. Then again, it is mostly fish. Hope it's not radioactive.* She gripped the Mossberg tight, trying not to feel too sick to her stomach with worry. Randomly deciding to hop on a trip out of town could be the dumbest thing she'd ever done... besides possibly being talked into shoplifting by this girl Denise as a 'coolness' test. Needless to say, she'd failed—and never spoke to her again.

Cliff's gonna be pissed at me if this goes wrong. He's probably still going to be mad at me for not asking him first. I'm eighteen, dammit. Stop thinking like a child.

Harper sat in silence, jostled by the occasional swerving motion whenever Rafael dodged an obstruction in the road. The others didn't talk much except for airing their curiosities about what to expect at the Army camp. They hadn't heard much about it, but assumed they'd find a giant field of tents. Annapurna wanted to drop off the cargo and get out as fast as possible.

"Umm, guys? Do you think you could give me a few minutes to ask around about my friends? I swear I'll go as fast as I can."

"Yeah, sure." Deacon extended his fist back over his shoulder. "This ain't a long trip."

Harper stretched forward to bump knuckles. "Thanks."

She spent the remainder of the ride either looking out the side window at the passing ruin of cities or staring at the shotgun, mentally asking her father to keep her safe and get her back to her siblings—and Logan.

The van eventually slowed to a stop. Rafael rolled down his side window.

"What's your business here?" asked a man outside.

"Dropping off food from Evergreen. Check with Colonel Fowler. Arranged the deal a couple months ago." Rafael pointed over his shoulder with a thumb. "Don't have much gas left. Be nice if we could unload and get going quick."

A woman in desert camo peered in the right side windows, nodding in acknowledgement of Harper's wave.

"All right," said the soldier by the door. "Looks legit. They let us know you would be stopping by at some point. Go on in."

"Thanks." Rafael drove forward.

A chain link gate topped with razor wire went by the window seconds before the van swerved to the left and then the right. He stopped, backed up a short distance, then killed the engine.

"Go on and ask about your friends. We can do the unloading." Deacon opened the passenger door and got out.

Harper shoved the side door open. She jumped down, stretching away the discomfort of sitting in such an awkward, cramped pose for about an hour. Once her legs decided to cooperate, she slung the Mossberg over her shoulder and took in her surroundings.

A dusty breeze rolled in from the east toward the mountains, noticeably warmer than up in Evergreen. The place had the look of an *Indiana Jones* movie set in the Egyptian desert, only without the sand dunes. A tall fence, mostly chain link but with some solid metal parts, encircled a massive tent city. Rafael had stopped the van close to the front gates in a sort of courtyard formed in the middle of several Quonset-style buildings arranged around an open space. Watch towers of portable scaffold stood at all four corners along the outer fencing, each manned by two soldiers—one with a machine gun. Rafael had backed the van up to one of the larger huts. To her left, twenty rows of canvas tents stretched off more than a football field's length into the distance.

People milled around in the 'streets' between tents. Laundry hung here and there, boxes and crates formed improvised tables where men played cards or checkers. The scene appeared reminiscent of some nonspecific Middle Eastern city slum, the buildings rendered in canvas instead of stone. The air reeked of body odor and ass, likely due to the two large latrines standing at the edge of the courtyard— both apparently way overused.

Harper turned in place, then approached the nearest guy in a uniform. "Excuse me?"

He took a step back, putting his hand on a pistol at his belt. "What are you doing with a weapon? You gotta turn that in."

"Umm. I'm not moving in here. We just dropped off food. Going right back out. While I'm here, I wanted to find out if maybe any of my friends had been relocated here. Sergeant Clarke said something about a commandant?"

"Oh. Uhh, good luck with that. I don't think they really keep track too well of who's here. Your best bet at finding someone is going to look around. But..." He pointed at the Mossberg and her .45. "You can't take weapons into the tent city."

Harper squeezed her hands into fists, trying to keep a calm face. No way would she surrender her weapons—especially Dad's shotgun

—to the Army. They would probably make up some excuse not to give them back to her or claim they'd been 'lost.'

"Easy, kid." The guy, Morton, J according to the name stenciled on his shirt, pointed at the white van. "Just stash it in your vehicle. It's a little rough among the tents. Tensions are high, so Colonel Fowler ordered that no lethal weapons go deeper than the courtyard."

"Okay. Thanks."

Deacon, Rafael, and Annapurna stood by the back of the van talking to an older, almost fiftyish, guy in camo. His field cap had a black bird insignia on the front, so she figured he'd be the colonel. While they discussed the shipment, Harper leaned in the side door of the van. Rafael's AR-15 remained in the sling. Deacon had left his leaning on the dashboard. Evidently, they didn't worry about anyone stealing the weapons. Somewhat more confident, she slid the Mossberg under the passenger seat, then stashed her .45 beside it and covered them both with a nearby oily towel.

Maybe it would be a good thing to leave them here. The tent city looked cramped. Someone could quite easily grab her from behind and take the guns. Without time to really think, since the others wanted to leave as fast as possible, Harper hoofed it across the courtyard to the rightmost 'street.' The outside row of tents had been put up with mere inches between the canvas and the fencing. No one could walk easily behind the tent row.

She steeled herself, then proceeded to walk into the camp.

The smell of humanity thickened, nearly watering her eyes. People looked up at her, most with guarded expressions, some pitying. One man jumped up and started running toward her with a desperate hopeful expression, but stopped a few paces away, looked disappointed, then trudged off.

Aww. Poor guy. Probably thought I was his daughter.

She stepped around people while peering as unobtrusively as possible into the tents on the way. They appeared identical from the outside, save for whatever random junk had been piled up in front of them. All were square and about the size of a large living room. Most contained three rows of bunk beds and footlockers, thirty people sleeping per tent. Each resident of the camp had little personal space and even less privacy. Clothing hung from lines strung across the tents or from the bed frames. Here and there, some of the people had made walls out of sheets, sectioning a tent into multiple rooms.

Everyone looked like they'd been wearing the same clothes for weeks, and the odor saturating everything proved it. Men, women, and children merely existed in suspended time, neither part of the civilized world nor part of what came after. A few, she suspected, might have been waiting for word they could return to their homes, word that might never come.

We didn't have a flood. We had a damn nuclear war.

A two-ish year-old boy in a red shirt and no pants watched her go by, his expression blank. He reminded her of that ad on TV where the celebrity wanted two bucks a month to feed the poor in some other country, only paler.

There aren't any diapers left.

At the end of the first row, she encountered another latrine by the fence that had *vastly* exceeded its capacity. The ammonia stench wafting from it ripped the breath out of her throat and burned her eyes. People had started pissing on the ground beside it to avoid having to open the door. Gagging, she hurried into the next 'street.'

People dressed in the tattered remains of Gap, A&F, Nike, and so on fixed her with challenging stares, like a thief come to mooch off their already limited supplies. Some women shot her nasty, territorial glares while others gave her looks that warned her to run away from this place.

Men both sitting outside and in the tents occasionally stared at her the same way the Lawless had, no doubt their brains racing with what they wanted to do to a cute, young redhead. At least six men watched her with unblinking, hungry stares, buzzards waiting for a chance. She rested her hand on the empty holster at her hip, regretting her decision to disarm.

If those guys try to grab me, I'm in deep shit. The others won't hear me screaming from all the way back here.

She walked faster, thankful that they made the run early in the day.

Had the sun been down, or even dim, Harper had little doubt those men would have tried to grab her. *Damn. Damn. Damn. Now I hope the guys* aren't *here.* This place is horrible. Desperate, she started yelling her friends' names.

Harper navigated another two 'streets,' calling out for Christina, Darci, Andrea, and Veronica. Once or twice, grown women looked up in response to a name, but not recognizing her, made no move to approach.

The next lane she went down between tents set the hairs at the back of her neck on edge. More junk than usual narrowed the walkable area, and unlike everywhere else, no one loitered in view. Harper kept walking fast, peering into one tent after the next. Here, she kept her mouth shut, no longer shouting for her friends.

When Harper peered into the second from the last tent on the left, close to the back end of the camp, a man grabbed her from behind and pressed something metal to her throat.

"Easy, girl," whispered the man. "Soldiers ain't watchin' right now. Be a shame to cut such a pretty throat."

Shit! Despite the utter panic exploding in her mind, she forced herself to keep an outward calm—mostly. The man pulled her backward across the alley into another tent where two other men appeared to be waiting for her. Despite the fifteen bunk beds being loaded with clothing and possessions, she found herself alone with three men. No one to help. No witnesses.

"Dibs," said a twentyish man on the left with shaggy hair.

"The hell you say," rasped the man holding her. "I'm takin' the biggest risk. I go first."

"Yo," said man number three, a pudgy biracial guy in his forties with droopy cheeks. "We all gonna get shot in the head for this, we should like flip a coin or something for firsts."

Damn right you're gonna get shot in the head. She tried to get her throat away from the knife edge.

The man holding her moved the knife away and gave her a little shove toward the other two, who surrounded her. Trapped in a circle of three guys, she whirled to face her abductor.

He pointed the knife at her face. "Strip. And do it fast."

Harper pretended to look down, still watching him through a curtain of her hair as she reached for her belt. The instant the knife guy looked toward her groin with hungry anticipation, she sprang forward and grabbed his wrist. Spinning under the limb, she torqued his arm around, bending the hand backward until pain involuntarily made him lose his hold of the weapon. Before the other two men could take a step, she finished the wrist-lock takedown, drilling the first guy into the ground on his chin.

A little bit of pressure in the right place broke his wrist and dislocated his elbow.

Knife Man screeched in agony.

As the other two ran in, Harper scooped the knife off the floor. The younger man grabbed her left arm, but a quick slash at the air made the pudgy guy back off.

"Bitch!" growled the man holding her arm. He swung her to the left, ramming her back against a bunk bed frame.

Adrenaline, fear, or simple refusal to be a victim blocked out any pain. Harper jammed the knife into his gut. He let go of her arm to grab his wound, stumbling backward. She rushed at him, shoving his shoulders while simultaneously hooking his leg with her heel. He fell, curling on his side, moaning and bleeding.

A blur came at her from the right.

Harper jumped away from it, slashing without aiming. Her attack left a shallow slice down the front of the pudgy man's neck. Blood streamed onto the front of his shirt, but the slash didn't look deep enough to be inherently life-threatening. However, the man didn't appear to realize this and started shouting in panic at all the blood before running out of the tent.

"Bitch stabbed me!" rasp-whined the shaggy man.

The guy who'd initially grabbed her dragged himself to his feet, his right arm hanging limp at his side. He glared at her, murder glinting in his eyes.

With the pudgy guy out of her way, Harper had a clear path to the exit—and took it. The guy might have only one usable arm, but he looked psychotic. That, and she had no desire to stay involved in a fight she could avoid.

She sprinted out of the tent, hooked a right, and ran to the rear end of the camp by the chain link fence, spinning to face the 'street' she'd come from with the knife up. Neither of the other two men chased after her. Harper stood there for a moment catching her breath, her arms shaking from excess adrenaline.

Dammit. Screw this. I gotta get out of here. The guys would have heard me calling for them by now. They're not here.

Knife concealed against her forearm, Harper fast-walked over one row. That street appeared noticeably wider than the last, and not only because it had less junk in it. Whoever put the tents up hadn't been terribly precise with the spacing. The extra room reassured her a little, but she still kept her head on a swivel looking out for anyone else trying to grab her.

She paused six tents away from the rear of the camp, right where the stink of the toilets started to lessen, at the sight of a child sitting on the ground by a fluttering flap of olive-drab canvas. The girl wore a long-sleeved pink shirt with a mermaid silkscreen and a denim skirt. Her white leggings ended in tatters at her ankles, feet bare. She clutched a Barbie doll in both hands, not really playing with it, not really doing much of anything but sitting there staring into nowhere. Her long, mouse-brown hair had become a rat's nest hiding her face. But that shirt looked really damn familiar. One of Madison's friends loved mermaids, and Harper felt certain she'd seen that very same shirt before.

After slipping the knife into the empty holster that usually carried her .45, she approached the girl, who appeared about nine or ten, and crouched. The kid lifted her head peering up with vacant brown eyes that seemed too large compared to her gaunt face. She had a distant, shell-shocked, expression, as if her soul had gone elsewhere on holiday for a while.

That's gotta be Eva. Maddie's friend. Oh, no. She looks so broken. "Eva?"

A glint of recognition lent a touch of life to her otherwise wooden features. "Harper?"

"Yeah."

Eva looked around, then back up at her. "Where's Maddie? Did she die?"

"No. She's fine." Harper bit her knuckle, barely able to believe the half-starved waif sitting there could be the same girl who used to be a screaming loud giggle machine that rampaged around their house. "Are you here alone?"

"Mommy's inside. Daddy is gone. Mommy's sick. She's got a baby and it's not Daddy's."

Harper patted Eva's shoulder. "Wait here a sec, okay? I'm going to go talk to your mom."

"Okay. I'm glad Maddie's alive. I miss her."

Barely able to hold back tears, Harper stood and crept into the tent. Eight women of various ages and ethnicities lay on bunks, some reading, one stitching patches on the knees of a pair of tiny jeans, another woman appeared to be sleeping. Two smaller children sat together on a bunk at the back left corner, playing with matchbox cars.

Harper had met Mrs. Parsons only once or twice, so didn't really remember what she looked like too well. However, only one woman in the tent—with the same shade of mouse-brown hair as Eva— seemed about the right age and had a small but noticeable baby bump protruding from under her pale brown Army style T-shirt. Her desert camo fatigue pants looked a little big for her, but also much cleaner than anything else the displaced survivors had been wearing.

Why does she have Army clothes? Harper approached that bed. "Mrs. Parsons?"

The woman snapped her head up, looking at her in shock. "How do you know my name? Oh, wait. I think I know you. There's something familiar."

Eva crept in and walked up behind Harper, clutching her Barbie tight to her chest.

"Your daughter's friends with my little sister."

"Oh. Yes. Nice to see another person we know survived... such as it is." Mrs. Parsons grunted, sat up, and swung her legs off the bunk.

"If you have anywhere else to be, you might not want to stick around." She rubbed her belly. "Or you might end up like me."

Harper gasped. "Oh, no…"

"Doesn't matter now. We're just circling the drain."

"Mommy's sad 'cause Daddy died." Eva brushed her hand over the Barbie's hair. "He got stabbed."

She's thinner than Madison was at the worst of the shortage. Harper wanted to pick Eva up and hug her, but worried she'd break. "I'm so, so sorry. My parents died, too."

Eva looked up at her. "Oh, no. They were really nice. That's horrible."

"Thanks." Harper squeezed her fists, heartbroken at the sight of her little sister's friend so wan, but she also couldn't pull her gaze away. "Mrs. Parsons, you should come back with us. I got the okay to bring my friends back, but I… don't think they're here."

"Back?" asked Mrs. Parsons.

Harper sat on the edge of the bed and explained in a relatively quiet voice about Evergreen. Eva grabbed her mother's arm, more alive than she'd been yet, begging for permission to go see Madison.

"What difference would it make?" Mrs. Parsons jostled side to side like a mannequin under Eva's tugging. "Die here. Die there. Craig's gone. Eva's sick. It's just a matter of time."

"I'm not sick. I'm hungry," said Eva in a near whisper. "And bored. And sad."

"Come on." Harper took Mrs. Parsons' hand and pulled her upright. "Grab your stuff."

"What stuff?" She kept staring at the ground. "This is it. I only had the one outfit I ran out the door in and that man destroyed it when he attacked me. The soldiers gave me this. They've been damn stingy with everything else, but I guess they couldn't have me running around naked. That would be a *distraction,* wouldn't it?"

"Okay then. Come on." Harper grasped Eva's hand as well and led the two of them out of the tent. "If you don't care either way, then I'm making an executive decision."

A trace of the former Mrs. Parsons emerged from her mental fog. "I don't remember you being so, umm... commanding."

"I wasn't. Before, I just tried to be nice to everyone. Guess I've learned that some people don't deserve to see my nice side. Seriously, come on. Don't give up. Eva needs you."

"C'mon, Mommy," whispered Eva. "Please?"

Mrs. Parsons shrugged in an 'okay, whatever' sort of way.

Harper led them outside down the lane between tent rows, trying not to make eye contact with anyone while watching every possible shadow in case those men tried to finish what they started before. While those men—indeed half the men in the camp—scared her, she felt guilty at not having the ability to take the entire refugee population with her. As much as she wanted to, this many people would overwhelm the farm and risk the safety and security of everyone she cared about. If she locked eyes with the wrong desperate person, the dam would break.

It had to be this way. She couldn't harm Evergreen, even for noble reasons.

Her new home couldn't handle an influx of thousands.

23

WASTE OF FOOD

E va clung to her mother until they made it to the end of the tent row and entered the courtyard among the Quonset huts. Once out in view of multiple soldiers, Harper allowed herself to relax a little. It didn't seem likely a man with a broken arm or a guy with a stab wound to the abdomen would come charging out into a crowd of armed military personnel and try to take revenge on her in broad daylight.

They probably think I live here and are waiting for dark. She sighed out her nose. *I should tell someone so a random redhead doesn't get murdered tonight.* As much as she had little interest in delaying the trip home, if those men attacked her, they'd attack other girls or women. *No. I can't keep quiet.*

Harper guided Mrs. Parsons and Eva over to the van, already empty of boxes. None of the soldiers made any move to stop her, or even looked at them longer than a passing glance.

"Wow, this place is worse than I imagined." Harper helped Mrs. Parsons into the van.

She eased herself down to sit on the floor behind the driver's seat. "A couple days after the strike, the Army rolled through, collecting survivors. They said we had to evacuate due to radiation. Loaded us in this big open-backed truck. We drove past crowds of people rioting and looting. The soldiers shot anyone who tried to run at the convoy if they looked aggressive."

Eva curled up in a ball beside her mother, a far-off look in her eyes.

She's seen people die. Harper clenched her hands into fists, once again lost to anger at whoever set off the war. This kid who used to hang out at her house all the time, any normal ten-year-old, now looked like a smaller version of a broken combat veteran. *Mrs. Parsons is in bad shape. She's so depressed I'm scared for that baby.*

"Never did figure out who stabbed Craig. He left the tent at night to go to the bathroom and didn't come back. They found him in the morning by the latrine. A few weeks after that... The man who..." Mrs. Parsons brushed a hand over her belly. "Damn soldiers didn't get there fast enough. I told them a man in a Rockies sweatshirt had... you know. They tracked him down, dragged him back to me and asked if he was the one. When I said yes, they took him outside the tent and shot him right there. No jail here."

Eva's expression hardened with angry satisfaction.

She watched it... or at least knows what happened. "I... wow." Harper bowed her head. "Don't know what to say. You need to get out of here. Evergreen is nice."

Mrs. Parsons looked up with a blank expression. "The Army is trying to discourage crime here by more or less shooting people on the spot if they believe they did almost any sort of crime. Even stealing food or clothes. I killed a guy by reporting what he did."

"No, you didn't. That guy got what he deserved. There's no prison anymore." Harper glanced back at the roughly one-fourth of the tent rows she hadn't checked. *Ugh. That's going to take too long. They'll leave without me. Maybe I should start shouting names from the courtyard? And crap, I still need to warn someone about the attack.*

"Waste of food," muttered Eva in a dead voice.

Harper gasped, horrified.

The girl looked up at her. "One of the soldiers said that after they shot him. I think they're right. Bad people shouldn't take food away from good people." The child's stomach growled.

"Yeah... Umm. You guys wait here a sec, okay? I need to go talk to someone."

Mrs. Parsons nodded and collected Eva into a hug.

Harper jogged around the van into the large Quonset hut. She stopped a short distance inside the big garage door, looking around at various soldiers at desks or tables in search of someone higher in rank than a private. Not that she really understood the insignias, but anyone who looked near in age to her would probably not be too high up the chain of command. When she spotted a stern-looking black woman wearing sergeant's stripes, Harper approached the desk where the soldier sat cleaning a combat rifle, its parts disassembled and arranged in front of her. She didn't look too much older than thirty, but practically radiated badassery.

"Excuse me, sergeant?" asked Harper.

The woman looked up, seeming about to snap at her, but held her tongue, her expression going from annoyed to concerned. "I'd say you're out of uniform, but I don't recognize you. Civilian?"

"Yeah. Well, kinda. Evergreen militia. I'm here with the people dropping off food."

"You'll need to talk to Lancaster for that."

Harper shook her head. "This isn't about the shipment. I wanted to go along on this trip to look for my friends who I thought might have been here. We used to live in Lakewood. Didn't have any luck finding them, but three guys dragged me in a tent and tried to rape me."

Sergeant Garner—according to her nametag—leaned back in her chair, making it creak. "Who did it? What did they look like? And... are you okay?"

"Yeah. I got away. Just rattled." She took the knife out of the holster and explained how the one guy grabbed her from behind, and she'd disarmed him as soon as he gave her the opportunity. "The guy who grabbed me at first has a broken wrist and maybe elbow. I heard it pop. The other guy grabbed me, so I stabbed him here"—she poked a finger into her abdomen, on the left side—"and he let go. Last guy, I just wanted him to go away but he kinda ran into me flailing with the knife and I cut him on the neck. Just a scratch really."

Sergeant Garner nodded. "Since you're not a resident, I'll assume you don't know their names. What did they look like?"

"Umm. I didn't really get a good look at the guy who grabbed me. Thirty or so, short black hair. Red shirt. The guy I stabbed was like twenty, shaggy brown hair and beard. Woody Woodpecker on his shirt. Last guy's like forty, kinda heavyset. Big droopy face, and he's like half black. The other two are white."

"Okay. Will you be prepared to make an identification?"

Harper bit her lip. She wanted to get back home as fast as possible, but if those men grabbed her... they'd attack any woman they thought they could get away with assaulting. "Yeah. I will."

24

BAD TRIP

Sergeant Garner instructed Harper not to leave the camp until they finished investigating, likely not more than an hour given that the injuries she'd inflicted on all three men would make them easier to identify.

Harper returned to the van to wait with Mrs. Parsons and her daughter, mostly so she could make sure Rafael and the others didn't leave without her. She sat on the floor in the open side, one foot up in the van, one on the ground outside. None of her militia buddies were anywhere in sight, perhaps still off with Colonel Fowler.

A few minutes later, Eva pointed out the door. "I've seen her before, at Maddie's house."

Harper looked.

Darci Sutherland emerged from the second to last row on the left, an area Harper hadn't checked. Her friend didn't look as much in need of food as Mrs. Parsons or Eva. Somehow, she *still* appeared to be strung out, either high on weed or desperately in withdrawal. Smudges of black lipstick marked her face, though the cosmetics had mostly been wiped away. Her former pixie cut had grown out to touch the shoulders her crop top exposed. Grime smeared her bare stomach above a dingy purple miniskirt. She wore fishnet stockings, but like Eva's leggings, they'd disintegrated below the ankles, likely from walking around outside with no shoes for weeks.

Despite her refugee wardrobe, she still had the same laid-back, 'whatever happens, happens' demeanor as always.

Transfixed, Harper simply stared at her friend as the girl walked across the open dirt.

Darci paused in front of her, thumbs hooked in the waistband of her miniskirt, bony hips peeking out the top. "Hey, Harp. I hate to ask, but you got any kush or something?"

Harper blinked in shock, not quite able to process seeing her friend behaving so... normally. "You look so weird without black toenails."

"Umm, what?" asked Darci in a sleepy tone.

"Sorry, I think my brain shut off. Dar!" Harper leapt to her feet and grabbed her in a hug. "It's good to see you!"

"Whoa. Calm down. You're acting like we almost died in a nuclear war or some crap." Darci hugged her back. "Oh, wait. We did."

Harper leaned back to arms' length and stared into her friend's sapphire-blue eyes. "Are you high?"

"No. That's the problem."

"Oh. My. Gawd!" Harper again clamp-hugged her friend. "Darci! You're alive."

The girl didn't embrace her back, standing there like a post. But she always did that. "Still kinda trying to figure that out."

"What?" Harper kept squeezing her.

"Not sure if I died in the blast and this is a weird afterlife thing or if I really am high as shit right now at home and seeing this crap."

Harper looked her friend over. The girl seriously needed a shower, reeking of sweat, BO, and even puke. "I'm sorry. It's real. You have any stuff in the camp? You're coming with us, out of here."

"Nah. Just what's on me."

"Cool." Harper pulled her friend into the van. "Is anyone else here?"

"Yeah. Lots of people."

Harper couldn't quite laugh. Darci may or may not have been joking. "I mean, Christina, Andrea, or Veronica."

"I haven't seen them. Been here for a couple months." Darci yawned, her bloodshot eyes struggling to focus on Harper. "You didn't mention Renee."

"Found her already. She's okay." Harper pulled the towel away from the passenger seat and recovered her weapons.

Eva gasped in awe. "You have guns."

"Yeah." Harper slung the Mossberg over her shoulder and stuffed the .45 back in its holster. "Things have... changed. I'm part of the militia now.

Darci laughed. "You? In a militia? Get real. You can't even step on beetles."

"Some people out there are lower than bugs." Harper sat in the van's side door, feet still on the ground outside.

"Have you actually shot people?" Darci opened her eyes a little wider, almost seeming awake.

"Yeah. But only when they were going to hurt me."

"Wow." Darci whistled. "How the hell did you wind up on a militia?"

"Dad didn't want to leave the house right away. Like two months after the strike, these bastards calling themselves Lawless broke into the house to steal our stuff—and probably kidnap me an' Maddie. They killed Mom and Dad. I choked and couldn't pull the trigger on a person, so I grabbed Maddie and ran. To make a long story short, a group of survivors going by about a month before that tried to talk us into following them to Evergreen, said it was safe there. After I ran, we made our way up there. They wanted me to give them Dad's shotgun for their militia to use, but I couldn't part with it. I had to protect Maddie. So, I wound up agreeing to join."

"Wow." Darci whistled. "I never pictured you doing anything like that."

"Heh. Neither did I." She stared down at her sneakers. "Doesn't matter what happens to me anymore. It's like all I care about now is keeping Maddie safe. And my two new siblings."

"More siblings? Your mom wasn't preggers." Darci scratched at her stomach. "I'm not either."

"Random much?" Harper smiled. "No. Found Jonathan on the way to Evergreen and Lorelei happened after."

"You had a baby?" Darci blinked. "Wait, no. That wouldn't be a sibling."

"Well, I'm basically her mom. She's six, adorable, and... brittle. Had a rough life."

"Oh."

"Gawd." Harper exhaled hard. "I'm so glad you're okay."

Sergeant Garner and about a dozen other soldiers carrying M4 carbines crossed the courtyard before breaking up into groups of three and entering the tent rows.

Guess they took me seriously.

Darci squinted at the sky. "Sorry about your parents. That's a total bummer. I was sleeping when the blast hit."

"Lucky you had a basement bedroom."

"Yeah. The whole basement. I had a big ass bedroom." Darci held her arms out to the sides, swaying as if still high. "At first, I thought Dad put a war movie on way too loud." Her dazed smile fell to a somber stare. "He never even woke up. Like, all this junk hit our house and some of it landed on him in bed."

"Oh, no." Harper covered her mouth. "I'm so sorry."

"I dunno what happened to the others. Veronica's probably kicking someone's ass right about now." Darci grinned. "Everything was so chaotic and fast. I don't remember too much about the first couple days. I just stayed home until I heard a lot of people outside. They were leaving in a group to get away from radiation."

Cross-legged, mellow as can be, Darci spent a few minutes describing walking past rioters, looters, Army soldiers shooting anyone with a weapon, small kids screaming for their parents, mobs hunting down anyone who looked Asian since everyone seemed to think China started the war.

"One old guy even tried to tell people we deserved the nuclear fire because of God or something... they beat him to death, too."

Harper shivered. "You look pretty healthy, all things considered."

"Yeah, food's a bit strict here, but I've found a trick to getting extra food."

"Trick?" asked Harper.

"Yeah. Guys will pay for sex with food sometimes, but I always make them give me half their plate first so they don't cheat me."

Umm. What? She stared in horror at her friend, more at the total blasé way in which she'd said such a thing. Darci *had* been the first of her group of friends to go all the way with a boy, but she never imagined the girl capable of basically turning into a prostitute. A cold chill spread over her insides. Harper pictured herself and Madison swept up by the Army and brought to a survivor camp like this. Faced with watching her little sister turning into a half-starved waif like Eva, she probably would've offered herself in trade for extra food, too.

Shit... that could've been me.

Overcome by grief, Harper grabbed Darci's hand. "You're getting out of here. Okay?"

"Sure." Darci shrugged. "This place is kinda shitty at night. I think the only reason I haven't been jumped is everyone knows I'll put out for food."

"Put what out?" asked Eva from inside the van.

"So, I found Renee," said Harper, trying to change the subject.

Darci laughed. "Cool. She still scared of everything?"

"Yeah, pretty much."

"How's she holding up with this nuclear bullshit?" Darci waved her hand about randomly. "This sobriety crap really sucks. Seriously, you got anything? I need to take the edge off, bad. I haven't lit up in months."

Harper smirked. "Are you for real? You're asking 'Follows Rules Girl' for weed?"

"Guess that's a no." Darci scratched at her bare midriff. "What about clothes?"

"That, I can definitely help you with... once we get to Evergreen. Did you leave your boots in your tent?"

"No. Someone stole them off me when I slept."

"Whoa." Harper tilted her head. "You slept in your boots?"

"Yeah."

"Why?"

Darci laughed. "So no one would steal them. Bastards nicked my coat, too. And my bag. I had most of a pound of kind bud left, too. Sons of bitches."

"She says a lot of bad words," whispered Eva.

"Yeah, I do. The world has become one big bad word. It won't care about a few more." Darci glanced at the girl. "Hey, that rugrat kinda looks familiar."

"I'm not a rugrat," said Eva in her toneless voice. "I'm ten."

"She looks familiar because you've seen her before. She's one of Maddie's friends." Harper cast a heartbroken glance out over the tents, thinking about her little sister trying to text the girls on a broken cell phone. She hadn't expected to find *all* of her friends here, but had hoped for more than just one. That only Darci had apparently survived twisted her guts into a knot. She clung to hope that the Army might have other camps, or maybe her other friends' families had taken shelter elsewhere. Evergreen couldn't be the only settlement.

Besides, at the end of this summer, they would all have gone in different directions for college, life, and whatever anyway. But that didn't matter. In this new world, friends stayed together. Kids born or living in Evergreen would likely spend their entire lives there, the same way people did in the old days. No one back then went out of state to school or moved out of their parents' home the instant they turned eighteen.

Anyone who still had parents and friends would keep them close.

Deacon, Rafael, and Annapurna emerged from the big Quonset hut and approached the van.

The big guy appeared surprised to find Harper there. "That was fast. Searched this whole place already?"

"As much as I could." She explained locating one of her little sister's friends, introduced Mrs. Parsons and Eva, then told them about Darci finding her. "Darce has been here for weeks. She's sure

Andrea, Christina, and Veronica aren't here. So, no point roaming around back there. It's kinda dangerous."

Darci patted Harper on the leg. "Her walking around is like waving meat at starving dogs."

"That bad?" Deacon looked out over the tents. "Damn."

"If they think they could get away with it, yeah."

Harper looked up. "Yeah… we can't quite leave yet."

"You got in trouble?" asked Deacon.

"Yes and no. I got in trouble in the sense that trouble found me, but I didn't do anything wrong."

Deacon, Annapurna, and Rafael crowded around her like a pack of protective older siblings.

"What happened?" Annapurna stared into her eyes.

Not wanting Eva to overhear, Harper nodded to the right then walked a little ways past the van. The other three followed. She went over the story of her attack. By the time she finished, Deacon looked ready to go help the Army search—and assist with the execution part.

"I think I need to start asking Cliff to show me some moves." Annapurna patted her arm. "Are you sure you're okay?"

"More or less. I'll be fine until I try to sleep tonight." She fidgeted. "Never had a knife at my throat before. Have you ever been so scared shitless you stayed calm? Like the needle went right past ten and broke. I think I'm still at twenty or something. If I randomly freak out later, that means I've calmed down."

Rafael chuckled.

A few minutes later, a large group of soldiers walked two of her attackers out of the camp at gunpoint. Shaggy, his hands bound with zip ties in front of him, still clutched his gut wound, barely able to walk, his weight supported by the soldiers ushering him along. They hadn't tied the hands of the guy with the broken wrist, probably since it had swollen up and appeared painfully unusable.

Another pair of soldiers dragged the pudgy guy with the slash on his throat out of a smaller Quonset hut bearing a medical cross on its front wall. They'd tied his hands behind his back, but he also had clean white bandage panels on his neck wound.

They bandaged him up only to execute him. Wonder what excuse he gave the doctor for how he got hurt.

A bald, confident soldier at the later end of his twenties approached her. Despite being thin, he stood half a head taller than Deacon. An insignia of a single black bar marked the center of his field cap. "Garner, is this her?"

"Yes, lieutenant," said Sergeant Garner.

"I'm to believe these three men attacked you with intent to commit a crime of a sexual nature?" asked the lieutenant, Boyd according to the name on his uniform.

They were going to kill me. Why do I feel guilty that they're gonna die? Despite her dread at what she expected would happen in a few minutes, Harper kept her chin up and tried not to appear nervous or guilty. "Yes, sir." She re-explained looking for her friends, being grabbed, and fighting clear of them. "These are the ones."

"Gotta be a special kind of stupid to pull that shit after what happened last month." Garner shook her head at the men with a glare that said she just waited for the lieutenant to give the order.

"You know how we deal with criminality here, miss?" asked Lieutenant Boyd. "Are you completely sure these are the men who—"

The guy with the broken wrist made a grab for the rifle of a soldier next to him. Both men holding his arms wrestled with him, trying to peel him away.

Amid that distraction, the pudgy guy screamed, "Get off me" and twisted his big body hard enough to hurl one of the men holding him to the ground. He started to run, but the other soldier still had a grip on his left elbow, and flung him to the ground, flat on his stomach. The big guy started to struggle, unable to get up with his hands tied behind him—but several of the soldiers near him riddled him with bullets.

Shaggy, his face pale as death, stared down. He appeared to expect death, but lacked the energy to put up a last stand—or care.

The soldier holding the contested M4 wrenched it away from broken wrist guy, then walloped him in the face with the stock, knocking him to the dirt, his jaw smashed.

Lieutenant Boyd drew a 9mm Beretta from his hip, aimed, and put one bullet into the forehead of the man she'd stabbed, then shot the last man while he lay dazed.

Harper didn't make an obvious show of cringing from the spectacle of death, but she kept her gaze off to the side, not looking at any of them. *Someday, we might have to do this in Evergreen.* Taking the life of someone trying to kill her in the heat of the moment while defending herself had become a necessary evil she could cope with. *Executions*, however, she couldn't handle. She hoped she would never change so much that she could bring herself to shoot a defenseless person, no matter what they'd done—except for a few atrocities that might break down the last barrier of her humanity.

She *really* didn't want to think about those crimes, as they involved Madison, Lorelei, and Jonathan—or any of the kids. Thinking of the man who shot Logan made her bite her lip. Technically, shooting an unconscious man had been an execution. But, she rationalized it as having happened within seconds of the attack. Not the same as staring into the eyes of a condemned person and pulling the trigger.

"Well." Lieutenant Boyd holstered his Beretta, emitted a pained sigh, then put back on his 'military face.' "I'm sorry that had to happen. This isn't exactly an ideal situation for anyone concerned, but given the state of things, we lack the resources for incarceration."

"I understand." Harper swallowed saliva. "Those three would've been a threat to other women."

Annapurna, Deacon, and Rafael took a few minutes to comfort her while the soldiers gathered up the dead and dragged them away. Lieutenant Boyd apologized to Deacon for the attack on one of his people, assuming him the 'person in charge' of the Evergreen crew. They shook hands, and the lieutenant walked off toward the big Quonset hut, hands clasped behind his back.

He hates having to do that, too. I hope karma is real. Whoever pushed that button deserves worse than death.

"Ready to get going?" asked Rafael.

"Sounds good to me." Annapurna pulled Harper back to the van, ushering her inside in to sit on the floor.

Mrs. Parsons looked up, her knowing stare tinged with jealousy—but not too much. More a 'good for you' sort of feeling than resentment at Harper for getting away. Eva, evidently oblivious to what just happened a few meters away, began peppering her with questions about Madison. To keep her distracted, Harper told her about Evergreen, that Becca had turned up as well, and both of them did fine.

Deacon climbed into the passenger seat.

"Hey, big dude," said Darci. "Shouldn't Harper sit there? She literally has shotgun."

Harper groaned. The men laughed.

Annapurna glanced around at everyone, confused. "What does that have to do with sitting up front?"

"It's just like something people say when they wanna sit in the passenger seat." Darci shrugged.

Cliff would know why they call that 'shotgun.'

Rafael grasped the key. "If anyone here has gods, might wanna ask them for a hand."

Everyone—even Eva—held their breath.

He turned the key. The starter emitted a labored *whirr-whirr-whirr.*

A desperate scream built up inside Harper's lungs, but before she could shout at the van to start, it did just that.

Whew.

25

REVENGE IN SMALL DOSES

Annapurna stretched tall to peer out the window as the van exited the camp gate.

"What?" Harper clutched the Mossberg tighter. "You look like you're expecting a problem."

"Hoping not, but... I am somewhat surprised they aren't giving us trouble for taking your friends out."

"It's a survivor camp, not a prison," said Mrs. Parsons. "We can leave if we want, but there's nowhere to go. Sometimes, I think we would've been safer out there on our own."

"Trust me, not really." Harper shivered. "Especially around Lakewood. A gang's taken over that whole area. They're the ones who killed my parents. Cliff thinks they started off as a band of former convicts. Right after the war, we hid out in our basement. Dad didn't want to go outside yet because he worried about fallout. I think his plan was to give it six months if we could find enough canned food, but the gang attacked us after only two. If you see anyone wearing a scrap of blue cloth like a necklace, run the other way."

Darci nodded. "Oh, yeah. I saw some of those dudes before the Army found me. They kicked in doors across the street. Remember the 'secret base'?"

"Wow... I haven't thought about that in years." Harper pictured Darci's basement bedroom, specifically, the unfinished part in the back containing the hot water heater and furnace. A small hole in the brick wall led to a dirt-floored crawlspace they used to play in years ago.

"I hid in there while they raided my house. They took everything from the kitchen, even the ramen. Got a real bad feeling from them, so I stayed hidden and got the hell out of there once they left." Darci rubbed at a small cut on the side of her foot. "Is it weird that I don't really miss being home? Like, I'm more upset that someone stole my damned shoes than I had to leave my house. Like who does that? Takes someone's shoes."

Eva wiggled her toes. "Someone stole mine, too."

"What?" Harper gawked. "Seriously?"

"Yeah." Eva frowned.

"Maybe someone else with a child who didn't have shoes. Guess they saw her and decided their kid deserved them more. Some people." Harper sighed.

"It didn't happen at the camp." Eva shook her head. "Someone tried ta pull me off the Army truck by the legs."

Mrs. Parsons squeezed her daughter in a hug. "Our truck had so many people in it. Piled on top of each other, hanging on the sides. They kept trying to climb on, throw people off to make room. Didn't care if they tossed a little girl or an old person to the street to make way, just blind panic."

"Like rats trying not to drown," muttered Darci.

"The Army man hit the guy who grabbed me in the face with his gun, but he took my shoes when he fell." Eva frowned, picking at the tattered white fabric around her ankles. "My leggings wore out. I gotta shower with Mom now 'cause there's not enough water. They don't let us wash clothes either."

Heartsick, Harper stared at the rail thin phantom who somewhat resembled Madison's friend. She'd have felt happier about bringing the girl to Evergreen if not for the dozens of children left behind at the Army camp. She couldn't take them away from their families, and she couldn't bring that many people back with her. Both because the van didn't have enough room and the town's food supply might not be able to tolerate such an increase in population. Next year perhaps if the greenhouses worked.

To distract herself from her inability to help everyone, she started talking about Evergreen, trying to cheer the Parsons and Darci up a bit. Though, her friend didn't act too much different from how she remembered. The girl had always been overly mellow. Christina once joked that her reaction to the end of the world would be 'wow, that sucked.' From the look of it, she'd been right.

Of course, Darci dealt with the death of her mother eight years ago to cancer. Even then, she hadn't been overly emotional, though her interest in the goth thing intensified after that. Harper figured her frequent use of weed, ecstasy, and whatever other 'light drugs' she could get her hands on had something to do with losing her mother so young. Darci's father had been awesome, so no one could blame 'daddy issues.' In fact, Harper credited him with her friend only wanting to get high on softer drugs as an escape rather than obliterate herself with stuff like heroin or meth. The man didn't deserve to be crushed in his sleep by flying concrete.

The more Harper spoke of Evergreen, the more Eva seemed to crawl out of the mental cocoon she'd been hiding in. It seemed as though she'd started off in black-and-white, gradually shifting to full color. A hint of happiness in her eyes made her gaunt appearance even more alarming, but offered hope she hadn't suffered *too* much mental damage.

Kids are resilient, said Tegan in her mind.

"Shit!" screamed Rafael.

Before Harper could look up, the van swerved hard to the left. A couple of gunshots went off outside, but nothing hit the van. Eva screamed and went rolling into the passenger side wall. Harper fell over onto her back, feet in the air. Darci slid into the rear doors while Mrs. Parsons crashed over onto Harper, squishing her.

Oof. Ouch.

Deacon fired out the passenger side window, empty shell casings jumping over the seat. Harper raised her arms to shield her face from the flying hot brass. The van straightened out with enough of a rebound swerve to fling Mrs. Parsons away and propel Harper into an upright sitting position. Eva tumbled into the middle of the cargo area, flat on her back. Deacon pivoted to his right as the van accelerated, snapping off a few more shots at their attackers.

The engine struggled to respond to Rafael stomping on the pedal. When it started to chug toward an imminent stall, he eased back and erupted with Spanish cursing.

"What's going on?" shouted Harper.

"Lawless." Deacon fired one more shot. "Bunch of them jumped out on the road in front of us."

Harper moved up to one knee so she could see out the windshield.

They rumbled down a four-lane street, two in either direction separated by a narrow concrete island. A Diamond Shamrock station went by on the left before they crossed a bridge with metal arches on either side. The street past the bridge went downhill at a relatively steep angle, offering a panoramic view of a small town that had been smashed by a nearby nuclear blast. Traffic lights up ahead draped down on their poles like candles left too near an oven.

"Where the heck are we?" She whistled. "This place doesn't even look worth scavenging from."

A liquor store went by on the left, all its windows missing. Cars in the lot had been reduced to bare frames sitting in puddles of once-molten plastic and rubber. Trees, street signs, lamp posts, and telephone poles all canted to the right, toward the West, away from the source of the blast.

"Golden," said Rafael. "Washington Road. Gonna try to loop back to 93 on the other side of town."

As soon as he said it, she spotted a small "Welcome to Golden" sign coming up on the island in the middle of the road. She held onto the passenger seat for stability as the van slalomed abandoned cars as well as a corpse or three. Buildings on both sides had suffered significant damage from heat, their surfaces charred or melted, large swaths having burned to the ground.

"Stay down." Harper balanced on her left knee, right leg stretched out for stability, and aimed the Mossberg at the window. They couldn't open more than tilting out an inch or so, but if she had to, she'd blow out the glass to keep everyone safe.

Darci draped herself over Eva, holding the girl down. Mrs. Parsons did her best to lie flat. Annapurna covered the driver's side, rifle poised. Harper focused on the dark spots between and inside the blasted buildings going by. She eyed a building with a sign that read 'Mountain Toad bar.' She kept aiming around at openings, alleys, broken fences, and debris hurled from across town like she played *Call of Duty*, expecting Lawless to ambush them at any second. Some of the concrete chunks looked bigger than refrigerators, embedded in the craters they made when they came down.

Most of the smaller trees here had vanished, incinerated in place or knocked flat and burned to ash. A few thicker ones still stood like charred matchsticks in a field to the left. A statue in the middle of the road depicted a cowboy with a little girl sitting on his shoulders. Rafael drove onto another bridge with four metal framework towers, one at each corner, supporting cables—half of which had snapped— connected to brick columns along the sides of the roadway.

Harper's stomach twisted over in worry, dreading the bridge would collapse out from under them... but it didn't. The next intersection offered a view of a big mesa to the left, beyond a parking garage. Up ahead, a brown arch spanned the road with a larger 'Welcome to Golden' on it in yellow letters. Rafael drove under it, accelerating along the relatively open street in the downtown section.

The scenery reminded Harper of World War II movies showing bombarded Europe. Many of the close-packed buildings had disintegrated to shells of crumbling concrete. A large brownish building on the right still had a 'Vital Outdoors' sign near the peak of its roof, but the stores themselves looked as if a tornado had blown through already. Whether looters or nuclear wind did it, she couldn't tell.

Sudden gunfire came from up ahead. Harper shrieked and ducked as the windshield exploded inward, a burst of glimmering snowy fragments dusting over everyone. Several *clanks* hit the frame and a loud *boom* accompanied the vehicle lurching left and down.

"*Mierda!*" shouted Rafael, stomping on the brakes.

Harper rocked forward. Tires screeched. The Darci-Eva bundle slid into her from behind, knocking her over on her back. Mrs. Parsons steamrolled Annapurna into the driver's seat.

Wham!

The van slammed into something hard, coming to a full stop. The hit flung Harper into the passenger seat, squishing Darci and Eva. Fortunately, Rafael had slowed enough that the crash didn't hurt too much. She scrambled upright, instinctively pointing her shotgun at the side windows and scanning for danger.

They'd hit a parked sedan on the left side of the road in front of a place marked 'Woody's Wood-Fired Pizza.'

Rafael grabbed the AR from its sling and fired out the broken windshield, shell casings landing almost perfectly in the center console's cup holders. Deacon jumped out the passenger door and charged forward to take cover behind a half-melted pickup truck sideways across the road. Several Lawless returned fire from positions behind cars a little more than a block away.

Annapurna aimed between the two front seats, shooting at the thugs.

Eva screamed, "Behind us!"

"That's not good," deadpanned Darci.

The back doors swung open.

Harper swiveled to her right. Two men wearing blue sashes started climbing into the van; the near one pushing the doors wider, the guy right behind him raising a handgun. As reflexively as tagging flying plates on the range, she shot the gunman first and the lead man second in the span of not quite two full seconds.

Seven.

They fell to the road, revealing three more Lawless about thirty yards away coming up behind the van, all with guns drawn. Without even thinking, Harper screamed a war cry, leapt to her feet, and charged out the back. She fired at the closest man despite the range, mostly to call attention to herself and draw incoming fire away from a pregnant woman, a child, and her friend sitting in a metal box with nowhere to go.

He howled in pain but didn't go down. Harper sprinted as hard as she could run, bullets whistling by and clicking off the road behind her. She veered left and leapt behind a burned out SUV in the middle of the road, hunkering down as incoming shots *clinked* and pinged off the wreck.

Six.

Rapid fire came from her right side. A man somewhere to her left and in front let out an *oof.*

Footsteps scuffed closer. Harper swiveled left, raising the Mossberg barely a second before a big man in a motorcycle helmet and Kevlar rounded into view past the end of the SUV, a large hatchet in each hand. She shifted her aim down to avoid an ineffective strike on armor, blasting him in the groin from four feet away.

Five.

The man emitted an awful howl and doubled over forward, dropping his axes and grabbing the bloody ruin between his legs. Harper pumped two blasts into the helmet point-blank, shattering it apart into a spray of bloody foam chunks and plastic shrapnel.

Three.

The man stopped screaming.

"You're clear," shouted Annapurna.

Harper glanced to her right. Both Annapurna and Rafael aimed out the back of the van, the likely source of the barrage seconds earlier.

"Clear on this side," yelled Deacon.

"Anyone hit?" called Rafael.

"I'm good," said Annapurna.

"*Estoy bien,*" said Rafael.

"I'm okay." Harper didn't like how much her voice quivered, but she didn't feel scared… merely shook from adrenaline. She stared down at her hands, then at the van twenty or so feet away across completely open road dotted with white marks where bullets had chipped it. *Oh, damn. What the hell did I do?*

Three rounds left. She flipped the Mossberg over and fed it six shells from her hip bag, then crept back to the van, her hands still trembling.

"You okay?" asked Annapurna.

"No, not really. Having a 'holy shit I can't believe I did that' moment."

"Damn girl." Deacon trotted over. "Why the hell did you run like that?"

Harper glanced at Eva clinging to her mother, Darci staring at her in total disbelief. "I didn't want those f—those... bastards shooting into the van. Bullets would go right through it and hit them." She couldn't help but laugh. "I just killed three Lawless and I can't make myself drop an F-bomb. How messed up is that?"

"Dude!" Darci gestured at her. "Someone stole Harper and replaced her with a legit badass. Did you like blow the faces off three damn people?"

Harper cringed away from the corpses on the road beside her. "Don't remind me... and those bastards with the blue sashes aren't people anymore."

"Umm." Eva poked her finger into a new bullet hole beneath the side window. "Can we please stop being inside a video game? I don't want to be shot."

Darci looked at Harper the same sort of way her classmates had in the dream, freaked out that someone she knew killed people. But, rather than accusation, the girl's expression gave off awe. "You okay, Harp?"

"I don't know." The shotgun seemed to grow heavier in her grip. "What even *is* okay anymore? Lawless. Just lawless. Not people. Yeah. I'm good."

Mom? Dad? If you're out there somewhere watching me, I paid a couple more of them back for you.

26

MASTER KEY

R afael, AR-15 in hand, walked around to the back of the van. He didn't look *too* worried, but his expression remained far from pleased.

"How bad is it?" asked Deacon.

"Biggest problem is replacing the tire. Doesn't look like the engine took any hits. Ain't no fluid rainin' down to the street at least. We swap the tire, we should be good to go. But, I ain't gonna fight with this engine too long. If that gas quit, we'll be better off walking home."

"Rafael." Harper gestured at Darci and Eva. "They don't have shoes. And Mrs. Parsons is pregnant."

He set his hands on his hips. "So? Lotta people walk without shoes. Just gotta be careful where ya step. An' the woman is pregnant, not crippled. Not saying we gotta *run* back to Evergreen. But standing around here fighting with an engine that's choking on dead gasoline is just gonna get us shot when more of them bastards come back."

"Yeah. Ain't no thing." Deacon smiled. "I can carry the kids if need be."

"I can walk," said Darci. "Unless there's like a shitload of broken glass on the road."

Annapurna glanced at the Woody's Pizza building. "Just in case more of them show up, let's take cover inside, away from the van."

"Sounds good." Darci hopped down to the street and padded over to the restaurant, stepping around bloodstains and debris.

Mrs. Parsons carried Eva out the side door and around the front end to prevent her from seeing the bodies. Deacon grabbed the men each by one ankle and dragged them to the opposite side of the street, concealing them in a dirt lot to the right of a big building made to look like adobe. Scorched letters over the doors read 'Table Mountain Inn.'

Harper faced the pizza joint and noticed it connected to another building on the left at the corner, a Starbucks. Despite her temptation to check for coffee, she followed the others into the pizza restaurant.

The interior looked like a smaller nuke went off inside it. Sparkling flecks of broken glass glimmered everywhere on the floor, a beautiful—but painful—sight that kept Darci from going farther than about two steps. Mrs. Parsons, who still had her sneakers, crunched in among the tables until Eva abruptly screamed. She pivoted to look toward what made the girl shriek, and recoiled.

Harper hurried over, shotgun ready, but lowered it at the sight of long-dead bodies, little more than charred bones and puddles of dark purple-black rot. Eva cried softly, whispering about not wanting to see dead people anymore. The sight of the child clinging to her mother sent Harper's emotional rollercoaster on another free-fall dive. In the absence of a hormonal storm, she managed to keep the sudden, painful grief for her mother off her face. She looked away, not truly jealous of Eva for still having her mother, but that didn't mean she wanted to watch such a glaring reminder of comfort she'd never have again.

Deacon walked in, picked Darci up, and carried her in to a safe glass-free spot.

"Maybe this isn't such a good idea." She looked around at the floor, curling her toes. "If I gotta run out of here in a hurry, I'm gonna shred my feet."

"We ain't fixin' ta be here that long." He smiled at her, then approached Mrs. Parsons, holding out a handgun, grip first. "You ever fire a weapon before?"

"Once, a couple years ago." She set Eva down seated on a table and accepted the gun. "Like riding a bike, right?"

"That's a gun," whispered Eva, eyes-wide.

Harper bit her lip, worried that arming a woman who'd stopped caring if she lived or died might not be a wise idea. With any luck, the woman still had enough drive to protect her daughter, and possibly hope in Evergreen, to hang on.

Out of habit, she walked past an aisle of partially melted tables and checked the kitchen for canned goods. The Lawless, or someone, had already cleaned the place out, so she returned to the front room and stood by the front window, gazing out at the obliterated city. Rather than give in to sadness, she felt only anger at the people who caused such destruction.

A '*ka ching*' made her turn.

Darci hovered by the cash register, its drawer open, gathering the paper bills in a wad.

"The hell you bothering with money for?" asked Deacon, chuckling.

Darci shrugged. "Seems like a waste to just leave it here."

"TP is worth more than that cash." Harper sighed. "Mostly because it's wider and softer."

"Yeah, I know. But, still. Have you ever held like a thousand bucks in cash before?" Darci grinned, flapping bills at her. "I feel like Randy now."

Harper started for the back room again, inspired by thoughts of finding TP. "I never did trust that guy."

"No one trusts dealers. Not even the people who buy from them." Darci glanced down at her miniskirt. "Crap. I don't have pockets. Oh well."

After a few minutes of rummaging, Harper scored two large cardboard boxes of cheap toilet paper as well as a couple bottles of bleach and some other cleaning supplies the Lawless had no interest in. She lugged her haul to the van, then searched the bathrooms, taking all the TP and paper towels from there as well.

Outside, Deacon and Anna collected the dead Lawless, stripped them of anything useful including weapons, ammunition, and clothing not too bloody to be saved. Harper stashed the last of the TP in the van and gave in to the temptation to check the Starbucks.

The huge window along the front of the coffee place had melted into a bizarre puddle that looked more like spilled epoxy resin than glass. A streetlamp nearby bent over backward like a limp hose, flat on the road.

She rummaged the machines, shelves, and cabinets out front, having no interest in gift mugs or cups. Alas, it appeared that someone already cleaned the place out of coffee and food, so she ignored the main area and headed for the back. There, she discovered a storage room secured with a gouged padlock. The previous looters had evidently attacked it with a hatchet or hammer but failed to do enough damage to break it open.

For a minute or two, she weighed the gamble of wasting a shell on a padlock that could turn out to be guarding nothing. The idea of seeing Cliff's face if she brought back coffee—plus wanting some herself in a bad way—convinced her to burn a shell. She backed up a few paces, leveled the Mossberg off at the padlock, and fired.

The padlock and its bracket exploded in a shower of metal parts.

Eight.

Harper nudged the door aside and stepped into a small room with shelves containing about a dozen cases of coffee beans prepackaged in one-pound bags. "Yes!"

Deacon ran into the front. "Harper? You okay?"

"Fine!" she shouted. "Back here."

He rushed to the storage room door, aiming around with his AR-15. "What are you firing at?"

"Sorry. Just needed to use my master key to open a lock." She pointed at the coffee. "Help me grab these?"

"Aww damn." He laughed. "Sure."

27

PRIORITIES

Harper and Deacon loaded the coffee into the van with the TP and cleaning supplies, then went back inside Woody's Pizza. Eva whispered to her mother, asking when they could eat something. Darci paced around her relatively small area of safe floor.

"Where's Rafael?" asked Harper.

"No idea." Annapurna shrugged.

Harper bit her lip and hurried to the window, looking out at the road. Anxiety built minute by minute. *Dammit. Why did I go on this stupid trip? Madison is gonna kill me if I get stranded out here.* She peered back at Darci and Eva, hung her head, and sighed out her nose. *Okay. That's why.* Restless, she paced around by the front of the room, glass and wood fragments crunching under her sneakers.

Minutes of awkward silence later, Rafael hurried in the door.

Everyone jumped.

"Okay. Found a donor van for a tire." Rafael smiled.

"You shouldn't have run off alone," yelled Annapurna.

He waved dismissively. "Just scouting around. Easy to run from any problems. Gonna need someone to watch my back while take the tire, though."

"I'll go." Harper started for the door. "Let's just get it done quick."

"Whoa, Harp." Darci whistled. "When did you turn into Miss Rambo?"

She swept her hair off her face. "It's a long damn story. I'll tell you about it once we're home."

"You're going back to Lakewood?" Darci cringed. "That's not a good idea."

"No. That place is dead." *There's nothing left of the past. It's all gone.* "I mean my new home. Evergreen." Harper walked outside.

Rafael hurried over to the van, grabbed some tools from under the driver's seat, and rushed off past the Starbucks, around the corner to the right. Harper jogged after him. They went one block down before turning left past a brick red parking garage that had mostly collapsed in on itself. Soon, they passed a post office on the right. Rafael kept going straight at the next intersection, hurrying along the side of a big building with a rounded corner and lots of missing windows, half shattered, half melted. He ignored another parking garage entrance on the left and went straight to the end of the huge building and into the parking lot behind it, bee-lining to a Chevy conversion van that had been partially shielded from the thermal blast by the building.

Maybe twenty feet ahead, the street ended at a T in front of a big apartment complex, the left side curving around the five-story parking garage. Harper gave a quick look around, saw no Lawless—or anything else moving—and hurried to catch up to Rafael.

The spare on the back and the two tires on the passenger side had melted, but the rear driver's side tire remained intact. He crawled in one of the missing windows and came back out carrying a small jack.

"Okay. This is gonna take a few minutes. Cover me."

"Right." Harper stood behind him, looking around at the apartments and the streets.

A few dead people lay on the sidewalk behind the big office building, beneath the yawning metal frames that once held two-story-tall windows. The corpses appeared rotted to the point where she couldn't tell how they died, other than they hadn't been vaporized by the nuclear flash. *Sorry.* Shaking her head, she gazed up at the building. Someone's sports car had ended up inside the third floor, upside down, smashed like a stepped-on soda can.

Rafael set up the jack and started cranking. "Yanno, I'd been pretty damn close to opening my own garage. Lot of years busting my ass, saving up, earning certifications. Had like ninety grand in the bank, and a decent shot at getting approved for a business loan. Was finally gonna pull the trigger in January."

"Sorry," whispered Harper. "That sucks."

"Well, at least my training isn't totally going to waste. Never thought I'd be stealin' tires off parked cars, though. I don't miss having my own garage as much as I miss Marissa. We were gonna get married once the dust settled from opening the garage." Creaks and groans came from the van, its weight shifting onto the jack.

Harper kept looking around, alert for danger. "Is she, umm...?"

"Don't know. I haven't seen her since the blast." He stopped cranking the jack and gestured at the corpses on the sidewalk. "I think the people who got vaporized are the lucky ones. All their problems went away in an instant. They don't gotta mourn no one or figure out how the hell to survive." A tool clattered to the pavement with an almost melodic metal ringing.

"Aww, don't talk like that. People lived without technology for a long time. We're the lucky ones because we survived the worst war ever in history and have a reasonably safe place to call home. Yeah, it's not easy, but... we're still here."

Rafael grunted, leaning all his weight on the tire iron to break a lug nut's hold. "You really believe that? You don't sound so confident."

"Mostly." She turned toward him, head bowed. "Sometimes... okay, a lot of times, I feel guilty because I'm still alive. Dr. Hale said it's 'survivor's guilt,' and it happens all the time. People who go through something like a plane crash, sinking boat, natural disasters, whatever... and survive, feel like they aren't worthy to live when other people died. It's not easy to deal with. I can't even imagine how many people died because of that war. Smart people, important people... my parents. Who am I to still be here? But... I'm still here. I might not be a genius doctor or PhD or anything, but Maddie, Jonathan, and Lorelei seem to be happy I'm still around."

"Meh. I still think it's easier on the poor bastards who never even knew what hit 'em." He grunted louder, straining. The lug popped with a *clank*. "*Ahí tienes, hijo de puta.*"

"What if there's nothing after death? Maybe there is, maybe there isn't. But I'm not in any hurry to find out for sure. What good would it do to give up? I've got Maddie to think about. And Jonathan, and Lorelei. Those people who rode wagons out to the Old West couldn't possibly miss the Internet or Starbucks or video games because they never knew anything like that existed. The war absolutely sucks, but I gotta deal with it for the kids I'm playing mom to now." She huffed. "And I don't even like calling what happened a war. We didn't suffer a war, we suffered a bunch of arrogant, idiotic assholes having a temper tantrum."

Rafael laughed. "Yeah, I guess. I spent my whole life working to become a mechanic. Pretty soon, the world won't need me anymore. I'll be useless."

"No way, man. There's more than cars that need fixing. Pumps, generators... you're trying to get that biodiesel going right? There could still be cars if you make them exist. What if you're the guy that makes a working engine with sustainable fuel, you could be the Henry Ford of the apocalypse."

He laughed.

"I mean it. The world needs people like you to get back what we were stupid enough to throw away. I gotta believe that things will eventually get better. It might not happen in our lifetime, but it's not like all modern knowledge was wiped out. We didn't literally jump back to the 1800s. People back then could never have imagined computers or SUVs. We remember what used to exist, so we'll have an easier time getting back there. There's books."

"If we don't all die."

"When did you become such an optimist?" She puffed hair off her face.

A dull *thud* came from the road that curved to the left past the parking garage.

"Crap. Someone's there. Be right back." Harper raised the shotgun and hurried out of the parking lot and across the street.

When she reached the parking deck, she crept up over mulch and bushes, past the incinerated remains of tiny trees. Huge rectangles of steel gridding, a safety barrier spanning the second-to-fifth stories, hung between columns on the otherwise wide-open parking deck, the metal drooped from the heat blast.

Someone or something grunted and scuffed about on the street past the corner, sounding close.

Harper peered around, but an extension of the parking deck blocked her view of the street, so she scurried up to the next wall and peeked around it.

A shirtless man in dark grey pants shambled in a zombie-like gait up the sidewalk on the opposite side of a narrow street running between the parking deck and five-story apartment buildings. Bloody fluid leaked from numerous sores on his back and arms. He'd swollen to almost inhuman proportions, his left hand dark red and blown up like an inflated rubber glove. No hair remained anywhere on him.

There is no way in hell he's a literal zombie. Oh, crap! That's radiation poisoning. He's gotta be radioactive as hell. This whole place could be freakin' glowing. She aimed at his head, but hesitated, unable to murder someone who presented no threat to her or anyone else. *He's gonna be dead soon anyway. That's pretty bad radiation sickness.* As swollen and delirious as the man looked, he couldn't have much time left to live. Days, maybe hours of misery left.

Please forgive me. She pulled the trigger.

Blam.

His head exploded like a watermelon.

Rafael cursed. The distant clatter of a tire iron hitting pavement echoed back.

She ran to him, shaking from fear of radiation. "Hurry up. We have to get out of here *now*."

"What the hell?"

"This dude looked like a damn zombie. All swollen up and purple. No hair. Didn't seem like he had any intelligence left either. He couldn't have been exposed to that much radiation during the initial blast, or he would've been dead months ago. He got a fatal dose recently. There's serious radiation around here somewhere."

"Shit." Rafael spun the tire iron rapidly with one hand. "Keep an eye out in case someone heard that shot."

Harper stood watch, shivering with dread. "C'mon. C'mon."

"I'm going as fast as I can." Rafael removed the last two lugs, then handed her the tire iron. "Here. Hang onto that."

She grabbed it, stuck it through the belt loop of her jeans, and resumed looking around for danger.

After gathering the lug nuts into his pocket, Rafael yanked the tire off the van, hefted it up over his head, and ran back the way they'd come from. She jogged after him, her head on a swivel, alert for any Lawless—or more radiation victims. When they made it back to Woody's Pizza without seeing another living soul, she finally allowed herself to breathe.

Maybe only a few of them came here? Do the Lawless know there's dangerous radiation close to here? Stop panicking. It can take hours sometimes for symptoms to appear. He could've been miles away when he got irradiated and wandered here.

Rafael grabbed the jack from their van and raised the front end. Deacon and Annapurna walked outside to help stand watch. While Rafael changed the tire, Harper explained about the man she'd seen suffering bad radiation poisoning.

Annapurna fidgeted, her face paling a shade in response to the story.

"Anyone feel any tingling or anything?" asked Deacon. "The kind of radiation that's fatal in a real short exposure, you can feel it."

"No," said Harper. "I hope. Nothing I noticed."

Annapurna slung her AR-15 on its strap and helped Rafael pull the dead tire off. She dragged the bad one away to the side while he mounted the replacement. She returned, starting the lug nuts with her fingers while Rafael tightened them using the tire iron. As soon as he got three all the way tightened, she lowered the jack and packed it away in the van while he continued putting the rest of the nuts on.

Harper ran inside the pizza place. "C'mon. Time to go."

"Umm…" Darci held up her bare foot. "Glass."

Mrs. Parsons carried Eva outside.

"Grr. You need shoes."

"No shit. Got any in your pocket?"

Harper ran over. "Get on my back."

"Where's the big dude?" asked Darci.

"Standing guard outside. Trying to save time here. Come on. We gotta go."

Darci hopped on.

"Oof. You're a bit heavier than I expected."

"You're a bit scrawnier than I expected."

Harper raspberried, making Darci laugh. She almost made a joke about everyone being short on food, but what her friend did for enough to eat sapped any sense of humor from the idea, so she trudged outside without a word. Once they reached clean ground, Darci let go and scrambled into the van.

"Okay. Moment of truth." Rafael reached in and turned the key.

Labored whirring came from the starter.

"Crap," whispered Harper. "Please, no."

"It ain't that bad a walk. Twenty to twenty-five miles. Maybe ten hours on foot." Deacon shrugged.

"That's bad. It would be dark before we got home." Harper lightly banged her head against the side of the van. "And we'd have to abandon all the TP and coffee."

"Is that coffee radioactive?" asked Annapurna. "This place looks pretty bad."

"Umm… the storeroom didn't look damaged. No windows." Harper bit her lip. "Does that matter?"

Rafael tried to start the engine again, but it only whirred. "This gas is probably jelly now."

Deacon punched the side of the van. "C'mon you thing. Start. And the coffee's probably no more radioactive than everything else around us now."

"Sec." Rafael hopped out, opened the hood, and fiddled around. "Gonna give this another ten minutes before I declare it a lost cause."

"Are we gonna have food?" whispered Eva inside the van.

"Yes, honey. Soon." Her mother stared out the window at Harper with an accusing look that hit her like a slap. The Army camp had been bad, but still better than being stranded out in the middle of nowhere.

Harper walked around to the side door and got in. "There's food in Evergreen. We just need to get back there. Didn't bring any supplies for a long trip because we thought this van would work and it's only like an hour by driving."

"Okay… here goes. Last try." Rafael climbed into the driver's seat. After muttering softly to himself in Spanish for a moment, he cranked the ignition and feathered the gas pedal.

Whirring came from the starter.

The engine chugged, then died with a loud backfire.

He turned the key again—and it started.

Everyone cheered.

Harper damn near cried tears of joy. Deacon and Annapurna jumped in. Rafael backed away from the wreck they'd hit, cut the wheel, and drove onward.

"We're not clear yet." Deacon aimed out the passenger door window. "That group on 93 didn't chase us into town. Stay alert."

Mrs. Parsons flattened herself out on the floor with Eva. Darci also hit the deck. Harper kept watch on the right side, favoring the rear while Annapurna covered the left. Rafael nursed the van along at a frustratingly slow pace, but they still moved faster than walking, or even running. After a harrowing few minutes, he took a right turn onto a larger highway. Enough spaces existed between the ruined cars that he could accelerate up to about forty and have no trouble weaving among them. The engine rattled and gasped like it would quit at any second.

Once it seemed highly unlikely that the men who initially attacked them on Route 93 would be a threat, Harper relaxed and flopped to sit on the floor, shotgun draped across her lap. She didn't know if the close call had been a warning from the universe that she shouldn't gamble with leaving Evergreen again, or if going to look for her friends had been the right thing to do.

Eva lifted her face away from her mother's shoulder to smile at Harper. Even Mrs. Parsons appeared to have finally set her apathy aside, appearing almost to be in a good mood. Darci lay flat on her back, staring at the roof, her expression unreadable.

Okay. Maybe going to Eldorado was a risky idea, but a good one.

"What are you thinking, Dar?" asked Harper.

"I really want some damn weed."

Harper laughed. "At least you got your priorities straight."

"Damn right." Darci grinned.

28

DANGEROUS

T he most difficult task of Harper's life waited for her upon returning to Evergreen: not telling Madison that she had found Eva right away. She hadn't intended to turn it into a big surprise on purpose, but she wanted to sleep that night. The doctors would be busy with the girl and her mother for the rest of the evening, and Harper needed sleep. Madison basically stayed up all night when she looked forward to something the next day. It took a nuclear war to get her to fall asleep on Christmas Eve for the first time in her life.

They'd returned a little past the time the kids had gotten out of school, and dropped Darci, Eva, and Mrs. Parsons off at the med center first thing. Considering the child's malnourished condition, Tegan wanted to keep her there for at least a few days under observation. Both doctors, as well as Grace and Al Gonzalez, appeared shocked at the Army allowing the girl to get *that* thin. Harper suspected Mrs. Parsons' depression more than the soldiers might have had something to do with it. Hopefully, the woman would improve in better surroundings.

When Harper returned home, all three of her siblings swarmed her, making it clear she knew how freaked out they'd been when she didn't show up to walk them home. Carrie had stepped in to keep an eye on them. As expected, Madison gave her grief for leaving town, but upon hearing *why*—likely the only chance to ever check the Eldorado Army Camp for her friends—her little sister stopped being angry. Instead, she fired the guilt cannons: getting clingy and telling her how sad she'd be if something happened to her.

Cliff's reaction to her going with them on the trip made her feel like she'd snuck off to a party after her father told her not to. Only, she didn't end up grounded. He merely looked at her with a 'do you have any idea how worried I was' expression. With Cliff, Carrie, and all three siblings staring at her, she relayed a simplified and kid-safe version of the trip (that left out finding Eva and Mrs. Parsons). The description of the camp conditions caused Madison to cling even tighter, curled in a ball beside her on the couch. As soon as she mentioned encountering Lawless, her little sister fell quiet.

Harper spent the rest of that afternoon and evening worried and guilty, and almost caved in about mentioning Eva. She didn't want to because Madison would demand to go straight to the med center, and the doctors may or may not let them have visitors yet. The girl would either have a screaming meltdown or spend all night bouncing around like a chihuahua on ten espresso shots.

Board games made for a decent time kill, and also gave Harper a chance to spend time with the kids. Later that night once the kids went to bed, she stayed up a little longer to talk with Cliff and Carrie about the trip, with full detail. Carrie gasped at the mention of what happened to Mrs. Parsons.

"She's gonna kill you." Cliff chuckled.

Harper exhaled, not quite able to smile. "Hopefully, she'll be happy enough not to think that I didn't say anything tonight. Planning to take her to visit in the morning. How radioactive do you think the place was? That guy I saw... did I do the right thing?"

"Bloated, purple, and moaning? Yeah, I'd wanna be shot in the face, too." Cliff shivered. "Whatever exposure he already suffered killed him the instant he soaked up that many rads. Even if real hospitals remained working, they couldn't have done anything for him other than make him comfortable for the last few hours or days he had left."

She sighed. "Thanks. Still feels like I killed a guy."

"That's understandable, but know that you didn't. He was already dead... just didn't realize it yet."

"Heh. So, umm... Eva like hugged her mother and I, umm..."

Cliff held his arms open.

She clung to him, letting her guard down for a few minutes so she could enjoy the feeling of having a dad. His embrace soothed the part of her not yet ready to be an adult, the inner child she had to tuck away in an armored bunker. "I'm *so* glad you're teaching me that hand-to-hand stuff. I don't wanna think about what would've happened otherwise."

"Did you honestly expect me to let you be on the militia *without* showing you that stuff?"

She pulled her hair off her face, managing a weak smile. "No, not really. But thank you for teaching me."

"However, you did scare the crap out of me." He patted her back. "Thought you were just going to ask them to keep an eye out. Didn't expect you'd end up going on the trip."

"Neither did I. Kinda all happened at the last minute. I started trying to describe my friends, and Anna kinda got overloaded and suggested I go with them. Wow, that place was horrible. I guess it's better than starving in the ruins of a city... but holy crap. Walking around those tents was almost as scary as my first couple days running around Lakewood alone with Maddie. I never want to go back there."

He patted her shoulder. "So, don't."

"Not planning to. Oh, Dad?"

He glanced at her.

"Check that cabinet." Harper pointed.

Cliff narrowed his eyes in playful suspicion. "If something comes flying out at my face..."

"Swear." She held up a hand.

He maintained his challenging stare for a few seconds more before relenting and taking the two steps across the kitchen to open the cabinet door—revealing twelve one-pound bags of Starbucks dark roast. Cliff's expression shifted to worshipful awe.

"You look like you're peeking into the Ark of the Covenant." Harper chuckled.

"That wouldn't be this impressive." He plucked one bag, cradling it like a newborn infant. "Where'd you find this?"

"Looter's privilege." She grinned, and explained finding twelve cases in the storeroom. "I had to. Call it thanks for getting my stuff back. Though, I dunno if that'll make you cry."

"Damn near might." He fake sniffled.

Harper chuckled.

He set the bag back in the cabinet and winked at her. "Thanks."

She exhaled. "Okay. Gonna go to bed before Maddie and Lore drag me down the hall."

"Night, kiddo."

Harper stuck her tongue out at him. He returned the gesture with a 'nyah' sound. Trying not to laugh too loud, she headed down the hall to get ready for bed. Three steps later, the emotional weight of the day crushed the humor straight out of her. She grabbed her nightie from the bedroom, went into the bathroom, and stared at the tub.

I can't stand in a shower for as long as I want to right now.

Instead, she soaked in a hot bath, letting her mind drift from horror to horror as it cared to. She watched herself mercy kill the irradiated man between replaying the men attacking her. Somehow, despite what they wanted to do to her—had likely done before, and would do again—she couldn't feel pleased with their execution. Relieved, yes. Pleased, no.

The hot water leeched the soreness from her muscles. She didn't bother with soap as that would require moving. Each passing minute lessened the tension in her body. Being disgusted with the world seemed like the natural reaction to the day she'd had, but the world had been plenty horrible before. The worst parts of it—school shootings aside—just hadn't occurred anywhere inside her bubble of awareness.

People suck.

Right as she started to slide down a black well of thinking that the annihilation of eighty percent or so of the world's population had been an improvement to living conditions, the door creaked open.

"You comin' to bed?" Lorelei poked her head in. "Baf time?"

The innocent face framed in platinum blonde felt like the hand of an angel pulling her back from the precipice of apathy. "Not really. Just sore and needed to soak a bit or I'd never be able to go to sleep." *Okay. Most people suck, but not the ones here.*

Lorelei walked in. "Gotta pee."

"Knock yourself out." Harper closed her eyes and let her head rest against the back of the tub, debating sleeping there the whole night. But… the water would eventually become cold, not to mention neck cramps.

A moment after the toilet flushed, the shower curtain pulled aside. Lorelei grinned at her. "Please come to bed. I need hugs."

"Okay." Harper patted her on the head and sat up. "Give me a bit to dry off."

"Yay!" Lorelei bounced on her toes, then ran back to the bedroom.

SLEEP TOOK ITS SWEET TIME ARRIVING THAT NIGHT.

Harper expected a dream about zombies, and her brain didn't disappoint. Perhaps since she'd been ready for the sight of hundreds of that irradiated man chasing her around Golden, what might have otherwise been a nightmare ended up merely depressing.

She awoke to Madison and Lorelei arguing over underwear. Apparently, Lorelei didn't want to put any on because 'they all smelled.' Madison kept insisting she had to and she should pick the least stinky ones. Harper sat up and glanced to her right. Both girls had on dresses so dirty her mother would've freaked at sight of them. Of course, post-end-of-the-world, they looked about normal.

Eagerness to reunite Madison with Eva obliterated the last of Harper's fatigue. She hopped out of bed, walked straight past the great underwear debate of 2019, and headed to the hall closet. There, she retrieved an unopened packet of undies that would've fallen straight off Lorelei a few months ago, but should fit her now that she had improved from severely underweight to simply underweight.

"Here." She tossed the pack to Madison. "Those should work. I'll do laundry this afternoon."

"Have you been hoarding clean underwear?" Madison blinked at her. "I've been wearing the same six pairs for months."

"No, just a couple packs a little too big for her before. Excuse me." Harper scurried into the bathroom.

Madison followed, but hovered outside the door. "Can you maybe do laundry more often? Yeah, a nuclear war happened, but do we have to be disgusting? Seriously, we—Lore! They don't belong on your head!"

Lorelei giggled.

Harper face-palmed. *She's doing that on purpose to make us laugh.*

After she finished in the bathroom, Harper got dressed. True, she *had* let the laundry go a bit too long. Rather than spend half the day wearing a towel, she'd stop by the quartermaster's and try to find a plain dress or something for herself and the girls so she could wash all the dirty stuff at once. Her least funky outfit had probably been worn six or seven times since the last time it saw hot water.

Oh, holy crap. The machines might work again. She blinked. *I might not have to scrub crap by hand in the bathtub. Whoa. Laundry might not be an all-day project.*

Buoyed by that awesome thought, she hurried to the kitchen for a breakfast of toast with orange marmalade. The taste of it momentarily made her sad at the thought she might never see oranges again in her lifetime. They wouldn't grow in Colorado and nothing even close to interstate cargo transport existed anymore. All rumor suggested the East Coast had been pummeled beyond recognition, so any produce growing in Florida for the next hundred years would likely glow in the dark.

When they finished eating, the kids scrambled out to the backyard. Harper cleaned up the dishes since Cliff had to run off for a patrol.

Until or unless Cliff made things official with Carrie, Walter considered Harper responsible for the three kids, so she got to stay home to watch them on the condition she be prepared to respond to any emergency air-horn blasts. If the day ever came where her more-or-less parents made things legal, Carrie would assume responsibility for the kids while Harper went out on patrol. She didn't mind that idea, either.

Deciding to roll the dice of chance, Harper put all her clothes in the first load of laundry along with as much of the girls' stuff as would fit and wore a towel. The clothes Cliff had brought back from her old home still stank like mold and wet dog, and a hint of dead person. They'd have to be washed before she'd be able to bring herself to wear them. She nearly jumped right out of it in a celebratory dance when the machine worked. After scurrying to the living room to grab *The Secret Garden*, Harper spent the next hour or so sitting in the laundry room since she had only a towel on, reading. Within minutes of her taking clean stuff out of the dryer and getting dressed, Becca, Mila, and Christopher showed up. Perhaps due to the warm day, none of them bothered with shoes. All four girls wore simple dresses, making the kids look like a scene out of a movie set somewhere in 1930s rural America: a bunch of innocent, slightly grubby, happy children running around outside to play in a time before video games or scheduled youth sports.

Harper threw the kids' clothes into the washing machine, then headed to the bedroom to grab the Mossberg, slung it over her shoulder, and returned to the kitchen. She opened the patio door. "Maddie? Becca? Come here a sec please."

The kids all froze, staring at her. Following a brief pause, Madison and her friend walked over.

"What?" asked Madison.

Harper motioned for them to step inside. "I need you two to come with me real quick."

Becca's eyes widened. "I didn't do it."

"No, this isn't bad." Harper laughed. "Just a little walk to the med center."

"I feel fine." Madison folded her arms.

"So do I." Becca tucked a lock of her yellow-blonde hair behind her ear. "And shouldn't my parents be taking me?"

"Please? It's nothing medical. I promise you guys will thank me." Becca fidgeted.

Madison huffed. "Okay. Fine."

"They'll be back in a little while," called Harper.

Mila, Jonathan, and Christopher resumed playing Frisbee.

The girls followed Harper out the front door, constantly giving her suspicious glances. She led them down Hilltop out to 74, hung a right turn, and walked to the med center, barely able to contain her excitement.

Ruby waved from the counter as they entered. "Morning, girls. Everything okay?"

"Yep." Harper crossed the room. "How's things here?"

"Good, good." Ruby smiled at the girls. "Are you two enjoying your first day off school?"

"Yeah." Becca smiled.

"I don't know yet." Madison narrowed her eyes at Harper. "I'm waiting to see what sort of treachery awaits me."

Harper cackled. "Come on."

She headed down the hall to the patient room. Mrs. Parsons sat in a chair beside a bed containing Eva. The girl appeared happy despite being hooked up to an IV line. The pair of them also looked almost normal again, having cleaned up and been given new clothes. Of course, the girl remained far too thin, but not quite as bad as Lorelei had been upon her initial arrival in Evergreen.

Madison stopped short in the doorway. She looked at Eva, up at Harper, back to Eva, and burst into tears. Harper squeezed her shoulder.

"Oh-Em-Gee!" squealed Becca. She ran over to the bed.

At the outburst, Eva glanced toward them. "Maddie! Becca!"

Madison, still sobbing, sprinted to the bed, half climbing into it to hug her friend. A few minutes of happy crying soon became laughing and an explosion of three tweens talking, peppered with 'Oh-em-gees' and multiple squeals or gasps. Madison and Becca both fussed over Eva for being so skinny, and gushed at Mrs. Parsons for having a baby. The woman kept on a pleasant face and accepted their goodwill despite the circumstances of her pregnancy.

They'll be occupied all day.

Harper walked over to Logan's bed, leaning down to kiss him.

This, of course, set off a chorus of 'ooohs' from the girls.

"Heard you did something risky." Logan grinned. "Your sister stopped by yesterday to inform me how unhappy she was that I didn't stop you from leaving town."

"Sorry. So, umm… how are you feeling?"

He squeezed her hand. "Still hurts when I breathe, but it's gone down from 'gah, holy effing crap' to 'ouch.' Dr. Hale said I can probably go home next week, maybe as early as Wednesday."

"Nope." Harper shook her head. "You're gonna stay with us until you're back to normal. I don't think three other guys from the farm will be too interested in looking after you."

Logan shrugged his right shoulder, not moving the injured side. "I'm not one of those guys who gets a cold and acts like he's dying."

"So you're the type of guy who gets shot in the lung and plugs it with bubble gum thinking you don't need a doctor?"

He laughed. "Not quite that bad, but yeah. That's closer to the truth. I can manage."

"I don't want you to 'manage.' I want you to get better. If you try to do everything yourself, you're going to take forever to mend."

"Okay, okay. Fine. But Troy, Ed, and Juan are going to be heartbroken I'm not there."

"Totally." She faked a serious face.

They looked at each other for a moment, then cracked up.

"Do you think this is going to work?" She fidgeted her thumb across the back of his hand.

"Are you asking me about *us* working, Evergreen working, whether or not humanity will rise from the ashes… or me recovering at your place?"

She blushed a little. "Mostly option two but some option one. I'm not sure what I'm doing since I've never like been in love with anyone before."

"Never?"

"No. I mean… there have been boyfriends before, but I never felt like losing them would be the worst thing in the world."

"Wow. But none of them got shot after a nuclear war though."

"Don't be a jackass." She poked him. "Do you think we'll have a future together? And I mean us as well as this town. So many things could go so wrong, I can't even figure out which ones to worry about."

Logan pulled her hand up and kissed her knuckles. "Well, I can say for sure we won't have nukes fall from the sky again in our lifetime."

She laughed despite shedding tears. "I said don't be a jackass."

"Hmm. Was that a laugh I just heard?"

"Yeah."

Harper lifted her gaze off the floor to meet his, speaking in a whisper so Madison didn't hear. "The other day when those two guys started shooting at Marcie, one of them was this guy Scott who used to work at the Starbucks we always went to. He didn't seem to recognize me at first. I'd seen him three or four times a week for like two years. And there he was with a gun, maybe even shooting at me."

"Maybe?" Logan tilted his head. "How can someone shoot at you and you not know if they did?"

"They'd gotten inside a house, and fired at us from a window. Too dark to see anything inside and I had been ducked down behind a tree at the time. He missed."

"Obviously." Logan squeezed her hand, worry radiating from his eyes. "I don't want anything to happen to you."

"Good. That makes two of us. I really don't want anything to happen to me either."

"Jackass." He winked.

"You started it." She stuck out her tongue.

"So mature."

She raspberried him.

"It's not really surprising." Logan grimaced while shifting his weight. "That guy had to see thousands of people every day. Easy for faces to blend into each other. Different for you because he'd always been the one behind the counter."

"Well, he did say 'skinny mocha' right before Roy shot him. I think he might have been willing to surrender, but they didn't give him the chance." Harper sighed. "But, for all I know, he could have shot me anyway. What happened to people?"

"The guy probably snapped. The hockey team was on the road stupid early that day. We left the hotel like ten minutes before we saw the first nuke light up the sky. The driver slammed on the brakes and cut off the road to put us under an overpass. Might've been the only reason we made it. We all huddled there in the bus for hours, dreading the instant any of us moved, another explosion would go off. It took me a while to believe it really happened." Logan let his head fall back on the pillow, staring at the ceiling. "I lost my parents and little sister. Might have lost my older brother and sister, too. I still don't know. Might never know. Every day I wonder how I didn't just say screw it and give up."

"I'm glad you didn't."

He brushed a hand over her cheek. "You had Maddie to protect. I didn't. Just me. None of us on that bus had any hope our families in Springs survived. But, I dunno. We still had each other and this silent 'we have to survive' team mentality took over. Even Zach and Kirk stopped with the Mexican crap until we got to Evergreen. Guess this place made them feel safe again."

"Maybe. We're like in a nowhere world between terrifying danger and any ordinary day." She exhaled. "I really hope we live to see a day where things are kinda back to civilization. Why are there so many lunatics?"

"People are wired differently. Maybe that Scott guy had a wife or kids or something and he couldn't handle losing them. Maybe he just had cats or even suffered a psychotic break over losing access to WoW."

"Huh?"

"It's an online game. Players can be really addicted." Logan shrugged. "Trying to make a joke."

"Sorry. I played some games, but not all that many. I used to read more than anything."

He raised both eyebrows. "So, I'm dating the smart girl? Cool."

"What if I snap?" Harper paused, glancing over at the tweens sitting cross-legged in a circle on Eva's bed, chattering away like they used to do. "I don't know how much longer it will be for me before I do. I've killed people. Four more yesterday. And it's freaking me the hell out that it's *not* freaking me the hell out. Have I already snapped?"

"You seem fine to me. Lawless?"

"Three. One was…" She shuddered. "Some poor guy with bad radiation poisoning."

Logan grunted from the pain of sitting up. He pulled her close, cradling her head to his shoulder. "Please tell me you didn't get irradiated by something out there. I can't lose you. Not after I've lost everyone else I've ever cared about."

"No… I'm okay. He must have been wandering." She hugged him back, choked up at the vulnerability in his voice. "Now, lay back before you rip open your stitches."

He relaxed, and let her ease him back down. "Tell me what happened?"

"Okay." Harper twisted a lock of hair around her finger continuously while explaining everything about the trip.

He scowled off to the side when she mentioned the three guys grabbing her. "They got what they deserved."

"It's bothering me to think that I'm less dangerous to a random bug in the house than I am to people."

"That bug in the house didn't attack you. It's just being a bug, doing bug things… not wanting to hurt anyone. Now if you ran into a scorpion trying to sting you and stepped on it, that would be entirely different."

"She'd still try to save it," called Madison from across the room.

Becca and Eva laughed.

"Yeah, I guess you're right." Harper let out a long breath. "So… assuming I don't have a mental breakdown in my future, how do you feel about *us*?"

"How do I feel about you? Or us. Hmm. I've been thinking about it a lot since I have so much time in here to do nothing but think about stuff." He beckoned her closer with a finger, whispering, "This isn't for little ears."

Harper smirked, but leaned closer.

"This is how I feel about *us*," he whispered, before sitting up and kissing her.

Not wanting him to strain his injury, Harper pushed him back down, but didn't stop kissing him.

A chorus of "awws" came from the girls.

Harper muffled a laugh into Logan's shoulder.

He patted her on the back of the head. "I think we're gonna be okay... as soon as these damn stitches come out."

29

SCHRODINGER'S NORMAL

The ghost of dinner hung in the air as a fragrance, faintly meaty with hints of onion. Harper stood at the sink doing the dishes, occasionally glancing out the window at the kids playing in the yard. Madison and Becca wanted to return to the med center after eating, but reluctantly accepted that Eva needed some quiet time.

She suspected the dinner Cliff cooked had been made with something other than the chicken he claimed it to be, potentially rabbit or squirrel meat. It didn't taste quite like chicken, but she didn't mind the flavor. Even though Madison largely abandoned vegetarianism in the interest of not starving, she would probably have still objected to eating bunnies or squirrels. While the girl didn't only want to save the 'cute and fuzzy' animals, her degree of upset at people hurting animals grew according to the cuteness of said animal.

I'm kinda glad he didn't tell us what we ate. As long as it's not cat or dog, I'm okay with it if I don't have to picture the poor critter. Oh, ick. It might've been frog. She chuckled to herself thinking that Madison would have been bothered by frog meat less than either squirrel or rabbit.

Regardless of what they'd had for dinner, Harper smiled at Cliff going next door to spend time with Carrie alone. Though the electricity had been stable all day, she sincerely doubted they planned to watch movies.

Though it hadn't started to get dark out, the sun burrowed itself deep into a thick wall of clouds in the west. A hint of wood smoke carried on the breeze, likely from cook fires going on in the southern parts of town where electricity hadn't yet reached. Outside, the orangey light cast everything in a surreal glow, dim enough that her reflection appeared on the window.

The young woman gazing back at her wasn't entirely Harper Cody. The girl had the same red hair, same general features, but her blue eyes didn't hold a sense of perpetual shy anxiety. Her jaw had a firmer set, chin higher, more confident. She no longer looked like the sort of person who would quietly walk the other way to avoid a loud or uncomfortable situation. Mom and Dad probably wouldn't even recognize her at first.

But… she also looked happy. Or if not happy, at least content.

Maybe I'm not as messed up as I thought.

Once she finished cleaning the dishes, Harper headed to the living room and picked up the cursed book, *The Secret Garden*. She considered it jinxed because every time she tried to read it, something interrupted her. She flopped on the sofa, held the book up in front of her, and stared a challenge at it.

"I don't care if it's one paragraph a day, the only way to break your curse is to finish you. Game on."

A pleasant two-ish hours allowed her to make a good deal of progress before the kids spilled inside. They clustered around the television to use the PlayStation, taking advantage of it before the town's power grid breathed its last gasp or the system itself crapped out. Jonathan found a few other titles installed that worked without an online connection. Tonight, they took turns with a racing game involving flying hover-glider type vehicles in a futuristic city.

Harper kept reading, not wanting to look at the science fiction scenery. The idea of a reliable working car and grocery stores felt like they'd become luxuries of an impossible future, forget flying cars and cyborgs.

The kids rotated turns. When Becca and Mila had the controls, Jonathan and Madison decided to do a few dance stretches. Lorelei, not terribly interested in the video game at all, played with her dolls on the sofa beside Harper.

"Why are you guys bothering with that?" asked Becca. "No one cares about dancing anymore."

Madison reached up with both hands and grasped her right foot which hovered over her head, her leg up behind her back. "I did dance because it's fun. Never wanted to become a pro. It's exercise and I liked doing it."

"But we play outside all the time now. We don't have to go to dance class or gymnastics to get exercise." Becca reached up and tickled Madison's defenseless stomach.

Squealing, Madison lost her grip on her foot—nearly kicked Jonathan in the head—and fell seated on the floor, laughing. "We're not outside right now. And, again, I like doing it." She stood again and pulled her other leg up behind her.

Jonathan copied the maneuver. Harper cringed at the sight of a boy stretching like that. It somehow just didn't seem right, or comfortable—or possible.

"When's Eva gonna leave the hospital?" asked Becca.

"Soon. Maybe even tomorrow." Madison grinned. "She's not sick, just hasn't had enough food."

"Nice." Becca grinned.

"Not having food is bad." Lorelei shook her head hard. "People shouldn't do that."

"What about Melissa?" asked Becca.

Madison glanced at Harper, her smile fading. "I dunno. Ask Harp."

Becca paused the game.

"Ack!" yelled Mila.

"Sorry." Becca twisted around with an expectant look.

Harper stuck the folded paper back in the book and closed it. "I didn't see Melissa at the Army camp. She's probably at another one."

Madison's mood crashed. She lowered her foot to the floor and stared down. "Do you think the gang got her?"

"No," answered Harper without hesitation. "Most of the people who lived around us evacuated fast... within a couple days of the attack. Those idiots didn't show up for two months."

"Yeah. We were kinda dumb." Madison sighed, her mood improving from sorrow to blah. After standing there for a second or two, she ran over and curled up beside her on the couch, leaning her head on Harper's shoulder. "We should've left. Is it okay if I'm mad at Dad for making us stay?"

Harper brushed her sister's hair with her fingers. "Yeah. It's okay. I'm sure if ghosts are real, he'd be angry with himself for deciding to stay, too. But... I'm sure he'd be happy we're okay."

"Yeah." Madison clung tighter to her arm. "I'm not mad at you anymore for going to the Army camp."

"Good." Harper kept stroking her hair.

"Now I'm mad at you for not telling me you found Eva as soon as you got back." Madison stuck her tongue out, but the gesture seemed more playful than anything.

Harper chuckled. "Yeah, I figured you'd be upset about that. I also knew you wouldn't be able to sleep last night if I'd told you, since the doctors wouldn't let anyone see her."

"Okay. That makes sense."

Carrie, next door, made a noise loud enough to hear over the video game.

"Is Aunt Carrie in trouble?" asked Lorelei, wide-eyed with worry.

"Umm." Harper's cheeks burned red. "No. She, umm... probably just saw a mouse."

"Had to be a really big mouse if it made her scream," said Madison.

Harper blushed even harder. Fortunately, the innocent look on her sister's face proved she hadn't meant that the way it sounded. "Could've been a rat. Don't worry. Cliff's there. So... tomorrow's Saturday. You guys wanna go back to the pool?"

"Yeah!" cheered the kids in unison.

ACTING WEIRD

S aturday passed in a pleasant blur of swimming, hanging out with Darci and Renee—who reacted to seeing Darci almost the same way Madison had reacted to Eva—and unwinding. True to Madison's guess, the doctors allowed Eva to leave the med center that morning, and she joined the kids to play. She wound up swimming in her dress since Renee hadn't had a chance to make a suit for her.

That afternoon, Cliff and Carrie watched the tween squad while Harper slipped off with Renee and Darci to Earl's—at Renee's insistence. She spent a while talking about her now-official 'job' with the quartermaster, dealing primarily with sorting, repairing, storing, and assigning clothes. Once the farm began producing materials, she would start working on manufacturing cloth from scratch and sewing new garments.

Darci had—somehow—located weed, and sparked up a joint right in the middle of Earl's.

Renee and Harper declined her offer of a toke.

"Where the heck did you find that?" whispered Harper.

"Oh, chill out. Nothing's illegal anymore."

"Uhh, Darce…" Renee nodded at Harper. "Harp's basically a cop now."

Darci burst into laughter. "Yeah, well. I'm sure they don't care about a plant."

Renee fidgeted.

"No, not really. Though, I am curious how you managed to find it." Harper waved the smoke away from her face. "And please puff that the other way."

"Some Spanish guy has a hydroponic thing in his basement. Had a whole bunch stashed away. Dude kinda looked familiar."

"Lucas Garza," deadpanned Harper.

"Yeah, that's him." Darci snapped her fingers. "Nice guy."

"He was in movies or something, right?" asked Renee.

"Something like that. Might've been a made-for-TV movie or a series. Nothing I ever watched though. Used to be a rich celebrity, but not like *super* big." Harper sipped her beer.

Darci's eyes opened to normal human width. "Wow. Seriously? I was chillin' with a legit celebrity?"

"Yep." Renee laughed. "You finally got to meet someone famous, but they weren't a musician."

The door opened.

Harper looked up to glance at who walked in and gasped at the sight of Logan not-quite-limping in. She jumped out of her chair and rushed over to help him to the table, letting him have the booth spot where she'd been, then dragging a loose chair to the table end.

"I'm not supposed to have beer since I'm on pain meds. Just needed to get out of that place and be social."

Renee's cheeks reddened a touch.

"No wonder you insisted we go here." Harper looked around. "Damn. No pretzels to throw at you."

"Sorry," whispered Renee.

"Naw, it's great. Thank you."

"Not bad." Darci looked him over. "So you're the one Harper's stupid for, huh?"

"Something like that." Harper grinned.

"Umm. She's not blushing." Renee blinked. "Or denying it."

Darci took a few seconds to react, again opening her eyes all the way. "Wow. Now I know the aliens stole Harper and replaced her with a pod person."

"Naw. I'm still me. Just… I guess I decided to stop worrying about trivial bullshit since there's actual *deadly* bullshit to worry about now." She took another sip of her beer. "And you know what's really worrying me?"

"Killing people?" asked Renee.

Logan rested his hand atop hers. "Madison?"

"You don't wanna die a virgin?" Darci grinned, leaking smoke between her teeth like some kind of Cheshire dragon.

"All of those things bother me to some degree." She held up the beer. "But what's bothering me right now is that this stuff doesn't taste overly strong to me anymore. Maybe I should lay off. I don't wanna turn into a drunk."

Her friends chuckled.

THAT NIGHT, HARPER SAT ON THE SOFA BETWEEN LOGAN AND RENEE while Jonathan and Madison clobbered each other in *Mortal Kombat*. Lorelei played with an Etch-a-Sketch the kids had found in a closet earlier while going house-exploring among the unassigned homes.

The power flickered, but didn't falter enough that the game quit. Everyone looked up at the lights. Another power dip happened a few seconds later, but the game didn't seem to care.

"So eerie," whispered Madison. "I hope they aren't dropping more bombs."

"Is it ghosts?" Lorelei gasped, then clung to Harper.

"No. The electrical system we have is so iffy right now, if a bird lands on a wire somewhere, the lights flicker." Harper stared at the floor lamp by the front window, daring it to flutter again.

"Reminds me of my old apartment," said Cliff from his favorite recliner.

"Hah." Carrie—in a second recliner beside his that appeared in the house that afternoon—laughed. She told them about her younger brother's house in backwoods Virginia. Whenever it rained, snowed, or did anything else but be sunny, he'd lose power for days. "That town probably had one guy with one truck and the electricity stayed off until Jim-Bob whatever felt good and ready to go out there and fix it."

Cliff couldn't stop snickering for far longer than that deserved, evidently struck funny by some mental image.

Harper, Renee, and Logan talked, mostly Renee about how weird she found it that Darci seemed to be the same person, unfazed by even the end of the world.

"'Nee, Darce has smoked so much weed she probably still hasn't realized the war happened. It'll probably hit her in about three months."

Renee chuckled, but it sounded sad. Logan said 'wow' with his eyebrows.

"I'm kidding." Harper sighed. "She knows. Just handling it in her own way is all."

"Cool." Renee nodded. "Least wherever she was, she had enough food."

Harper squirmed. "Yeah. She did."

Cliff, in whom she'd confided that particular truth, glanced over his book at her with pity and a bit of anger—probably directed at the war itself.

"Can't think of what to talk about. Usually, I always talked about movies, but there aren't any good ones coming out this summer," said Logan.

"Yeah. Guess we better grab books on how to live like the 1800s and start talking about that stuff." Harper let her head flop back. "Ugh. But hey, we're alive, right?"

"I'd rather be bored than terrified." Renee managed a weak smile.

Harper and Renee exchanged a meaningful look. Between Darci's experience in the survivor's camp and Renee being held captive by the Lawless for a few months, Harper couldn't decide which one had sucked more. Both Darci and Renee had lost their parents as well, then had to endure even more awfulness. Compared to the two of them, it sure felt as if she and Madison got lucky.

We're all broken a little bit. But, at least the glue seems to be holding the pieces together for now.

Eventually, it got late. Harper reminded the kids of it being Saturday night, time for baths. Jonathan ran off to hop in the shower. Madison put the PlayStation away and spent the next twenty or so minutes playing dolls with Lorelei until the boy finished. As soon as Jonathan exited the bathroom, Harper assisted Logan down the hall to his room. Jonathan had agreed to share the room, relinquishing his bed to the wounded and using a sleeping bag on the floor for the duration.

The girls ducked into the bathroom and shared the tub. While Madison washed Lorelei's hair, Harper scrubbed Madison's. The six-year-old mostly played with her boat, only half paying attention to any effort to teach her how to wash herself. When the bath ended, Harper dried Lorelei off, then herself. They all put on their nightgowns and clustered at the sink.

She felt a bit strange standing there with both of her sisters, all brushing their teeth at the same time as though they'd become rural farm kids who'd never known about cars, electronics, or air conditioning. The modern world she'd once lived in increasingly felt like some strange dream that couldn't possibly have been real.

Teeth done, they crossed the hall in a group and crawled into bed together, Lorelei on her left, Madison on her right. A few minutes passed, Harper staring at the ceiling. Nothing particular worried her awake, merely the general anxiety of wondering what messed up thing would happen next.

Am I going to wind up getting into a gunfight with one of my old teachers? The way things are going, next week Mrs. Carroll, that nice old crossing guard, will show up and try to burn down the quartermaster's building.

"Harp?" asked Madison.

"Yeah?"

"Eva's acting weird. She's real quiet now. You'd always yell at her to quiet down since she was really loud."

And you used to be goofy and bubbly all the time. "Yeah. I remember. She saw some bad things."

"So did we," whispered Madison. "I'm acting weird, too. Aren't I? Not being silly like I used to be."

"You're doing great, Termite." Harper squeezed her close. "We saw some real bad stuff, too. You know I wish the war never happened. It's awful and horrible, but maybe it's time we stop thinking all the time about the bad stuff. There's still some good here."

"Like what?" asked Madison.

"Me." Lorelei grinned. "Mommy didn't want me. Now I got a family who loves me."

Harper kissed her atop the head. "Absolutely. And, now, we'll stay a family like people used to do long ago. I won't be moving to college or getting my own apartment somewhere far away where we'd only see each other once or twice a year on Christmas and Thanksgiving. That's not so bad, right?"

Madison hugged her. "Yeah."

Eyes closed, Harper allowed herself a moment of hope. Lorelei's soft breaths brushed warmth over the left side of her neck while Madison's head rested on her right shoulder. Sure, a semi-automatic shotgun leaned against the wall in easy reach, but their bedroom felt safe and cozy. She lay there trying unsuccessfully to fall asleep for several minutes until the unnatural silence of a world without cars or airplanes started to pull her under.

"Harp?" whispered Madison.

"Yeah?"

"It's okay if you wanna go out with Logan. He's nice. But, he's gotta stay here so you don't go away."

Chuckling, Harper squished her with a one-armed hug. "Slow that down a bit, Termite. Not like I'm gonna marry him next week."

"So, two weeks?"

"Bit slower than that, but things might possibly end up that way."

Madison let out a bright, chirpy giggle… the way she used to when something hit her funny, but not quite so funny that she doubled over in laughter. The girl hadn't made that sound once in the past eight months.

Hearing a trace of the old Madison watered Harper's eyes. She stopped trying to fall asleep so she could stay awake and enjoy this quiet time with her sisters.

For the first time since her father dragged her out of bed a few minutes before six in the morning the day civilization died, she dared to believe that happiness might still exist in the world.

fin

ACKNOWLEDGMENTS

Thank you for reading *The Lucky Ones – Evergreen #3*. The story of Harper and company will continue… soon.

Additional thanks to Lee Sheridan for editing and Alexandria Thompson for the wonderful cover art!

ABOUT THE AUTHOR

Originally from South Amboy NJ, Matthew has been creating science fiction and fantasy worlds for most of his reasoning life. Since 1996, he has developed the "Divergent Fates" world, in which *Division Zero, Virtual Immortality, The Awakened Series, The Harmony Paradox, and the Daughter of Mars series* take place. Along with being an editor at Curiosity Quills press, he has worked in IT and technical support.

Matthew is an avid gamer, a recovered WoW addict, Gamemaster for two custom RPG systems, and a fan of anime, British humour, and intellectual science fiction that questions the nature of reality, life, and what happens after it.

He is also fond of cats.

Visit me online at:
   Facebook: https://www.facebook.com/MatthewSCoxAuthor
   Amazon: https://www.amazon.com/author/mscox
   Pinterest: https://www.pinterest.com/matthewcox10420/
   Goodreads: https://www.goodreads.com/author/show/7712730.Matthew_S_Cox
   Email: mcox2112@gmail.com

OTHER BOOKS BY MATTHEW S. COX

- Prophet's Journey

Divergent Fates Anthology

(Fiction Novels - Adult)

The Roadhouse Chronicles Series

- One More Run
- The Redeemed
- Dead Man's Number

Faded Skies series

- Heir Ascendant
- Ascendant Unrest
- Ascendant Revolution

Temporal Armistice Series

- Nascent Shadow
- The Shadow Collector
- The Gate to Oblivion

Vampire Innocent series

- A Nighttime of Forever
- A Beginner's Guide to Fangs
- The Artist of Ruin
- The Last Family Road Trip
- The Phantom Oracle
- How Not to Summon Demons

Standalones

- Wayfarer: AV494
- Axillon99
- Chiaroscuro: The Mouse and the Candle
- The Spirits of Six Minstrel Run
- Sophie's Light
- The Far Side of Promise anthology
- Operation: Chimera (with Tony Healey)
- The Dysfunctional Conspiracy (with Christopher Veltmann)

Winter Solstice series (with J.R. Rain)

- Convergence
- Containment
- Catalyst

Alexis Silver series (with J.R. Rain)

- Silver Light
- Deep Silver
- Silver Quarrel

Samantha Moon Origins series (with J.R. Rain)

- New Moon Rising
- Moon Mourning

Vampire For Hire series (with J.R. Rain)

- Moon Master
- Dead Moon

Maddy Wimsey series (with J.R. Rain)

- The Devil's Eye

- The Drifting Gloom
- The Dark Mercy

<u>Samantha Moon Case Files series</u> (with J.R. Rain)

- Blood Moon

Immortal Operative series (with J.R. Rain)

- Broken Ice

Young Adult Novels

The Eldritch Heart Series

- The Eldritch Heart
- The Cursed Crown

Evergreen Series

- Evergreen
- The World That Remains
- The Lucky Ones

Standalones

- Caller 107
- The Summer the World Ended
- Nine Candles of Deepest Black
- The Forest Beyond the Earth
- Out of Sight
- Evergreen

Middle Grade Novels

The Adventures of Ubergirl series

- My Dad is a Mad Scientist

Tales of Widowswood series

- Emma and the Banderwigh
- Emma and the Silk Thieves
- Emma and the Silverbell Faeries
- Emma and the Elixir of Madness
- Emma and the Weeping Spirit

Standalones

- Citadel: The Concordant Sequence
- The Cursed Codex
- The Menagerie of Jenkins Bailey

www.ingramcontent.com/pod-product-compliance
Lightning Source LLC
Chambersburg PA
CBHW031705170626
46808CB00005B/1615